MY RUSSIAN

Books by Deirdre McNamer

RIMA IN THE WEEDS

ONE SWEET QUARREL

MY RUSSIAN

# My Russian

DEIRDRE McNAMER

HOUGHTON MIFFLIN COMPANY

BOSTON · NEW YORK

1999

For information about permission to reproduce selections from
this book, write to Permissions, Houghton Mifflin Company,
215 Park Avenue South, New York, New York 10003.

Library of Congress Cataloging-in-Publication Data

McNamer, Deirdre.
My Russian / Deirdre McNamer.
p.     cm.
ISBN 0-395-95637-4
Title.
PS3563.C38838M92     1999
813'.54—dc21     99-19140     CIP

Book design by Anne Chalmers
Type: Linotype-Hell Fairfield and Caravan

Printed in the United States of America

QUM 10 9 8 7 6 5 4 3 2 1

To Bryan

For their insight and support, I thank Connie Poten, Megan McNamer, and Pat Strachan; Jacqueline Carey, Fred Haefele, and Patricia Goedicke; Sarah Chalfant, Jin Auh, and Andrew Wylie.

For his wisdom and wit over the years, I am deeply grateful to Leonard Wallace Robinson.

# MY RUSSIAN

# 1

ELEVEN BLOCKS from this darkened room, I have a husband and a handsome house. My bathrobe hangs from a hook in that house; my gardening clogs rest by the door; my furious son goes in and out, his demiwife in tow. In a drawer, in a desk, in that house, an itinerary tells them I fly home in a dozen days. The date is highlighted and starred.

When I leave this room, I wear a wig and some odd clothing I bought in Athens. Just like that, I've become a person who no longer fits the shape and color of my absent self, as it exists in the minds of my husband and son. They would look straight at this version of me and see no one they knew. I'm quite sure of that.

I am here to assess the situation. I'm here, let's say, to spy on my waiting life.

The couple next door in 202—pastel knits, running shoes — left this morning. They were here for a visit with a floundering daughter whose house is too cramped for guests. They liked the motel better anyway, because they could talk about her when they returned to the room each night. And the father could cough at alarming and luxurious length and no one would glance sideways, no one would prescribe. His wife stopped doing that decades ago.

They are the sort of old ones who seem to be melting — all the corners growing rounded, the head sagging forward, the body folding into itself in a whispery version of the way the lit-up monks folded themselves into their brilliant oblivion. Such a thing to think! But they keep coming to me, these illuminations of the ordinary people I call to mind. At this moment, yes, those old people sit on the edge of a bed worrying over a restaurant receipt, their white hair beginning to smoke.

Yesterday on the elevator they introduced themselves as Mary-Doris and Ed and told me the outlines of the situation with the daughter. Mary-Doris confided that she wouldn't mind walking around town a bit, get the kinks out, but Ed wouldn't do it. He has to drive everywhere. The rare times she gets him out walking, all he does is complain about the kinds of pets people keep, and the kinds of yards, and all the foreign cars. He worked for GM in Detroit for forty-five years and still wears his GM baseball cap.

As she told me about him, he watched her mildly, hands in his pockets. I seemed to know, looking at him, that he had no intermediary zone between his social self and his stark 4 A.M. self, no place in his mind to keep company with himself. You see these people on planes. They try small talk with the person next to them; it doesn't work; they eventually pick up the airline magazine and flip through it as if it's something that fell off the back of a truck.

Mary-Doris said that she had been a housekeeper for a family in Grosse Pointe for almost twenty years, that she had retired last year and what did I think they'd given her as a going-away present? Some stocks, I said. A gift certificate. A toaster oven. No, none of it. They had given her a papered bloodhound, worth a lot. But this dog ate so ravenously and was so nervy and big that she'd sold it for seventy-five dollars when they moved to their retirement house in Arizona. They called the creature the Disposer.

This morning I put on my taupe pantsuit and my walking shoes and my black wig, and I knocked at 202. I'd heard them moving around since six. I asked Mary-Doris if she wanted to go for a walk. She'd be good cover. She'd make me fully invisible.

I'm here, let's say, to correct the course of my life.

We walked slowly south, away from the Trocadero Motel and the interstate, and made our way into the university area with its spreading maples and its old Colonials, Tudors, viny bungalows. There stood my big house, windows flashing in the morning sun, the sprinklers sending up neat water fans. It looked serene and polished in that early light, as if it had never known trouble or had locked it away. The lawn was freshly mowed, and the clematis bloomed on the trellis. Behind the trellis stretched my landscaped yard, so carefully wild. The work of my Russian gardener.

He made a new yard, and then he was gone. And now it is up to us.

"There's a pretty place," said Mary-Doris, squinting for a longer look at my house. "That trellis looks a little raggedy, but nothing a few minutes with the snippers couldn't fix. Of course, these people hire the work done. Someone to design it all — someone to keep the weeds pulled." Then she told me about the rock garden she'd made around their modular house out there in the desert where they lived now. And I told her that I too hoped to have a garden someday, when I got my life back on track. She studied me.

"I'm in the middle of a nightmare divorce," I improvised. "My whole life has turned on a dime."

Mary-Doris nodded gravely.

"My cousin's a lawyer, and he's going to make sure I don't lose everything to my ex in Wichita. He lives here, this cousin, the rising star of the family. We meet this week and get down to brass tacks." I sounded insane to myself.

Mary-Doris sighed. "My daughter's husband's a certified maniac," she said. "Tore the screen door off this time. She's got an order. But a piece of paper doesn't stop a man like Toby Hennepin."

"No," I agreed.

I steered her across the street from my big house to the park. We sat on a bench near the pigeon-spackled soldier. Mary-Doris wore new shoes too. We rested, our blazing white feet stretched out before us.

I uncrossed my ankles, and it seemed a signal for my husband to emerge slowly from the side door of our house, the one to the wraparound deck. He wore his maroon jogging outfit. His silver walker seemed to pull him toward the patio chair. They got there, and he let himself down. He lifted the walker off to the side, then sat still, a hand on each knee. He could have been a parent, waiting for a naughty child. He could have been a criminal, waiting for the sentence.

"The man of the house," Mary-Doris said.

I felt utterly sheepish and wrong at that moment, like someone in a clown suit robbing a 7-Eleven.

My husband's name is Ren. Renton William Woodbridge. Nothing about the worst of this story is anything he deserved.

"A car wreck would be my guess," said Mary-Doris. "He's not that old." She sighed. "Sometimes the fatal mistake is to wear that belt. You try to be safe and buckle the thing, then the car takes the wrong kind of flip and there you are, hanging upside down with the blood supply cut off. For as long as it takes them to get to you. Which is anybody's guess, depending on where you are." She rummaged in her purse for breath mints and extracted one for each of us. She sighed again. She wanted to go home to the desert.

The door swung open, and Elise Prentice, our next-door neighbor, came out of my house. She carried a coffee cup and something on a plate. Her dog, Roberta, a dilapidated schnauzer, pattered arthritically behind her.

"The missus," Mary-Doris announced, squinting over the tops

of her glasses. "She'll give him a nice breakfast and they'll read the paper, and it could be ten, maybe noon, before they get into gear. Those people don't punch clocks. They have no place they have to be at any given moment in time."

Elise wore a short-skirted suit with a checked scarf knotted buoyantly at the neck. Her wine-colored bob glowed in the sun. She set the plate down and handed my husband a cup of coffee and brushed something off the shoulder of his sweatshirt. She is a pretty woman, with bright, efficient movements. On the shuttle from the airport, I saw someone who reminded me of Elise as she would look in fifteen years. Even in repose, the woman on the bus kept a smile on her face, as if she had decided somewhere along the line that the purpose of smiling is to coax happiness, not respond to it.

Elise bent over and gave Ren a long, searching look. She said something. He nodded. Her schnauzer sat down hard and hoisted a leg to scratch an ear.

"What if she isn't his wife?" I said.

Mary-Doris squinted at me. "Why wouldn't she be his wife?"

Elise touched my husband's shoulder and walked smartly down the steps, her dog at her heels. Then, oddly, she stopped. And Roberta trotted rapidly in our direction, as if I'd called her. I slumped and looked away. The dog planted her legs and barked happily at us, a middle-aged woman and her stooped mother. My face grew hot. I was furious that I hadn't thought of this possibility, and scrambled to think what I would do if the dog trotted over to say hi. But dog and owner just stood there for a few moments, and Elise waved apologetically.

"She appears to know us," Mary-Doris said dryly. We watched Elise guide the dog by her collar to the Saab parked in the driveway of the house next to mine. They both got in. Mary-Doris leaned forward. "Why is she taking the neighbor's car?" she demanded.

Elise backed her car out of her driveway and pulled it into

ours. Ren tipped his head back. His springy gray hair made a halo. Then he pulled the walker to him and hoisted himself to his feet. With Elise at his elbow again, he walked himself to her car and slowly got in. Elise put the folded walker into the back seat with Roberta and backed the car onto the street. We watched them as they drove away, and then the street and its houses seemed very quiet. Mary-Doris shrugged elaborately and offered me another mint.

The day before I left for Greece with my tour group, I sat with my family on our deck. Ren walked slowly around the yard with his walker, examining the flowers and shrubs as if he actually noticed or cared about them. He climbed the four steps up to the deck, to Mack and me, and it seemed to take forever. He sucked in his cheeks with the effort. He had begun to wear an ascot around his knobbled neck. For six months Ren had spent several hours a day in physical therapy. He was getting better, but slowly, so slowly.

He hauled himself up the stairs and Mack and I made conversation, rigorously not watching him. Mack wore his fedora and he sat tipped back in his chair, hat pushed back like a reporter's on the old-movie channel. It was the time of day when the light begins to fall sideways and so many of us feel that shifty unease of the day-wane, the urge for consolation and muffling.

Elise stopped by to see if we needed any help. Our trouble had brought color to her face, a spring to her walk. She scanned a newspaper ad, then made a phone call while she watered my geraniums. "It's available?" she asked someone. "That's wonderful." She switched the phone off and turned to us. "I love it when things are available," she said.

Ren told them that the intruder was masked, that he hadn't recognized the person who crept into our home that night of the freezing rain, whose fingertips pressed the four numbers that de-activated all the alarms. Ren trusted his security system. So when he heard the fractional squeak that began his own disman-tling, I know he glanced happily at the small red eye on the wall, ready to be reassured.

The eye had turned green. Someone new was present. He muted the Raiders game and pulled himself upright on the couch and tried to think. Our son was at his girlfriend's. I was at my friend Siobhan's in Seattle. This was someone new.

He reached behind his head — he told them he found this odd, later on — and dimmed the lamp; just dimmed it, as if he could soften what was going to happen next. He listened. He heard the blood in his ears, the grumble of a passing car. He got to his feet and walked, jelly-kneed, to his big desk. And then he fumbled at the back of the file drawer on the right side for the pistol. He held it in two hands, chest high.

His football game flickered silently. His shoes were off. A beer was poured. He'd tried to have a casual evening, a bachelor evening. He'd been working too hard. He'd looked forward to this.

That's the vision that cracks my heart, Ren. Your stocking feet, a little pigeon-toed, and that gun in your quivering hands. The flash of your wedding band. The avid green eye, watching you.

Mary-Doris and I walked from the park to the university campus, an amiable jumble of stone and brick around a grassy oval, and padded around it like someone's relatives. The bells clanged. A couple hugged on a bench. The faces of the students we passed, some of them, were pinched. I wonder about this. It's an era, I think, when too many kids wake up every day feeling they've slid a notch.

Mary-Doris's feet began to ache and so we made our way back across the grassy oval, across a practice field and a bridge, along a street where the houses shrank and the yards got weedy and the sound of freeway traffic began. Ed sat on a low wall in front of the Trocadero, his GM cap pulled low over his eyes.

"Pack your things, Mary-Doris," he said. "We're going home."

She raised her eyebrows. He shook his head. "Seems Toby Hennepin is back," he said. "Seems the big emergency is over and the next few days are for them to get to know each other again. Quote." He shooed her impatiently with his hand.

"What about the kids?" she cried. "What about Jennifer's birthday?"

"Get your things," he said. "I'll tell you all the gory details when we're on the road."

They turned to me. We said it had been nice to meet each other, and we hoped everything would work out for each other all the way around. I went to my room. Ten minutes later, a toilet flushed, their door clicked shut, and they were gone.

For meals, I walk to the fast-food places, order, and leave. My face is only briefly at the counter, and the workers there wouldn't know me anyway. I don't eat fast food in my waiting life. I buy lots of fresh vegetables, the best olive oil, good breads, and I make imaginative low-fat meals for my husband and, when he's around, my son, Mack. I arrange fresh flowers on the dining room table and roll antique linen napkins into monogrammed silver rings, even when it's only the two of us. Sometimes we invite our neighbor Elise to join us.

Now my wig sits on the second bed. My orange juice, my fishwich, my large coffee, await. It's dusk. The room smells of food wrappers, of tartar sauce. The curtains glow red. On the television, a woman is decorating a very tall wedding cake. She playfully jabs her finger at me. Anyone could do this at home, she says as she peers sideways at the alignment of the layers. It's a matter of patience and confidence, she calls out as she pipes a garland of perfect roses around the edge.

I tried CNN, but they were talking about manatees dying mysteriously off Florida. "Everything about her looks fine," a pathologist said, squinting down at one of the huge motherly bodies. "She's got plenty of fat. She's just dead."

Mack, my son, is seventeen. Two years ago, when he was not yet my height, he began to have a sexual relationship with a girl named Tamara Klemenhagen. Before that, he seemed an ordinary kid in every way. He wore jeans and T-shirts. He told corny jokes.

On October 16 of their freshman year, he and Tamara went to a movie together. Each month after that, on the sixteenth, they celebrated their "anniversary" with a candlelit dinner at her house. Her parents, a minister and a Montessori teacher we've known for years, absented themselves. I found all this out at a later date.

This past year, Mack began to wear a suit to school. He bought two suits, in fact, one at the Goodwill and the other at a place called Second Thoughts. They are both baggy-panted with large padded shoulders. At first he wore them with a T-shirt; then he replaced the T-shirt with a white shirt and a tie; and now there are French cuffs and cufflinks too. Sometimes a terrible tie clip, a flag or a jumping trout. He rinses the shirts out by hand and irons them himself.

Tamara has little-girl hair, that glossy pelt you never have again after twenty, a pure chocolate color. She wears long floral skirts and cotton sweaters or simple white blouses. She looks and smells impossibly clean. Her hands are baby hands, boneless, and she wears silver rings, thin as thread, on each index finger.

The two of them have developed an elaborate pattern of fighting and making up, as if their own bodies, their own running blood, isn't quite enough to sustain their passion and they must, so soon, resort to the devices of the long linked. They must deliberately court estrangement so it can be overcome in a rush.

There are tears then — hers and his — and a protracted making up over the phone, through notes, through intermediaries, and then they are serene for a while. He in his suit. She in her prissy blouses. I imagine her donning a long white nightgown and he some Fred MacMurray pajamas before they pull out the daybed in her parents' basement and her baby hands run down his chest, their filmy young skins slide against each other, their fingers lace. They pant like running children, and the only thing very old about them is their minds. Maybe. I don't know. There is something about them that is either more sardonic or more naive than I can bear to think about.

Ren and I let them have their affair, though "let" isn't the right word. We didn't raise serious objections, in part because we were so vehemently confused by the two of them, from the very beginning. I sometimes felt something like hatred for Tamara. I felt she had reversed her life and was starting out, in her dresses, her monogamy, her antiseptic sweetness, where I had ended up. She would get all the simple forms and alliances out of the way early and then her life could flare outward. I saw the mathematical sign, the horizontal V, between her and her future. Tamara now is less than she will be down the road. My sign, in those poisonous green moments, was reversed.

Three o'clock in the morning and I can't sleep, can't sleep. Soon I will do what I came here to do. It's a half-baked plan I have. I know that. If I'm caught, I will have nothing convincing to say.

"Hey there, hon," says Gerrald, the night manager. I help myself to a little Styrofoam cup of the rancid lobby coffee. In my waiting life, Gerrald would have called me ma'am.

Gerrald is pale and ageless. He could be twenty-five or fifty. He has slick black hair with comb lines in it.

"Three years ago, I would have been passed out right now," he said, as if I'd asked him a question. "Would have somehow got myself home from the bar and be flopped on the couch." He spoke as if he disdainfully examined his own flopped form.

He was watching television when I came down the stairs — a tiny little set with a tortured-looking antenna and some screaming laughter inside. His back looked very frail, the wings of it showing through the white cotton of his starched shirt. His cufflinks were tiny golf clubs.

"It's a pretty good system," he continued. "I come to work about the time I would have been going to the bar. And I finish up" — he looked at his watch — "with AA at nine A.M., nonsmokers' at the Elks."

It was the most I'd ever heard him say.

"Then feed the cats. Then breakfast, a couple videos, sleep, eat again, show up back here."

Here is another world: these graveyard shifts, these Gerralds. The lights at 3 A.M. make the parking lots blue. A truck gears down to climb the freeway ramp. Waitresses have a wordless smoke. Water plinks in a rusty pan. Muffled televisions shriek and scream. Gerrald's big eyes veer over to mine.

"There's cocoa too, hon," he said. I made some, stirring it with a plastic wand. "Pull up a chair," he said.

I pulled up a chair and sat with Gerrald.

A person in the television fell backward over a plaid couch.

2

Our town was once, those millions of years ago, an outlandish lake. Now the banks are mountains and the floor is dry, except for the rivers. One tumbles in from the north, another from the south, and they join the broad and calmer one that bisects the town and moves west to the Pacific.

The banks rise several thousand feet from the valley floor and are tawny and unrocked. Two of them have large white initials on their flanks. One is an *L* for a high school. One is an *M* for a college. They are town mountains. Domesticated. Though it is true that on their upper reaches, elk stride in ghostly packs through deep winter. An avalanche buried some boys.

In the summer, hang gliders run off the tops of the banks and float to the bottom of the empty lake. We watch them, tiny humans hung from bright sails, on evenings when the thermals are good.

In the part of town where I live, there are mountains at the ends of the streets. Even in the broader parts of the valley, the long flats, the eye stops at mountains. We live in a cupped hand. Or a greenhouse — the way a campus is like a greenhouse. You're nurtured and sealed off at the same time. You're supposed to thrive.

There are many trees. There is little or no wind. In winter, fumes from the paper mill and the exhaust of cars and the smoke of stoves get pressed down to the lake floor by warmer air, and then you breathe your own stale exhalations, your own quiet flatulence.

We're sixty thousand, give or take, and friendly in a western sort of face-to-face way. Rhetorical politenesses are not yet considered lethally inefficient, or even insincere. "How you doin'?" the grocery clerk asks. "You bet!" she says when you ask for a paper bag.

During the holidays I ran into a woman I know slightly who is active in various enlightened causes. "Have a reasonable New Year," she said to me, pleased at the unreasonableness of everyone except herself. "You bet!" I said.

It's a town that encourages a certain flamboyance but keeps you safe from any sybaritic fanning out into endlessness. Because you hit the banks of the former lake if you do. You stay or you leave, but there is no bank-scrambling in any sweaty sense.

Part of the way up one of the town mountains is a restaurant with a deck to sit upon at dusk. And then it's the sky that's the predominant presence, streaked and vast and who-cares, and down below on the lake bottom, a carpet of small orange and white lights, breakaway schools of them swimming down the valley, up into the gullies, up the big flanks.

Sometimes I see the lake coming back. One of my little visions. It is low and mostly invisible, and it is beginning to rise. Slowly, it lifts the glitter-fish. Slowly, it lifts us all. Soon we will stand on new ground, unsure of how we got there, where we should go next. That's what I seem to see.

# 3

You should see me when I am Francesca Woodbridge. I look like an ad for an investment firm. The wealthy couple in their forties, having wisely parlayed their parents' money into a pile, ponder their next move. She always has smooth hair, worn up, and a cashmere sweater. Calm-eyed, good-boned. That's me.

Don't be fooled.

You know that drawing of a sharp-chinned hag that becomes, when you stare at it, a young woman wearing a plumed hat? The data remain unchanged but the information, in a shiver of the neurons, becomes entirely different. There is a different *seen thing*. I'm thinking of that moment when the image changes. There's disconcertion, almost betrayal, in it. For a while now, the way I see myself and the way I see what's around me keep flicking back and forth so rapidly — sharp-chinned hag, plumed-hat girl, sharp-chinned hag — that I seem most of the time to reside only on that border between the shockingly disparate. It's a vertiginous, wind-in-your-ears kind of place.

Nine days ago I met my tour group in New York. We flew to Athens and the next day climbed into a chartered bus for the Inland Tour of Classical Greece.

There we were at Delphi. The driver, Yannis, sat on the bus fender while the rest of us trooped up the path to the crumbled temple, the home of the babbling oracle. She babbled, they said, and she touched herself in lewd transport and swung her eyes around. And when she stopped, smoke skittered between her eyes and yours, and a priest translated the message. Or not.

There was a person in our group who was nearly blind. She could see only through very thick glasses, and only those objects she held a few inches from her eyes. She was a photographer, however. It was the way she saw the world. Blindly, she aimed her camera in the general direction of something she wanted to see — she sometimes invited total strangers to position her — and then she took the picture, seeing nothing. When it was developed, she had it printed large, and then she brought it up to her poor eyes and saw, for the first time, where she'd been.

I looked back at our silver bus. Through the dust and the gnarled olive trees, it looked like a time machine, fresh from the sleek future. Yannis lit a cigarette. He wore his aviator sunglasses, his tight white shirt with a company logo, gray knit pants, and tire-soled sandals. He spit at the ground. Another bus pulled in behind ours and disgorged its passengers. They filed obediently toward the museum, and their driver joined Yannis. They talked. Yannis pretended to grab a very large steering wheel and yank it back and forth. The other driver threw back his head in laughter. Yannis stubbed out his cigarette, leaned toward the other driver to say something out of the corner of his mouth, then executed a perfect imitation of the waddling walk of one of our party, a screenwriter-slash-painter named Lew Trapper. It was not an extravagant imitation, just a very good one — good in the sheer accuracy and restraint with which Yannis somehow replicated Lew's bowlegged, barrel-chested, dimwitted arrogance, the way Lew's very small head seemed to follow his body at a distance, squinting to see where the whole package was going. The spatulate hands, palms facing backward — he got that. Best of all, he got Lew's farsighted squint at a rigidly extended

wrist, as if his huge Rolex were issuing complicated instructions.
The riff took just a few seconds. It changed our group from the
girl to the hag. One moment we were powerful pale Americans in
linens and sandals, striding intelligently and bright-eyed through
the remnants of antiquity. The next we were clueless loonies, the
aides laughing indulgently behind our brittle backs.

Our guide, Janine, an art-history person from Arkansas, never
stopped talking. I heard her in the distance, a high drone. She
produced words so relentlessly that they seemed to function as
her tensility, her uprightness. Poor Janine, I thought. She is exhausted already. If she stopped talking, she'd fall over.

I think about the metallic hand of the Greek sun, whirring cicadas, impossible chunks of ancient stone, graves and battle-
ments; about Janine's insect hum, the clicks of our cameras, and
the refrigerated bus that waited to transport the shiny and chattering pack of us to the next timeless place.

I think about the back of Yannis's head, the passing glint of his
sunglasses in the rearview mirror, and the way I seemed then to
feel a lover's hands run slowly up the backs of my bare legs. He
would squat to the ground and very lightly grasp my Achilles tendons with thumbs and index fingers, the signal, the pause, then
flatten his hands to run the leathery palms up the backs of my
calves, my knees, my thighs, until he stood too. Then he drew his
tongue across the hollow of my throat and stretched his fingers to
meet at my liquid seam. I sank a little, just rested into it, and he
pulled me open, infinitesimally slowly, an increment at a time.

It had nothing to do with Yannis directly, except as a person
can become an instigation. He gunned our cool capsule through
the crackling silver hills and I'd try to think about what I saw outside those smoky windows, but my eyes would close, and all I
could do was remember. All I could want was to want.

They were the neon thoughts of a leavetaking. That was clear to me. There was an exhilarated impatience to them, like the way travelers wave, so fervently and indefatigably, when they know they aren't coming back.

Back in Athens, we gathered for drinks on the terraced roof of our hotel. The plan was to board a ferry the next day for Naxos, our first island.

It was a blurred and fumy evening. The thin screams of motorcycles floated up to us. The Parthenon stood in the distance, tired-looking through the orange sun.

Lew the screenwriter explained his profession to the almost-blind woman, June. He talked a lot because he was getting a divorce and silence made him confused. He was trying to elucidate the difference between making a movie for the screen and making a movie for television. Take Vietnam, he said to June. Vietnam for the big screen would be panoramic, would be filmed on location in the jungles, the rice paddies. Vietnam for television, in contrast, would be "a burning palm tree with uniforms running back and forth in front of it." His words.

I sat at a wrought-iron table with Bonnie and Frieda from New Hampshire. They made me remember a story I read in a newspaper. A middle-aged man had taken off from Long Island in a little plane, his white-haired mother the only passenger. An airplane ride on a sunny day. Something happened and he passed out at the controls. For two hours — *two hours* — she talked to towers, talked to pilots who were tailing her, followed their instructions. But she had never flown a plane. She didn't know what to do. And there was her son, slipping down in his seat, groggy, passing out. And she was trapped above New Hampshire, the fate of them both in her hands.

I reminded Bonnie and Frieda of the story.

"More things happen in New Hampshire than most people think," said Frieda, carefully tasting her retsina. She wrinkled her nose. "What this is, is wine mixed with gasoline," she announced loudly.

The mother seemed to grow tired before she crashed. Her voice faded. Maybe they both had carbon monoxide poisoning, or food poisoning. She made some good competent turns, but then she seemed to grow confused, and her head, like his, slipped below the controls. And the little plane bore both of them in its silver body down to the ground.

As I finished, my voice caught.

"Lucky it didn't hit a school," Bonnie said.

"It seems to me there is everything in that story about being a parent," I ventured.

"Or about giving up," said Frieda, the brisk one. She slid her glass of retsina over to Bonnie. "Here," she said. "You're the world explorer."

I thought then, I have come to Greece to give up. I have prepared for it, and now I am about to do it.

"I should tell you, I'm going to go off on my own," I said to Frieda and Bonnie. "For a while — maybe until we all fly home." They looked at each other for verification. They looked back at me. I rose to find Janine and tell her my plans. "So I guess I'm saying goodbye and good luck, for now," I finished brightly.

They didn't get up. The almost-blind June leaned over from the next table. "You're leaving us?" she said. She retrieved her camera from her big bag and gestured to Lew's empty chair. He had wandered off somewhere. She took my photo, in order to see me later. I made a big smile.

The next morning I converted all my traveler's checks to cash, went to the ferry office on Syntagma Square, consulted the schedule, and picked an off-the-track island that had a boat leaving for it late that afternoon. I didn't think tourists would be there in any numbers — not yet.

Then I went to the American Express mail pickup, showed my second passport — the one I carried inside a small bundle of paperbacks in my suitcase — and retrieved a package addressed to Jeanne Thompson.

In my guidebook I found the name of the single hotel on my island, and I faxed the address to my husband and son. "New plans!" I scribbled. "I'm going island-hopping on my own for the next little while. Will arrive home on schedule. Keep you posted!"

That's how I talk at home.

On the open deck of the ferry, I read an article in the *Herald Tribune* about what makes music interesting. Early exposure to music sets up certain expectations in our heads, it said. "When the brain hears, say, ten notes of a melody, it will predict the eleventh note based on these stored connections." If the eleventh note isn't what we expect, we are jarred, but very often pleased. The subtle violations are the ones that particularly please.

Sea and diesel. Gulls flying like blown leaves in our wake. Kids at the rail, shouting at the glittering sea. Sun and blue. I was launched.

A boy, a young man, slept on a nearby bench, his face in profile. He was perhaps nineteen and very beautiful, his eyebrows an angry brushstroke, his hairline precise as a map.

Leaning against the rail, a round-shouldered man in a pink shirt and khaki shorts told an animated story to a young couple who surveyed him benignly. The fingers of his right hand were missing. He had only knuckles and a thumb. His right foot constantly tapped the deck. He jammed the fingerless hand into his back pocket and threw back his head to laugh at his own story. The young ones smiled. I saw now the interesting part of him. He wore a wedding ring on his left hand. It revised him in an instant. He changed from the lone wounded goof into a man with a wife, a man with a woman who loved him, with children who called him papa.

And then I thought, No. The ring could be a prop. A rather brilliant one. It could be the way he has found to block the pity of others, for isn't that partly what marriage does?

A woman eyed me as I walked past her. She had a girlish build, well-cut blond hair. All her clothes were just right; that is, they looked as if she knew how to travel. A black cotton skirt, a short-sleeved T-shirt, a cotton vest — all of it serviceable, chic, grown-up. A jaunty straw hat with a fresh flower in the band. She smiled a traveler's smile at me. I sent a small one back. A few minutes later, she walked over to the rail and struck up a conversation with a silver-haired couple. Her slim arm flew out in a competent palms-up gesture.

She looked casual, clear-eyed, happily on the move. But there was something else there, right from the beginning, something studied and frail. The combination of that fragility and her aloneness made her interesting to me.

She went back to her bench and retrieved a thick paperback from her bright little knapsack. She crossed her legs, smoothed her skirt, and read diligently. From time to time she looked up helpfully, as though someone had called her name.

I introduced Jeanne Thompson, my new self, to her.

"I'm happy to meet you, Jeanne," she said, shaking my hand.

She motioned for me to sit down on the bench across from her, putting her book away as though it had accomplished its job.

In perfect accented English, she told me she was on holiday from her job as a social worker at a halfway house for addicts in Switzerland. She was returning to Greece after an absence of twelve years. She had first visited with her husband, who was no longer in the picture.

As she talked, I could see her vision of what Greece held for her now. It was a place to reenact feelings of possibility. A dozen years before, she had traveled to Greece with a man who loved her. She had arrived with a slim, unlined, taut, sun-forgiving body and an advanced college degree and a man who shared her flair for fun. Night after night they drank at the perfect taverna on the perfect little beach. The taverna was festooned with hundreds of tiny lights, the beach was a pale bar of light stretched calmly beyond the laughter. It was the essence of the word "holiday," and it was what she had come back for, alone now, but hoping.

She looked older up close. Up close, she was in her mid-forties, and she had the papery skin blondes sometimes develop. There was a sorrowful tinge to her voice — sorrow at the transgressions of others, the disappointments they had produced in her. Her name was Ursula.

Some people seem to think that if they keep describing a self, they will create it. Ursula was like that. "Sugar is not me," she said, declining my offer of a mint, and I thought, Her addicts must hate her, those alcoholics and binge eaters trying to get through the next fifteen minutes. Up there in the Swiss halfway house, Ursula lays out her clothes for her holidays while one of her charges slips into the kitchen in search of ice cream, vanilla extract, who knows. Small points of red on Ursula's cheeks as she agonizes between the black skirt and the more casual khaki. Which one will say, I am Ursula? Which will catch the eye of the new man who surely waits for Ursula on a sunny Mediterranean isle?

She had a lilting disingenuous laugh, too girlish. It was the laughter of a child responding to the adoring parents she didn't have.

"I had to put a lock on the refrigerator," she said sorrowfully. But the sorrow was not for her addicts; it was for herself, the fine-boned child in a brutish world.

She began to irritate me, to scare me. This is one version of aloneness in middle age, I thought.

She got off the boat where I did. It was near dark. After the brief bustle of the docking and the departures — the pop of exhausts, the cycles whining off into the hills, the supply truck rumbling up the road — it was quite dark.

Ursula and I took a cab to the town on the other side of the island where the little hotel was. We were both too tired to talk. She offered nothing toward the fare.

The cabdriver pointed up a cobblestoned walk and left us. We hauled our suitcases-on-wheels for a long time, it seemed, and then the little hotel was there, white and glowing, its veranda draped with bougainvillea.

Ursula haggled about the price — it was a very low, shoulder-season rate — and grudgingly signed on for one night. As if she had an option. The town was asleep. We walked in separate directions down a short whitewashed hall. By then, I couldn't bear her.

The next morning I found a lovely rental room attached to the house of an old couple named Kouki. It was at the top of a very long hill embedded with 239 whitewashed steps. I returned to the hotel for breakfast on the porch under the pretty vines.

Ursula came lilting up the cobblestones as I sipped my third cup of coffee. She wore a simple white dress and her straw hat and carried a poppy, which she presented with a flourish to me.

"I have decided where I will stay," she announced, pointing on her map to a beach town six or seven miles away by bus. We would go check it out together this afternoon?

Gracious because of our coming separation, I agreed to take the bus with her to the beach town for lunch. It turned out to be a scrabble of frayed buildings along the curve of a small bay. There was a minuscule gift shop where the bus stopped and a cluttered little restaurant with a veranda where we ate fried fish and tomatoes.

I remember the sound of a generator, and the flies, and the sad waiter in heavy rubber sandals who waved his big hand down the beach and said there was an old man there with rooms to let. Very nice beach that way, he said, nodding. Reasonable price. Ursula looked around happily, as if she saw some other beach behind this beach. She tilted her big hat lower on her forehead.

"A tanned face is not me," she said.

And there were rules of behavior too. She did not believe in returning from holidays with too many good things to say about the trip, because those left behind would then feel deprived.

The first room is not the one to rent, she said. Never the first room.

Tsatziki? The garlic did not agree with her stomach. It was not Ursula.

We talked about the group I'd sent on to Naxos without me, and I mentioned the blind photographer. Ursula's ex-husband was a photographer, she said, and for many years she thought always in terms of photographs and movies because he did. Everything she saw, she saw through a lens.

She cupped her freckled hands around her eyes and pointed them at a black cat who sat washing herself on the cracked white step, flicking her nervous tail across the tops of two red poppies.

"Click," she said. And the girlish laugh.

Below the veranda on the beach, a plump woman in a black bikini placed oblong rocks on top of each other, balancing them in a way that seemed purely impossible. She worked very slowly. We watched her, waiting for the rocks to tumble, until they finally did.

Then three darkly tanned men in tiny swimming trunks bounded onto the beach as if someone had whistled for them, and put up a net and began to toss a volleyball vigorously across it. The woman in the black bikini took off her top, as if it constricted serious play, and joined them.

A couple, their skin burned deep pink, wandered onto the veranda, lugging their sunning mats, a boombox, a small cooler.

They spoke to each other in French. The woman was unremarkable in every obvious way. Not old, not young. Not slim or fat. Brown lank hair. Some kind of knit top and shorts and marshmallowy moccasins. The man was large and furred. They sat at their table watching the volleyball players.

The woman ordered a frappe, and when she bent to the straw, her tongue flicked like a lizard's. I saw it in profile. There it went again. The man didn't notice, or was used to it. He was trying to be bored by the nearly naked volleyball girl. At his side, his companion did it again.

I tried to catch Ursula's eye. She was lifting a tomato slice as if it hid something dead.

The topless girl raced a sheepdog down the beach, breasts leaping. She had rehearsed her cavorting and she was quite good at it. The furred man meditated on a sailboat, three hundred yards out to sea at anchor and beginning to glow in the slanting light. His companion watched the volleyball girl from beneath her eyelids, finished off her frappe, and lizard-tongued the straw.

"Music!" Ursula called suddenly. "Music at the beach is what I would like!"

I caught the bus back to my inland village, leaving her to find her room at the beach, her music, her holiday.

The next morning I descended my 239 steps and breakfasted on beautiful yogurt at the little hotel. A Scandinavian couple in their sixties, new arrivals, huddled over a map of the island, planning their rigorous day. The man looked like David Niven in lederhosen. The woman looked as if she had washed in peppermint and smacked herself all over with linden branches. I felt strangely protective of them, of their simple yodeling health, maybe because the morning was so lovely and limpid, exactly the right temperature, with a little breeze that smelled of flowers, baked thyme, and the sea. Or so I decide now.

In Greece, every sound on the early edge of the day floats in the air separately and whole: the brass of the chapel bells, a goat's small bleat, the mosquito whine of a moped topping one of the island's gentle hills, the falling cry of a mother calling a son. *Vassily. Vassily!*

Very early that morning I had watched the sun electrify the houses scattered like dice across the hillsides below. The sea out there had seemed to buoy all of us on its back — all the small morning sounds, the chalky houses, the sleepy men holding the tails of their donkeys as they trudged between the houses, up the stony white steps to their hilltop fields.

The second day on my island, I opened the package addressed to Jeanne Thompson and spread the contents on my nunnish white bed: a driver's license, a certified birth certificate, a credit card, a library card, a few business cards, a wallet with the initials JAT, and Jeanne's name and address on the ID card. A packet of eighty one-hundred-dollar bills, money I had essentially embezzled from the family accounts for months.

It was all there. I greeted my new self.

I packed a knapsack for someone to find eventually by the sea: sun lotion, a change of clothes, flip-flops, a towel, and a bottle of water. I added something more specifically mine — the stub of my airline ticket — hoisted the knapsack onto my back, locked my room, and put the key under a white rock near the door.

A road begins at the square and serpentines for two miles across the countryside and to a cliff above the sea. The sun got hot and then hotter. I passed a strange thing sitting there on land, far back from the sea: a little wooden skiff, weathered silver, with a broken oar. A piece of junk, really. The oar made a good walking stick.

The trail down to the water was rocky and hard to negotiate. I tripped a few times. My knee hurt. But finally I sat on a big boulder at the water, feet cooling.

In the shade of a gnarled cypress, I curled up and drifted or slept. There was a shushing breeze. There were the hot-grease cicadas. When I sat up, a canary-yellow sailboat emerged from the shadow of the next cove. It moved very slowly, that sailboat, and it glowed from within. It looked like a child's idea of a boat, the best boat. Someone waved at me. I waved back. It headed out to sea.

I scooped some dirt from beneath the big boulder and tucked my daypack into the hole. It fit in such a way that you'd have to be looking for it to see it. I planted the splintery oar.

This is what they would find, eventually. It would look as if Francesca Woodbridge had gone into the water, expecting to come out.

I ate at the hotel that evening, suspended in a nameless new lightness, and thought of my husband, my son. I mourned, with them, my absence, but also felt new, as if I had molted, shed my life and was now shivering damply in a strange and inevitable skin.

A hatted figure appeared in the near distance, backlit. It was Ursula. Gone were her light, crisp cottons. Now she wore a flimsy flowered dress and a limp macramé vest, elaborate sandals with many laces around her ankles, a necklace of wooden beads. She had tied a wafty scarf around the crown of her hat. She looked fussy and strange, like a child playing dress-up. Her skin was flushed. There were dark circles under her eyes. The flower in her lapel was withered.

"I have decided to try a new island," she announced, her voice a little shaky. "I do not like the fishing village." She looked ready to weep. Her room was filthy, it turned out, and there was no hot water, despite the hour-by-hour promises of the old landlord. In the morning, she had refused him a third of the payment, and he had turned his back on her and ordered her to leave. There was a large mosquito bite on her forehead. Her bony collarbone looked chafed. She had waited hours for the bus, she said. It did not arrive when it was supposed to arrive. The schedule was a lie. She would try another island. She wanted music in the evenings. She studied her tea mournfully. They had no tea at the restaurant at the fishing village, she added. And coffee gave her hives.

"Perhaps you would like to visit another island with me," she said. "Perhaps we will take the boat to Serifos and see if that is a good place."

"No," I said. "I'm here. I'll stay here for a while." She rubbed at a small spot on her dress. She said nothing. "I've heard Serifos is wonderful," I added.

Her straw satchel fell off the bench and some of the contents scattered across the floor. She moaned a little and squatted down to retrieve them. A pen rolled loudly across the floor and she scrambled after it, then furiously jammed things back into the bag. Breathing hard, she studied the tablecloth, stirred her tea. I noticed how thin and freckled her wrists were. Down in the square, the bus honked. Ursula looked up, startled, then stood. "Goodbye!" she said, hoisting her knapsack and straw bag. "I will go to Serifos!"

She walked quickly toward the square, her hand aloft. Then she began to run.

As I watched her, the owner of the little restaurant and hotel brought me a fax. It was from my son.

Mack is a computer kid who doesn't bother to spell-check. He's suspicious of words in general, prefers illustrations. His letter was written in the form of a huge thought bubble emanating from the brain of a whiskery cross-eyed fellow. Words were misspelled. Punctuation was dropped. Paragraphs ended with Mack's version of those horrible smiley faces — a pair of hands splay-fingered in shock.

What made its way out through all that winking and self-deprecation was a polite inquiry about whether I was glad I'd left my tour group to travel on my own; whether I was taking some good photos; whether this was the respite I'd wanted and deserved. That was the gist. That was his good manners, and I appreciated them.

Then this: "They took Jimster Reece in to question him about the Break-in." (Hands splayed in shock.) "They say he's the only one besides the Immediate Family who knew the security code. So basically they claim he shot dad I guess. My old buddy Jimster! I'm having some problems with this, like basically I don't think he would do something like that. What do you think about this turn of events?"

What did I think? I thought, I have been stopped in my tracks.

# 4

I HAVE NEW NEIGHBORS on each side. They pad around, cough, change channels, run water. One of them talks to himself. "Oh boy," he says. "Oh boy oh boy." It's a thin-walled place, the Trocadero.

I think now it was a mistake to spend time with Mary-Doris. She carries me to her house in the desert — a clear memory, a person — and I don't want that. Not now.

I wish I had told her more diverting lies. I like to lie, if you want the truth. I'm good at it. Sometimes I lie in such an elaborate and careful fashion that my stories jump up before my eyes, breathing on their own.

Just a few minutes ago, when I telephoned my house, I lied in a sideways sort of way to my son. His voice was cracked with sleep. My own voice was scratchy to my ear and I was fogged and headachy too, but this felt like the right morning to call and so I did. It would be Mack or the answering machine. Ren spends his mornings at the physical therapist. Elise had offered to drive him there when I was gone.

"I got your fax about Jimster," I said. "I'm going to travel around this area for the next ten days, but I wanted to talk to you first."

"You sound like you're just down the street," Mack said. "I thought there was supposed to be, like, a pause on the way down from the satellite or something."

"The fluid mysteries of space," I said.

A fire truck screamed up the street that borders the Trocadero. The Trocadero, as I said, is eleven blocks from my house.

"Where are you?" he said.

A pause. "Your fax," I prompted him.

"Jimster," he said. "My old buddy Jimster."

"Why?"

"Motive, opportunity, and, well, he's a bad-ass, ma'am," he said in his Sergeant Friday voice. I heard cold anger behind it, or thought I did.

"Where's your hotel?" he asked. "Is it near, like, the ruins or the temples or whatever?"

"Not really. It's actually by a river on the edge of the town. It's fine. The usual tourists. Plenty of hot water."

Mack grunted politely.

"Jimster," I said.

"Well, basically, he's the prime suspect in the shooting of your husband and my father, one Ren Woodbridge." He coughed. "As I told you by post." When Mack is upset he talks like that.

He told me that Jimster's "high profile" had alerted the cops. He'd been in trouble a few times during the past year, twice for shoplifting, once for possession of marijuana, and he'd also been questioned in connection with a burglary not far from our house and an assault with a baseball bat. Three masked teenagers had pummeled a young dope dealer in the mall parking lot. That last one made the newspaper, the police offering it as evidence of incipient gang activity that needed to be squelched at the outset. The boys who were eventually arrested were friends of Jimster's. He ran with a furious little crowd.

"Plus he has no alibi," Mack said.

Jimster had told the authorities he'd been at the movies that night, but no one had verified that. And, said Mack, there was the fact that Jimster probably knew the security code to the house. That was crucial. The person who entered our house knew that code.

"One night last summer, or maybe September, he came around," Mack said. "You and Dad were gone somewhere, and Tamara was at the Grand Canyon with Franklin and Krystal." Mack and Tamara both call her parents by their first names. "He came around in that old beater pickup with this girl in it, his girlfriend I guess, but I'd never seen her before. She had lots of white hair in a big tangle. Very massive white hair.

"And I got home about the same time and he said he wanted to ask a favor and he had to talk to me in private for a few minutes. It was raining and we didn't have jackets and I said, Well, whatever, sure, and I got the key from the rock and went into the house." I heard the scritch of a match, a grateful sigh. "And so, well, yes, the security system. The man of the house and his foolproof security system."

"Just finish," I said.

"We went into the house and I marched over to the alarm and punched the numbers?" His voice had risen a notch. "I sort of put my body close to the box and punched them fast, but who the hell knows? Maybe he was watching. Maybe I wasn't being totally careful and paranoid around this guy I have known since he was a little kid. Maybe so, maybe so.

"He was on probation for the pot thing," Mack added. "That's why I didn't say anything when they first came around with all their questions. I thought he'd just get hassled. But I've told them now." He took a long drag of his cigarette, hissed the smoke into my kitchen. I stifled the urge to console us both by scolding.

"What did he want to talk with you about, the night the girl with the white hair sat out in the car?" I asked, trying not to hear the bleakness in his voice.

"He just wanted a favor," Mack said, too offhandedly.

"What kind of favor?"

"He just wanted me to keep something for him for a while."

"Keep what?"

"I don't remember."

So Jimster Reece had come to our house last summer, a month before Ren was shot, and asked Mack to keep something for him. Stolen property, dope, whatever. Mack agreed — maybe because he feared Jimster and his friends, maybe out of loyalty, maybe both. And he had stayed quiet about Jimster and the security system. Until now.

"Why would Jimster do something like that? Just break in?"

Mack sighed, as if he were trying to be patient with a nagging child.

"Number one, you and Dad basically kicked him out of the house and told him you didn't ever want to see him again. He's majorly pissed. Number two, Dad's firm is defending the company that spilled all that pipeline shit and forced Jimster's old man to evacuate. They'll think Jimster broke into our house to trash something or take something. For revenge. Revenge of the clan. And things, like, escalated."

"That's ridiculous," I said wanly.

"Even if he gets a public defender who knows anything, he's gonna do some time, I'm betting," Mack said. "He's the only suspect they can put their hands on. He's got a record. He's on probation. He's got no alibi. He had some reasons. And they really want him." Now I heard misery in his voice. "I don't know why I said a fucking thing. I'm basically sending him to the farm. And I know he wasn't the one who broke in. I'm sure of it."

So why did you say anything? I asked silently.

When Mack was a baby, he used to tuck his downy head beneath my ear in a way I never saw another baby do — press his forehead to my neck and stay there for a while, just breathing my skin. As I listened to him, I thought about that.

"The first person they asked me about was the gardener," Mack said. Another scritch, another long sigh.

· 32 ·

"What about the gardener?" I heard the tightness in my voice. "He had a name, you know," I added. "His name was Yuri, and I don't know why they would be asking you about Yuri."

"Well," said Mack. "They said Yuri might have been mixed up with gang-type guys from Russia who are into robbery and shit, and extorting money from other Russians who are here. To finance their global operations or whatever."

"Oh, please," I snapped.

"I'm just saying what they said to me," Mack said patiently. "They can't find him to question him, but they said those people move around a lot, so that's no big deal. And anyway, why would the florist know the code to the house?"

"He wasn't a florist," I said.

I'd given Mack an opening, and he took it. "Well, what was he?" he asked quietly.

I should tell you something about Jimster Reece, a boy I've known since he and Mack were briefly on the same Little League team and became friends.

Jimster is two years older than Mack. He's a redheaded, volatile kid who was notable for his tantrums as a child and his mishaps all the way along. "Mishaps" is the wrong word. Trouble follows Jimster like a starved cat.

At three years old, he was bitten on the face by his mother's boyfriend's hunting dog. He'd tried to tickle the animal exactly the same way the boyfriend always tickled Jimster. The bite required nineteen stitches in a long sickle around his left eye, which was saved, and he wore that white scar until a couple of years ago, when we paid for him to get cosmetic surgery — paid to give him a face that spared him the curiosity and the outright inquiries of strangers. That was our idea, anyway, our good intention.

At nine years old, Jimster broke his tibia trying to jump an irrigation ditch and ended up, after surgery for the compound fracture, nearly dead from a staph infection. When he wobbled out that hospital door, twenty pounds lighter, skin like milk, his doctor called him a miracle on wheels.

When he was eleven, Jimster's mother sent him across town to live with the father he'd seen a dozen times in his life, and she rumbled off in a U-Haul truck to Boise, Idaho, to take computer classes and become the business manager of her latest boyfriend's lounge trio.

By this time Jimster and Mack were big buddies, and by the time Jimster started junior high he was eating dinner several times a week at our house. Often he spent the night. He loved meat loaf. I think now about how his face lit up when I set a meat loaf, that simple thing, on the table. And he drank gallons of milk. I doubled the amount of milk I bought in those years, the years when Jimster seemed to be growing almost visibly, day by day.

Jimster's father worked graveyard at the mill and slept all day on the couch in front of the weather channel. Jimster snuffed out the cigarettes burning beside his father's sleeping form and kept the freezer filled with TV dinners and the refrigerator filled with orange juice and beer and doughnuts, paid for with a wad of bills his father put in a jar at the beginning of each week. Jimster once wheedled an extra fifty and hired the Merry Maids to clean their mobile home down to its nub. But his father yelled that the cleaning products revived all his old allergies, and that was that for further upkeep. The place, Mack said, was a sty.

When Mack got involved with Tamara, Jimster no longer showed up so much at our house, though he and Mack occasionally disappeared into Mack's room for hours to play computer games. Mack said Jimster had a group of new friends. That he'd moved out of his dad's house and into an apartment with two of these new friends. That he'd quit high school and worked part-time at a record store, then got fired for shoplifting.

He seemed guarded about Jimster, Mack did, and I realized at some point that Jimster's life had entered some new orbit that Mack didn't think Ren and I could comprehend, or would want to.

Jimster dyed his hair black and let it grow long, then shaved it entirely and showed up one day with three silver loops through his eyebrow. He developed a curtness that was palpable. He didn't bathe much. His new body was lean and fast and twitchy.

On one of the last nights he spent at our house, he woke up yelling, "Fuck you! Fuck you!" And then he saw us standing in the doorway in our pajamas and realized where he was. I will never forget the look on his face. It was the imperious fury of a freak in a traveling show.

About nine months before Ren was shot, he and I attended a bar convention across the state. Jimster was eighteen then, and Mack had just turned sixteen. I had some trepidation about leaving the house to Mack all weekend, but was trying to coerce him into good behavior by the power of my understanding. If I conveyed trust, he'd have to give me a reason for it. That was the idea. It's what we do. Negotiate with our gangly, pimpled offspring as if we're all a bunch of diplomats. We keep scurrying after them, insisting we understand them, when we should probably just allow ourselves to be disdained for a few years. Our only job, after all, is to try to keep them alive and in possession of some future options.

However, there's simple cold power in drawing lines that are final — as we did with Jimster. And it's a perilous world out here.

When we came home, the house was empty. It was two o'clock in the morning. The familiar tick of worry began. Jails and emergency rooms. And then the anger. There goes sleep. Here comes an argument.

Ren was flying to Arizona the next morning to meet with a client and wanted to take his golf clubs. He went to the basement to find a putter his father had given him long ago, which he remembered as being better, weighted better, than the one in his own set. He stalked through the kitchen, clutching the putter, and tripped on the cat dish. "Christ!" he said, jabbing at the dish with his putter to push it back where it belonged. "I knew this was a bad idea. Those two."

The bar convention had been nonstop booze and chat. We were exhausted and befogged. He jabbed the putter at a denim shirt that lay on a kitchen stool and hoisted it aloft. "Jimster Reece's, I presume," he said. It was indeed Jimster's. I knew that shirt.

Ren began to march across the kitchen, the shirt on the putter like a wilted flag, when something fell out of the pocket and rolled across the floor. It was a cigar. A very good cigar. One of the bootleg Cuban cigars that a partner had passed around after the firm had won a round in the Recon spill case. The two hundred evacuees from the Homeview trailer court, including Jimster's dad, were part of a class action suit against the company.

Ren kept a box of the bootleg cigars in a humidor at the back of his desk drawer. He locked the drawer but left the key in it, for some reason I've never been able to fathom. Maybe simply to say, Only the key owner turns the key.

So there was a cigar from that drawer in the pocket of Jimster's grimy shirt.

Ren marched into his study and unlocked the drawer. He pulled it all the way out. He opened the humidor and verified the theft. "Well, shit," he said. He sat down at the desk, looking exhausted, the putter across his knees. I tried to smile in a sympathetic, cajoling sort of way.

"They were just messing around," I said. Ren looked at me.

"Granted, he shouldn't have taken it." I didn't know what else to say. "He probably did it on a dare. Mack dared him."

Ren got up, heaved a sigh, putted an imaginary ball across the rug. His movements were meticulous, controlled. I thought, incongruously, how handsome he looked in his good suit. How curly and thick his graying hair was.

"I don't care," he said. "I don't care what the reason was, what the hell transpired. And I really don't want to stand here listening to you trot out excuses for him. He turned the key in my desk drawer. He reached back and found that box and opened it and helped himself to one of my cigars. He put the cigar in his pocket and shut the drawer and locked it. What exactly is it that I have to understand here?" His voice was taut. "What do I have to understand beyond the fact that a kid who's eaten at my table, slept under my roof, borrowed my damn car — that he's willing to steal from me? What do I have to understand beyond that?"

I had nothing to say then. And I had nothing to say when the boys returned an hour later and Ren summoned Jimster out to the garage and Mack went to his room and slammed the door.

Jimster drove off in his pickup, very loudly. It had begun to snow lightly, and his pickup swerved a little as it took the slick corner. I said nothing to Ren. During the next few weeks I called Jimster's apartment, but never got an answer. I called a lot. And then I stopped trying.

I let him go. I let Jimster Reece go. I supported Ren in his dismissal of our almost-child, because I was too afraid not to.

Sometimes your life turns a long corner. While it's happening, you feel that your existence has inexplicably tipped up on its side as it speeds forward, and all you can do is hang on. Later, as if you watched an accident in slow motion, you see the beginnings.

It begins with Ren and me in a slow drift away from each other, a drift with the horrific dreaminess of a rip tide. You swim briskly toward shore, cheerfully and habitually and confidently, and notice that you are not advancing. You are, in fact, moving away, moving out toward the bottomlessness. Though all your motions say it should be otherwise.

We hadn't in a long time made love in any way that could be called a fervent hello. Though a routine of sorts, the motions, remained in place. Ren's erotic life was his work life. That's what aroused and amazed him. What fueled him. He and I, in my bitterest moments, felt like calisthenics. And none of the ways in which I tried to change that situation seemed to work. And so I stopped trying, because I felt amiably resisted, buoyantly snubbed.

It begins, then, with loneliness and a body growing cool. And with the looming prospect of a home without children in it. And with my first intimations that — how can I say this? — the guy wires had been cut. I began to sense that the wires had been cut and the ceiling of my life was floating upward, to become a speck, to disappear in a terrible blink, leaving me entirely unsheltered. That zing of new knowledge down the bones.

And then, late one afternoon, a week before Ren kicked Jimster out, the kitchen door opened and Jimster Reece was calling for anyone at home. And I was.

"Hi, you," I said, ushering him in. I sat back down at the breakfast bar, where I was sipping a glass of wine. That's part of it too, of course. Reaching a point where you have a few drinks in any case and come up with the reasons afterward.

Jimster had a springy, high-colored look that day. The anger, the outrage, was tucked away, maybe gone. His face had cleared up and he wore a new ski jacket and his eyes looked calm. He had roughed up his grown-in hair with some kind of gel. It sat atop his pale face like a bad wig, which I knew was the intent, and the comic vulnerability of it touched me.

This was not the kid who had gulped down cornflakes at our

table; who had slept on the plaid sheets of Mack's bunk bed; who had looked so hollow-eyed that first year after his mother took off in order for her boy, in her coward's words, to get to know his father. (What was to know? Sorrow, dirt, a snoring man on the couch, a jar full of cash.) This was a new adult.

"Nice hair."

"Why, thank you," he said disingenuously. He smiled. It was as if we both waited for an engaging Jimster to say his next lines.

"So," he said. "Is Mack around?"

No, he wasn't. He'd left a message that he was at Tamara's for the evening and maybe the night. That message was followed by one from Ren. Big strategy session. He'd be late too.

"You look like you had a bad day," he said. This was a new kind of thing for Jimster to say to me. I thought, He has a girlfriend. He is delirious with sex. He feels expansive, bold, adult.

I pushed back a strand of hair. It fell down again and I tried to tuck it back into my hairclip, but it wouldn't stay, and so I impatiently unclipped the clip and let my hair fall around my face and shook it. When I looked up, Jimster was leaning against the counter, studying me.

"When did you buy that pickup truck?" I said sharply. "Did you get a good deal?"

"Bought it from a friend. Outrageous deal." He stood up and stretched.

"Would you like a beer?" I said. He was grown. He could have a beer. I got up, filled with some kind of crisp and maternal verve, or so it seemed at the time, and I got a beer for him, though he hadn't said yes or no.

His fingertips rested for a moment near his eye, as if he were making sure something was there.

"It's almost invisible," I said. "They did a good job on that scar. It looks nice."

"How can something that's gone look nice?" he said.

"*You* look nice," I said, tracing the absent dog-bite scar with my fingertips.

His face flushed. I rested the flat of my hand on his cheek. His eyes closed. And then they opened, and Jimster Reece and I kissed briefly, then again, like longtime lovers.

# 5

H<small>E COULD HAVE</small> done it. He and Ren and that particular night — it could all be made to fit.

Let's say, for the sake of a scenario, that Jimster parked that old beater pickup in a pool of halogen light at Towne Square, a few blocks from our house. He parks the truck and walks briskly toward our hushed and leafy street. He wears running clothes and thin gloves and a watch cap, and now he jogs gently, a young businessman or a lawyer getting some oxygen after a day of deals. He has a bandanna around his neck. His feet slap the sidewalk quietly. A police car passes, and he puts his head down to look hard at his luminous watch, logging his progress.

Near our house he slows to a walk, cooling down, it would seem. He stretches. He looks casually around. Small warm lights glow in our windows, but he knows they are on a timer. He ambles up to the garage and checks the small side window. The cars are gone. No one is home. He doglegs around the side deck and ducks through the trellis into the back yard. It is raining lightly. The rain will freeze by morning. He hears the faint mumble of the television, some tiny cheers of a tiny crowd, and smiles, unfooled. He's done all this before, but not at this particular house, so familiar even in the dark. He finds the key under its rock and lets himself in and walks straight to the wall panel and punches the numbers. And all the little eyes turn from red to green. The house is breached. His shoe squeaks on the tiles.

What does he think at this point? That he is in a kitchen where he has sat so many times in the daylight, talking? Does he smell the coffee, my basil plants, and think, How did I come to be here in the night, my fingertips electric?

The television sound disappears. He exhales slowly.

And then, like an echo of his long breath, the light in the recesses of the house grows dimmer. A bolt of adrenaline shoots through him. He freezes. This is all wrong. This is not how it works. The lights go on, they go off; the television murmurs, then doesn't murmur. But not this. This is a human presence, this slow muffling of the light.

The creak of a floorboard. The slow sound of a drawer. His blood begins a frantic thumping in his ears. He pulls the bandanna over his lower face. And why does he not then simply leave? Go away? Leave the kitchen, the yard? Sprint down the alley and onto the street, bandanna down around his neck again?

Why does he not run lightly in the dark, back to his little truck? Is it because he is filled with hatred, the kind that can only advance?

He begins to move toward the person who has dimmed the light, who has opened the drawer. He slides along the wall of the dark dining room and peers across the foyer, and he sees Ren's back. Ren in his old gray cashmere, his slacks, his stocking feet, facing the direction from which he thought he heard the sound. The light from the television flickers across him.

Ren turns, the gun extended chest high. Jimster leaps toward him, and Ren is now toppled. The gun clatters off the coffee table, and they are both scrambling for it. And they both reach it, and it fires.

Red panic. Now Ren is no one he has ever seen. Ren is the groaning, bleeding stranger on the floor.

He runs, he fades into the dark, a huffing jogger again. Back in the battered truck, he tears out of the lot, cursing the loud muffler.

And where does he go then? Does he drive west of town on the frontage road, watching the speedometer, hearing tiny sirens on the edges of everything? Does he think, I have slept in that house? And does he then remember how he woke up disoriented and pulled the sheet up over his nose and it smelled good, like rich people's clothes dryers? And he thought, for just a moment, I am here where I belong. Then the next thought always came: This is not my home. And that was the one that always felled him, because he realized he lived the flip-side existence of the way a lucky person woke up. The lucky person's first thought: What awful place have I been? Then relief: I'm home. I'm safe.

For him, it was reversed. Waking produced fear.

And now there was a man on the carpet, bleeding.

# 6

A FRIEND ONCE TOLD ME about a man he knew in northern Minnesota who sailed iceboats — sailboats with runners. You catch the wind and the boat razors across the ice, the only sounds the scrape of the big blades, the flutter and snap of the sail.

This sailor had an uncanny ability to gauge the solidity of ice. He would start where the ice was firm, catch the wind, and race toward thinness. The big cloth grew taut and he leaned out for ballast, trying for the highest tension, the greatest speed. He tore through the metallic brilliance, nearly blind with wind and light. And as the iced thinned, the sound changed. He thought, Delicacy. The word was precisely the new sound. He heard it and tears crystallized in the corners of his eyes. High speed kept the boat just light enough to fly across the delicacy, the faintest sweep across a humming nerve. And then the firm, deep scraping began again, and he looked behind him to see the ice broken into shards. It was chunks of glass in black water.

One morning, not long after we banned Jimster Reece from our home, I stood on the back deck of our handsome house and I looked out over the yard and I realized that my interior self, the self I did not present to the world or even to those closest to me, seemed to have burned out. It was gray sticks and ashes. This happens. You thought there was a light under your bushel basket, but you were wrong.

The dead twigs, arranged in a small pile behind my breastbone, struck me in my better moments as a detail in a rather elaborate art installation. In one corner, the American family sits on a cedar deck at dusk, the father in his lawyer suit, the son in his own mocking suit, with his fake bride at his side, the mother with her heart of cool twigs. Not far away, the banned stepson. He looks hard at the mother; the mother looks away. Next door, an elderly man in a red baseball cap mists his lawn with weed poison. The poison floats upward and mingles with sound waves coming from a clock tower at Towne Square. The tower emits recorded bells, digitalized bells playing "Comin' Through the Rye." The gagged derivative riff and the weedkiller intertwine, and it all floats onto the little family on the cedar deck, the banned boy nearby. The mother tastes a metallic film on her teeth, and her voice becomes all hollowhappy like the bells.

Inside the house, on oak wainscoting, is a photo of the mother seventeen years earlier, her long hair flying. She kisses a wild-haired man with Ben Franklin eyeglasses. A windy kiss on an all-is-possible day.

The neighbor who is spraying his lawn just installed a burglar alarm that sounds like a barking dog. It goes off at odd times because the neighbor hasn't installed it right. Now, to the family, all barking dogs sound like burglar alarms.

Inside the mother's head are photos and newspaper clippings: a street child in São Paulo holds a cigarette and sucks a pacifier; parents of six-year-old autistic triplets petition to keep them together in a public school; "The teen suicide rate is 95 percent higher than it was in 1970," says the director of the Institute for Innovation in Social Policy at Fordham Graduate Center in Tarrytown, New York.

Mostly, though, she sees herself in a sunlit kitchen with her arms around a tall boy she is about to kiss in a way that is unforgivable. And she feels, watching that image, that her existence has become permeated by something very cold and very fast. The unlit killer-eye scans the deep water, hauling our lives behind it, an idea that makes her sad, makes her quiet. Makes her think about starting all over again, new.

# 7

At first it felt like a game, a peculiar combination of a scavenger hunt and a masquerade. More practically, I told myself it might be research. I would do it, then write about it, and perhaps sell the story to a magazine. At the time, I was working to complete a degree in art history at the university, and I also edited a newsletter for the local speakers' bureau. I wanted to branch out.

One day I drove down the long valley south of our town to interview a businessman from San Francisco who was scheduled to give a talk arranged by the speakers' bureau. He and his wife spend a week or so, now and then, in their log palace in the woods, a five-thousand-square-foot faux-rustic monstrosity. This was a man who had bought the right stock at the right time, married fortuitously, and now managed hedge fund investments for a big firm on the coast. He called the log palace his fishing cabin.

It was a tedious visit. The two of them made all the predictable just-folks kind of chitchat while they steered me among thousands of dollars' worth of custom-crafted pine furniture, Zuni pottery, Navajo wools, cathedral windows, multiple fireplaces made of local river rock. At the end of it, I drove through their two security gates, down the winding mountain road. A crew had torn up a portion of the road and I traveled for two miles through a cloud of grit. My contact lenses couldn't handle it and I pulled over, when the pavement started, to take them out and put on the eyeglasses I kept in the glove compartment and rarely wore. I felt filthy and red-eyed. I pulled my hair back in a knot, then tied a paisley scarf over it all.

In a town that lies on the valley floor about an hour south of my home, I bought a cup of coffee. Next to the coffee shop was a mom-and-pop mail shop, one of those places where you can package, copy, and mail. The hallway into the store had mailboxes for rent. I stopped there to buy some stamps and asked the woman at the counter if the boxes had a post office number or an address or what. It was an idle question. I think it was an idle question.

She told me the boxes were a mail drop and the address was a street address. "It's a service for our customers," she said gravely. "We have a lot of people around here who have their own good reasons for being, shall we say, somewhat out of touch. Somewhat hard to reach. They don't want the government, for instance, to be able to track them down wherever they go." She seemed to be trying to read my face.

"I imagine so," I said. "That's the valley, right? A lot of people from other places. A lot of constitutionalists, or whatever it is they call themselves."

"Your occasional bigamist," she said, a little smile playing on her face. "Your tax evader. Your loner. Your runaway father." She handed me a receipt. "Not that we encourage any breaking of the law. It's a privacy issue. Ours is not to ask."

She was a salty woman who looked as if she spent most of her time outdoors. Her voice was deep and gravelly and in some peculiar way comforting. It was a disappearing kind of voice, the heavy smoker's voice. In fifty years, I thought, that voice will be an artifact.

"I'm new to the area," I said, surprising myself. I do lie sometimes, but I rarely lie casually. "Can any regular nonprivate person rent one of these boxes just because she expects to have a few different addresses in the next year? While she's looking for a job and the right place to live?"

"Well, sure," the woman said. "It's just a more ordinary reason than some." We both laughed.

The next day I went to the library and looked through newspaper microfilms, reading obituaries. The one I found was two years old. A woman a year younger than I am had been killed in a car wreck over in the eastern part of the state. She had been born in our town, but moved to a ranch over east when she married at age twenty.

I went to the courthouse and told the clerk I was doing some genealogical research and wondered if I could get a copy of the birth certificate of that woman, who was a distant cousin. I acted apologetic for taking up anyone's time. The clerk said I couldn't get a photocopy, but six dollars would buy me a certified copy. Whatever, I said.

I walked out with a birth certificate for Jeanne Anne Thompson.

In her obituary photo, Jeanne Anne has a peculiar, acute look on her face, as though she is watching an oncoming truck but doesn't yet know what it will do. We know, of course, but Jeanne Anne doesn't. Not for a few more moments. I liked that look, her alertness, and I liked, more than that, her ordinary forgettable name.

A week after I got the birth certificate, I drove down the valley to the mail drop and rented a box for Jeanne Thompson. I paid in cash. "See you, Jeanne," said the raspy-voiced clerk.

I should mention that I looked that day the way the clerk had first seen me. Eyeglasses. A scarf over my hair.

On my next trip to the valley town, I parked my car and walked a few blocks to the Department of Motor Vehicles. I identified myself as Jeanne Thompson and told the clerk I had spent my entire adult life in Manhattan and was one of those people who had forgotten how to drive a car. Now I was here in the land of drivers, and I had to become one myself. I needed a learner's permit.

She didn't say much; didn't really seem to see me. Didn't seem to pay any attention to my too-eager smile. She gave me a form to fill out, reminded me that I must drive at all times with a licensed driver, and told me to come back when I was ready to take the tests. She glanced a time or two at the big clock. The place was empty and she was ready to close it up for lunch.

It wasn't as difficult as I'd thought it might be to create a new identity. And it was a thrill. Step by step, it worked, and I grew amazed.

When my next credit card bills came, I filled out the form to add a cardholder to one of my accounts. The new holder was Jeanne Anne Thompson. Now she was connected to me on paper. But not, I thought, for long. And I was right. Three months later, the company would write to Jeanne at the mail drop and ask if she wanted her own card. She did. When the new card came for her, I canceled my own, effectively breaking the link between us.

I had lost my own Social Security card, so one day when Mack was in the shower, I slipped his card from his wallet. I copied it, then whited out the name and number, typed new ones in, signed Jeanne's name, copied the copy, and laminated it. At dinner I handed Mack's card to him. This fell out of your wallet, I said.

In the used-book store downtown, I had found a little book by an author called Anonymous, which told about choosing phony Social Security numbers. You need to be careful. The first three digits are the code for the area where the number was issued. I wanted that to jibe with Jeanne's life, so I made it do that. The next two digits indicate, in a complicated and coded way, when the number was issued. I chose the middle digits of my own number, so I wouldn't be flashing a card that said I got the number before I was born, say. Our numbers to this point were identical. For the last four digits, I reversed my own. Easy to remember.

I bought a wallet and had it monogrammed: JAT. I filled out the ID insert with Jeanne's name and the address of the mail drop, all in backward-slanting block letters.

One afternoon I drove down the valley to the Motor Vehicles office, showed them Jeanne's learner's permit, and said bravely that I was ready to be examined. I took the written exam and the driver's exam, hesitating just a bit on the parallel parking without actually botching it, and scored respectably on both. I gave them the mail-drop address. My photo shows me in glasses, my hair slicked into a tight knot at my neck.

To celebrate after the exam, I had passport photos taken at a nearby print shop and ordered business cards for Jeanne. Just the name and address, I said. I'm between occupations.

I used Jeanne's birth certificate and driver's license and the photos to apply for a passport, and it arrived in due time at the mail drop.

Now I had these things in the name of Jeanne Thompson: a monogrammed wallet with an identification card, a driver's license, a Social Security card, a credit card, business cards, a birth certificate, and a document that allowed me to move, as Jeanne Thompson, anywhere in the world.

# 8

OUR YARD then was simply a swath of lawn with some bushes along the edges. One day I thought about a curving path, some raised beds, a small arbor. I saw myself, at the end of this project, in a richer, more complicated setting, and it was an idea I could like. Also, it had occurred to me that any rekindling of myself might involve some gestures of investment — taking extraordinary care of the ordinary. So I called a number I had seen on the bulletin board of the health-food store where I buy my produce. A woman rasped something to me that I couldn't understand, and then a man's voice came on in subdued, halting English. He was the yard person, the gardener. His name was Yuri Petrov. A few days later he drove up in a battered red pickup with no muffler. The noise was incredible.

He turned off the engine, jumped out, and silently faced the yard, squinting at the lawn, hand over brow. I greeted him. He looked to be in his late thirties, though he had an odd streak of white in his hair and the frank wrinkles of someone a long time in the sun. His smile was quite beautiful. His incisors were rimmed with gold. We shook hands vigorously, then moved to the deck and discussed the yard.

He crossed his legs like a priest. His pants were ill-fitting, un-American. He wore black socks, canvas shoes with thick soles, a plaid long-sleeved shirt. I thought of the group I had seen at the airport one day when I was picking up Ren from a convention in Maui. A half-dozen off-kilter people got off the plane to be met by a half-dozen more who looked just like them. They were Russians who had migrated to Ukraine in the eighties, then had fled when the Chernobyl nuclear plant exploded. They relocated in Italy first, then made their way to America, to new lives in the country of their old enemy.

Several of the older women wore babushkas, dark dresses, and grim shoes. Peasants on a jet, immigrating to our town. The young girls at first glance looked fashionably retro, with their plastic purses, dowdy dresses, poodle barrettes, white cotton anklets. Then I realized that they wore their clothes without irony. This was simply what seemed American to them and what they had been able to obtain. Unlike Mack and Tamara, they weren't commenting. Just watching them, I felt a small leap of relief.

Yuri Petrov came to our house three mornings a week for most of last summer. I talked with him often. Sometimes I sauntered out in the early sunlight to consult with him about what plants might go where. We sat on the deck and had coffee in oversized mugs. He smiled affectionately at their American excess. Like the people at the airport, he seemed both too young and too old for this world.

I could talk about this next part in the usual sorts of ways. The growing capillarian alertness, the unvoiced conversations, the urge to rerun small moments. That feeling of being watched and of watching yourself with a new tenderness and wariness.

I could tell you about a sweat-sheened neck and the way I wanted to rest my cool fingertips on a place that was beginning to burn. I could talk about physical eloquence, the way some people seem to inhabit rather than present their bodies.

I could say I became, in a matter of days and to my large surprise, extravagantly infatuated with the Russian in my garden.

Some kind of conversation seems to begin beneath whatever is being literally said. Our speaking voices go into voiceover and another conversation begins. It is the murmuring of calm, telepathic aliens. It's the real conversation and the only one, the way the semaphore, clear and specific, is the only real message, no matter how much the flag-holder also shouts.

Or so it seems. Though like everything about this state, embarrassment and chagrin are a hair away. You think it's a conversation, but it might only be your own underwater voice coming back to you. Quite possibly you're a fool. Quite possibly you're getting nothing back but your own signals, your own bat sonar. The bat-beeps assess the dimensions of the black cave and come back sounding like another's voice. You could mistake your own echo for a response. That's the fear.

There's that first moment, when the blinds on the eyes go away.

There's that second moment, when you look at him again and think, Oh. Light behind a shock of hair. A line from the eye, a squint line. You think, I would trace that delicate timeline with my fingertip, the line that started decades ago with a child's sun-reddened body splashing in the sea. His shouting laugh. His big, new-toothed smile.

You begin to imagine all his lives. There is the sunburned boy in the sea, and look at him: he keeps dunking himself just so he can come up shouting. There is a certain obsessiveness to it, a way of losing himself in the rhythm of his own plunge until he finally shakes the water off his head like a little dog.

There's the set of his jaw when a teacher chastises him, the way he listens to her papery words and to the bored singsong responses of his comrades, his thoughts fixed on a bird. The harpy eagle. He saw a harpy eagle in a book and is desperate to see one in waking life. He loves birds. He makes drawings of them that contain a confident swiftness, a kinetic accuracy no one quite recognizes but himself, the eight-year-old. He thinks about them: how a taloned eagle perches somewhere high on a branch where he can't see it but it can see him, and it feels a comradeship with him, an akinness, and he with it. But this is his secret, because others would laugh.

I'm forty-seven years old, I thought, amused and aghast. These thoughts, they're like the onset of a childhood disease like the mumps. Fierce and ridiculous in an adult. Silly and filled with danger. I batted them away at first. I tried to brush them off myself, those garish winged things that had mistaken me for their twig.

The tendons in his teenage wrist as he pitches a pillow, a rock. His young-man hands on a girl's hips, pulling her to him, leaning back to see how her face registers his hardness, his fluttering blood. Around the two of them, the modern little city Pripyat, full of engineers and pregnant women. All those babies, those prams, glittering on the surface of the creaking stone mass that is the Soviet Union, already fissuring with a hiss. Chernobyl, not far away, becomes a radiant clawing cloud, and long-legged Yuri is running, running, trying to lift off like his birds.

A wrist with fine dark hairs. The way a wrist can be intelligent. You watch a mouth talk, say something ordinary like Who knows? and your reply sounds so happy you scarcely recognize it, and you think, I could kiss you into stunned silence.

It feels true. True in the sense that what has dropped away seems untrue. True in the sense that the body comes alive in a way that is not easy to call insignificant.

Each gesture is a clue to the lexicon of the beloved.

Here is another country.

The yard took shape. We became collaborators, meeting at the beginning of each day to draw a new design. An idea for a particular corner. He and I talked often about an all-white flowerbed we'd planned for one corner of the yard — a grouping that would stay bright after dusk. We discussed the details of its long border.

We planned another bed of iris. Yuri would build a stone wall across the back of the yard with big river rocks in colors of dusty pink, muted green. In front of the wall, he would make a raised bed four feet wide, a bed that would catch most of the day's sun. The rock wall would be the backdrop for masses of tall white *Gypsophila perfecta,* which would stand behind drifts of bearded iris in shades of pale blue to darkest blue. Footing the iris would be a low spreading *Gypsophila* 'Pink Fairy'. A curtain of snow-in-summer would hang down over the bed's retaining wall to provide silver-gray edging.

"I can see this bed inside my head," Yuri said late one afternoon.

I went inside, needing something systematic and energetic to do, some equivalent of the job Yuri now took on, which was to dig up the sod where the raised bed would go. He dug vigorously, pushing his whole weight onto the shovel, wiggling it, lifting out a patch of grass and dirt, which he placed to the side. Each time he stepped hard on the shovel, his whole body jumped a little.

I chopped tomatoes and peppers for gazpacho, mixed a batch, and filled the sink to wash up by hand. This is the ridiculous, gothic part: thinking I was finished, I closed my eyes and felt beneath the suds for anything I'd missed, and grasped my big knife, hard, by the blade. The sink water very quickly turned pink.

I pressed a dishtowel against the gash, but the knife was sharp and the cut was deep. Blood quickly saturated the cloth. I couldn't make it stop. I grabbed another towel, pressed it to the cut, and ran into the yard, scared now. Yuri turned, startled, and I held my swaddled hand out to him. "It won't stop," I said. "I can't make it stop."

He cradled my arm, pressed his hand down hard on the towel, seemed to listen. "No," he said rather loudly, as if someone had called out a question. He retrieved a bandanna from his pants pocket and tied a tourniquet. He put my hand back on the towel. "Push again," he said. "I think we must visit to the hospital."

"I need to lock the door," I said. Which I did. Quite calmly I walked into the house, set the alarm, and locked the door on my way out — a precaution that struck me later as deeply peculiar. I think I had some idea that the dangers of that day, so suddenly manifest, could be neutralized by observing the forms of protection. Drops of blood fell on the kitchen tiles, on the deck, on the grass, but they were falling more slowly than they had.

Yuri had started his pickup. He pushed open the passenger door and I got in, and we roared away.

They stitched me up and gave me a shot. It seemed to take a long time. A man was raving in the next room, his shouts leaping across the murmurs of his attendants. He seemed almost to be barking. Finally he stopped. Finally they were done with my hand.

I walked into the lobby, looked around for Yuri, and spotted him outside. He sat on the fender of his truck, smoking a cigarette. He looked up as I came through the doors and watched me walk toward him. He looked at my face, at my bandaged hand, at my face again. It was a quiet blue evening, and the dropping sun made the windows of the hospital flare orange, like furnaces. He stood and I walked to him and he put his hand on my bare upper arm. I tipped my head forward and rested it for just a moment at the hollow of his neck. And then we got into the pickup and went to my home. We said nothing.

He parked his pickup. We both got out and I retrieved the key from its rock by the back step. Ren and Mack weren't home yet, but they would be soon. I unlocked the door, and Yuri and I walked into the kitchen. I went to the panel and punched the numbers that prevented the alarm from sounding, saying them aloud.

I wanted to offer him something. I know that now. I wanted to offer him access.

I took his hand and examined my dried blood on his fingertips.

"So," he said, a small crack in his voice. He ran a hand down the back of my head, and up again, his fingers combing my hair into strands that he could pull lightly.

A stepping back, both of us, to read the other's face. That silence. The sound of a long blade on breaking ice.

# 9

THERE IS A COPSE of quaking aspens not so far from the Trocadero lot, toward the river, and its birds make a small roar at dawn — the headmistress robins, the off-key chickadees, and, this morning, a couple of raucous crows, real screamers. I listened to them for a while, then took a shower and got back into bed to shore up my nerve. The curtain was open a little so I could watch the peachy sun pull its way up the sky.

I thought of the other people sleeping under this roof, finishing their last dreams. There would be a salesman somewhere down the hall, a guy in his forties, pudgy from all those hours in the car. Last night he saw something in a movie or a phone company ad that made him think how much he loved his wife, which was really another way of thinking about how much he needed to hear that she loved him. So he called her, and it was a hundred degrees where she was, and one of the kids had hit a neighbor kid so hard the kid had to have stitches. He found himself clueless about how to say how much he loved her, how even to offer some comfort, because he had been counting so much on tenderness for himself. So he said a completely maladroit thing, and she said a hasty and cruel thing, and they both hung up and sat for a while in their chairs, blinking back tears. He finally fell asleep during *The Guns of Navarone*.

A few doors down from him is a priest, perhaps. A silver-haired priest with a tan. He is in town to set up some kind of church conference, but the real reason is that the college parish has a new young assistant who radiates such joy, such untroubled sexuality, that the priest with the silver hair has become convinced, for the first time, that real happiness is possible on this earth, and that the younger priest holds some mysterious knowledge about how it is transmitted. He wants him with a hunger that cannot begin to be prayed away. But he tries, and then he gets drunk, and now he has passed out on top of the covers in a bathrobe his sister sent him. It has ships all over it and a crown on the pocket.

Next door to him is a young woman on her first trip as a sales rep for a pharmaceutical company. Mostly she sells antianxiety drugs and a new antidepressant that spares the libido. She is already up, and has pressed her pale cotton suit and tucked an extra pair of hose into her purse. She has taken a long bath. She has made her sales speech to herself in the mirror. She is giddy with her own prospects.

Last night she slept on her back, cool teabags on her eyes. Before sleep she watched a dumb movie and laughed out loud, just to laugh. She called her mother at their farm up by Canada and made little notes on the writing pad, a vision in her mind of a professional woman making notes. She wrote her mother's words, just to be using the writing pad: *Floyd. Bad axle. May. Jail. Check.* She is not vulnerable to any of it. And feeling her invulnerability, she is tender toward them all. She put the pad in her briefcase, where she will also put the miniature shampoo and the shower cap and the little soap. She practiced her signature, adding a new bit of flamboyance. Larger capitals. Yes. A large round *C*, warm but imposing.

And is it possible that Mary-Doris and Ed are back? Maybe they checked in late last night. Halfway home, they learned that the daughter's reconciliation with her husband was a bust and she has thrown him out for good. She's so distraught, she needs assistance. So here they are, ready to take the grandkids with them to the desert for a vacation from their hapless mother. The old people are exhausted already at the prospect. They lie on the big bed on their backs, breathing hard, dreaming their separate versions of a daughter who has grown so large and so hungry that they have to give her away.

I got up and dressed slowly and pinned on my gray wig. No lipstick, so my mouth looked tired. I shadowed the lines beside my mouth, between my eyes.

In the lobby, Gerrald surveyed me carefully. His skin looked bloodless.

"Hi, hon," he said.

"Are you all right?" I asked.

"Just tired as all holy hell," he said. "Need some iron in my blood or something." There were some envelopes on the counter. They were addressed to a dating service run by the weekly newspaper. The whites of his eyes had a pink tinge.

It was a pale morning, very quiet. I walked over the bridge and passed two joggers, one a girl of maybe twenty, black braid snapping up and down behind her like a pretty whip, and the other a crewcut runner about my age. He had the ravaged look of a marathoner. When we passed, he consulted his watch. I heard tiny little beeps. Had I looked like Francesca, I think he would at least have acknowledged my presence with a curt, athletic nod. Had I been a dog, I think he would have glanced at me. It's a revelation, the invisibility of age.

When I reached the university area, I slowed my walk. It was about ten o'clock. Ren is at therapy by nine-thirty on weekdays. I walked very slowly and added a small limp, a hitch really, that way of catching your walk just before the pain hits. Somewhere a few blocks away, a lawn mower droned. The maples were rustling and opulent.

The solid old houses were set back farther than I had noticed before, their eyelids hooded like those of sleek dozing cats. A tiny lady with a pink sweater and a white bun sat in a window of a rigorous Georgian I've always particularly liked. She sipped something from a huge fast-food cup. It seemed I should know who she was — she looked as if she had been sitting in that window for a lifetime — but I didn't. There are many people in my neighborhood who are strangers to me.

To feel more confidence, I concocted a scenario for myself. What was I? What was I doing here? Well, I was a caretaker for an old crippled woman who lived just a few more blocks away. I walked today because my car needed a tuneup and I needed the exercise. The newspaper said people with arthritic hips needed to keep moving, within reasonable limits, so I was. I felt the eyes of the woman in the Georgian appraising me. Stranger, her brain said. There she goes. All clear.

As I drew closer to my house, I ran down the checklist in my head. Ren at therapy. Mack at school, unless his motorbike was there. Elise at work. And the other neighbors? Dick Shields, the widower with the weed poison, went somewhere in the morning, most mornings. And the new couple left for work by eight-thirty. And the others on the block? A high school teacher, single, with a trust fund that had bought him the house — he would be gone. The retirees on the corner, Jack and Gladys Puermutter — they might be a problem. Jack was a raker. He has some kind of obsessive disorder and rakes when there are no leaves. Yes, there he was at the end of the block, raking. He raked very slowly, very beautifully, like the monks who rake the sand outside those big wats in Bangkok. I wouldn't be able to enter my front door. Not with Mr. Puermutter four houses away, raking. An old woman on foot walking right into the Woodbridge house might give even Mr. Puermutter pause.

I'd have to circle the house and enter the back door. I'd have to be rapid about this. Very brisk.

No motorbike in the driveway. Therefore no Mack.

But what if I walk into my house and there, somehow, is my son, eating toast in the kitchen? Or my husband, lying on the couch trying to be interested in a television show?

I can see the sheer fright, the panic, on their faces as they watch me enter my house, more than a week before I'm due, a lumpy old woman with a head of gray hair who speaks in the voice of the sleek Francesca Woodbridge. *Hello, my husband. Hello, my son.*

I watch their faces flicker in tandem through alarm, disbelief, defense, recognition — and what is that last expression, exactly? A kind of pitying shame. Estranged forever through pity, I will no longer be a decipherable person. I will be crazy beyond a doubt, and the crazy rarely get welcomed back. They've scared us too much.

My feet are too loud on the gravel. And now Roberta, Elise's dog, bounds stiffly over to the fence, her tail going like a metronome. She whines her greeting. I whisper urgently to her, asking her not to bark. Yes! I murmur. Nice day! Gotta go!

I take several huge gulps of air and walk rapidly across my back lawn and remove the key from beneath the rock, put it in the lock, turn it. Now I must keep moving. If the right numbers aren't pressed in fifteen seconds, the alarm will blare. The security team will come, fanning out across the neighborhood, and they will find me in this state.

Halfway across the kitchen to the alarm panel, my foot rockets ahead of me on a patch of grease. I flail and fall, smacking my elbow hard, twisting my knee. Almost in the same motion I'm back on my feet, scrambling. The seconds tick down. I reach the panel of buttons and stare at it. Think, I urge myself. My fingers are slick with sweat and they shake. I punch the numbers — Mack's birthdate — forcing myself to go slowly enough not to make a mistake.

Quiet.

I limp to the breakfast bar and sit down. I'm inside. An old woman, I am inside.

Some minutes pass. A shard of light slants through the window onto my foot, warming it. I move a little so that it falls onto my wrenched knee. It feels like a mother's hand. My motel room, its chill dimness, falls away. All my recent rooms do, including the one in which I imagine Gerrald at the end of each day. That one has a low ceiling, muddy colors, a couch with two cats on it, a big console television. Crooked shades. A plastic flower in a vase that was there when he moved in. Big boxes of catfood in the cupboard, and a case of Pepsi. The one light in the living room is too bright and makes every surface harsh, all the shadows inky. That sad room I seem to see.

But this room, this kitchen, is beautiful. It is cool and dappled and graceful. On the terra-cotta tiles, a rainbow quivers, shuts down small, opens up again. The cookie jar with the big chicken on it sits in its corner. It sat on a counter in my mother's kitchen out in the wheatlands when I was a child. My friend Siobhan and I — Siobhan, the computer whiz in Seattle — used to crawl onto the counter for cookies. Once, finding her favorite snickerdoodles, Siobhan put her arms around the jar and hugged it. "I love you, my big chicken!" she said.

Ren's father once walked through this door and sat at this breakfast bar in his suit. Mack, age three, came bounding in. This was his dramatic phase. He threw his arms out like an impresario. "You're just what I *wanted*," he cried to his grandfather, who looked the happiest, at that moment, that I ever saw him.

Once I filled a small clear bowl with plums and apricots — the plums dusky, the apricots humming with light — and Elise stroked them with the very tip of her finger as we talked about something ordinary. Her fingertip just brushed over the tops of them, steadily, unconsciously.

Sometimes when Ren did the dishes, he wrapped himself in his ridiculous barbecue apron and sang loudly, like he did in the shower. That was quite a long time ago, that singing — more than a few years.

The French doors opening onto the cedar deck make a wall of light. Beyond them stretches my smooth lawn and the raised beds. The walls of my kitchen are the palest lemon yellow, the white trim crisp. My box of herbs sits above the sink. I pinch off the thyme and smell Greece. The other faint smells: bread, fresh basil, coffee. My bird feeder outside the sink window, and on it right now a chickadee, its two-note call the essence of coaxing without expectation.

Perhaps I'll simply go upstairs, remove my costume and hide it, take a long bath with lavender salts. Put on my new silk robe and sip coffee with fresh cream from a cobalt-colored mug. My hand as I raise the cup to my mouth will smell faintly of lavender. The white robe will nestle me. The coffee will be heaven. On public radio, a pure-voiced boy will sing Mahler.

Oh, I will think, I lost the capacity to pay attention. I was not paying attention to all that was available to me.

I can do that. I can simply say, I came home early. I missed you. I wanted to be here and I came home. If I quickly go to my room and discard my disguise and put on something from my own closet, I will simply be here, my familiar self. It could be done.

My knee hurts. I limp through the hallway, past the long mirror, and catch sight of an old woman followed by a cat. Ragamuffin sashays up to me and throws her flank against my pant leg and rubs. She pivots and runs the side of her head along the same spot. Her throat rumbles voluptuously. "Hi, Rags," I say softly. She stretches languorously, deeply, then flops over on her back and stretches again, her white stomach offered to my hand. "You're so unseemly," I tell her. "You're such a strumpet." She sits up, pins her fluffy tail to the floor, and licks it furiously.

Sometimes it's as if there's a whole life going on down in the orchestra pit that's far more interesting in its details than all the posturing and speeches up on the stage. Plants are down there, and animals, and running water, and children talking to themselves. In her own system, Rags is very, very busy.

My house seems immensely solid to me, the walls extraordinarily thick. The furniture looks planted, inviting, the carpet warm. The details — photos, pillows, books — are vivid and energetic, the accents of interesting lives. I have lived here sixteen years. Under this roof with my husband and my son. We have slept more than six thousand sleeps apiece under this roof. That counts for something. Whatever else we are, we are each other's home.

The door to Ren's study is shut, and that isn't right. Every sound in the house now grows louder: the tock of the clock in the hall, the faintest *pling* of water dripping into the kitchen sink, the hum of the refrigerator. And behind those sounds there are breaths. Nearly imperceptible, but there. Steady breathing.

Against every instinct, I turn the knob slowly. I push.

Ren's study is lined with bookshelves, their interiors painted a dark green. His big desk faces the center of the room and sits at right angles to the couch. The couch faces the television and an angled wingback chair. A new rug has replaced the one that was stained when he was shot.

My son lies on the couch, deeply asleep, arms flung over his head. The room smells faintly sweetish, like cheap wine. He wears his suit, the necktie pulled loose. His hat is on the floor. It's a large couch, eight feet, leather. Mack is tiny on it. He breathes exhaustedly.

I can think of no reason. Did he come in just after his father left? Drunkenly make himself a breakfast? Pass out? Where is his motorcycle? No one has ever before looked so old, so young, and so lonely. But I don't plan to stay.

Ragamuffin pads into the room and jumps onto the couch and settles herself on his chest, purring loudly. He moans softly. I slowly, very slowly, walk backward. His arm rises from his side and he strokes the cat, and the arm falls down again. His breathing sounds a little lighter. His eyes stay closed.

A careful step backward, and another. I inch the door closed, watch my son's form go away, part of the big desk disappear. All that remains is the corner with the photograph of Ren and his parents the day he left for college. There is his mother, racked by multiple sclerosis, a bitter invalid in her chair. There is his kind father, who will later be shot by a stranger. There is Ren, wild-haired and hopeful, between them. And now he is the reincarnation of both of them. What defeat — to reach the time of one's prime and suddenly embody the saddest reversals of your parents.

Behind me, the phone rings. A bolt shoots through my body and freezes me. Two, four, five times. The answering machine clicks on. My voice: "Any messages for Francesca, Ren, or Mack? Leave them after the tone." She is so very sprightly, that person.

The caller seems to pause. Says nothing.

I listen for any stirrings from Mack. The house is a tomb.

In the kitchen is a shelf that is jubilantly strewn with souvenirs of our trips, a few photos, some carefully spontaneous clutter. And at the back of that shelf, almost hidden by a photo of Mack at a more exuberant age, his tongue stuck out at the camera, is a small silver box on four feet. I found the little casket at an estate sale and got it for a song, though it is real silver and quite old. It's filled with dust from the Mount St. Helens volcano — dust that chalked our town for days and that Ren scooped into a little bag for posterity.

This is what I need: something that is uniquely ours, something that looks somewhat valuable but wouldn't be quickly missed. This is what I will use to deflect attention from Jimster

Reece. The police will find this little casket in the possession of a better culprit.

I shove the box into my big straw purse. And then, my hands shaking so badly I can barely move my finger, I reset the security alarm. Out the back door. The key under the rock. I run, adrenaline erasing the pain in my knee.

A few blocks away, I catch a bus downtown and walk toward the Trocadero from there. By then the shooting pains are back. I'm exhausted. An elderly man sees my slow limp and offers me a ride. I take it, breathing raggedly. He seems relieved to deposit me and wishes me good luck with the rest of my life.

# 10

A MAY SOFTBALL GAME in 1980, the late day warm in the sun, cool in the shade. Lilacs in bloom, thwack of the bat, a big ordinary sky with oval clouds moving in busy silence, like dirigibles.

The field is on the north side of town, across the road from a small wooded cemetery, an almost hidden place. At the far edge of the cemetery, a steep incline ends in the freeway. On backlit evenings, the combination of molten traffic, shady graves, and young men engaged in sport creates a visual parable, difficult to articulate.

Ren is out there in one of his team's new T-shirts, bluebird blue, still creased.

Eight years after college, I quit my public relations job in Seattle and moved to our town to coordinate publicity for an environmental group that focused on local issues. I needed a change, needed a better home. My most recent relationships had been with an amiable painter who tended bar at a place called Goosey's, then a married engineer who spent a good portion of our brief affair reading me bad poetry that he had written late at night. I had begun to talk in a conversational manner with my cat.

Ren Woodbridge, a good friend in college, had gone to law

school at Cornell, then taken a job somewhere in the West, maybe Idaho. That's all I knew.

Several weeks after I started my new job, I got a press release from the university about an upcoming conference sponsored by the law school, the county health department, and an organization of public defenders. The title was "What Poverty Costs Us All." My contact was Ren Woodbridge. The number was local. When I heard his voice, so sly and warm, I was shot with happiness.

Someone hits a home run and I clap too hard because I'm agitated. Ren and I, long-ago pals, have become lovers.

Six weeks earlier, we spent an evening with some of his friends, drinking beer on a restaurant deck by the river. As Ren drove me home, he and I had an argument about something, I forget what, that caused my face to flush, his voice to rise. I remember how strong an urge I had to bait him, to win this one. He wasn't giving in.

Finally he walked me to the door and kissed me mockingly on the cheek and I kissed him back, on the mouth, some kind of taunting cap to the argument. And there we were the next morning, amazed at ourselves, uneasy and self-mocking, sleepy-eyed over coffee.

It felt almost incestuous, but like something not to stop. There was awkwardness, shyness in our new alliance, and a kind of giddiness that made us tell stories, that made us laugh a lot. We were carried away with ourselves and slightly aghast, too, in a way you are when a friend moves into a new category.

He was spending most nights at my apartment now. We went to movies together and held hands on the way out. I joined the wives and girlfriends in the bleachers at his softball games. It was a calm and easy thing to do after work. Have a beer, chat a little, soak up the simple warmth of it all.

That day in May. About a half-hour into the game, the sky in the west began to dim. A growing wall of gray went up before the sun. Here comes rain, someone said. The wall grew and darkened, and some of us noticed that it had a different look from weather, but it seemed silly to say so. We just cheered louder. It's going to rain like hell when it rains, someone said. Ren's team scored a come-from-behind win, and we all popped beers and glanced at the odd, thick sky, then decided we'd go to the bar where the bartender, Cherise, always bought a round for the winning team.

The bar was a relentlessly functional place, dim and windowless, scattered with daytime drunks who seemed to know us when we filed in loudly, who seemed to be amused by our numbers and noise. I remember the gurgling underwater bleats of the poker machine, and the steel-bikinied amazon on the pinball machine. How very dark and stale-aired the bar was, and how the industrial carpet gave up the scent of old smoke and spilled beer. How there always seemed to be a man in a dirty jacket at the pay phone, a trucker with a big belly and a wallet on a chain, who wrote numbers on the wall. And the back-and-forth motion of Cherise, her soothing choreograph of delivered drinks, brisk plunges into the ice bin, the swipe with the bar rag, the long pull on her cigarette, a businesslike roll of the bar dice with a customer.

The players congratulated each other and replayed key moments in the game. I talked to one of the girlfriends about the chief merit of cats over dogs, which is that you can't break their hearts.

We must have been there for about an hour. No one came in. No one left. The television was off.

Franklin Klemenhagen, Tamara's father, was on the softball team. He was a lawyer then. He and Ren were both public defenders, both working for pennies, though in Franklin's case a trust fund removed some of the sting. The two of them appeared on behalf of indigents charged with burglary, rape, assault, criminal drunkenness, murder. They were idealistic, and they were smart. Their clients got a very good defense.

Franklin was quite a lot thinner in those days, and he had a kind of Irish-setter eagerness that seemed to desert him six years later, when he became a man of the cloth. His father was the vice president of a huge coal company and a fairly successful inventor as well. It's a terrible combination in a parent: financial triumph plus demonstrated creativity. All it really leaves, as a way for a son to compete and triumph without seeming to, is altruism. Is that too cynical? Is it too cynical to suggest that Franklin's particular father, combined with his own temperament and the temper of his college years, left him no other option than to become a do-gooder?

When we met them, Franklin's wife, Krystal, called herself Christine. They had been married three years. She'd become pregnant with Tamara's older sister, Ariel, and they'd had a wedding in a mountain glade with the bride in white muslin, a daisy wreath in her hair. She is a pretty, long-limbed woman with a face so perfectly even-featured it's hard to retain it in your mind. In those early days she literally sat at Franklin's feet at parties, a wanton madonna, her long skirt and her shawl draped as languidly as her long hair. Later she finished her degree and co-founded the local Montessori school. Over the years her skin has become more tissuey, her blond hair dimmed by gray. She still wears it in a long ponytail, or a bun with pretty little Japanese sticks in it.

When Ariel and Tamara were little, Krystal — who had re-named herself when Tamara was born — made all those aggressive health-food things: the leaden muffins, the soy shakes. I remember her feeding Tamara little particles of muffin in her high chair. When the child screamed — the muffins wreaked havoc in her small stomach — Krystal played her a tape of Gregorian chants.

·  ·  ·

Ren left the bar to get the scorebook from his car so an argument could be settled about what exactly had happened at the bottom of the fifth. I was feeling bloated from the beer and ready to leave, and the butterfly feeling was back. I'm getting the flu, I think, I said to a woman named Janice. I always get the flu in the spring, I said. It was a deeply uninteresting thing to say, and her little smile let me know it.

Cherise had turned on the TV. Someone talked from a desk, then someone else gestured at the state of Washington with a stick.

We heard Ren's shout from the parking lot and went to the door to look. I hoped the bad tire on his car hadn't gone flat again. Every breakdown then was a financial crisis.

Outside, ashes were falling. Ren stood beside his car, his hand flat to catch the sifting gray. He looked like a figure in the aftermath of a disaster, trying to catch the burnt remains of his former world, the world in which he'd worn the creased new softball shirt of bluebird blue.

There was a film of gray on all the cars, on the ground. The sky was queasy, sulfurous. It looked poisoned. I thought, Hanford. The Hanford nuclear plant, near the Tri-Cities in Washington State, has blown, and we downwind have just been irradiated. And no one even told us it was coming. No one warned us.

I thought of Hiroshima. Of the silence afterward, which made all other silences fraudulent.

"Don't touch that stuff," Cherise's excited voice called over my shoulder. She stood in the door, knock-kneed in her miniskirt, her face light green.

"The mountain blew — St. Helens in Washington. Blew its damn stack," she crowed. "Brush that stuff off your car and you'll scratch the paint to shit! It's like ground-up razors."

All color had fled. During that night and the next day, our town seemed to die. The trees turned gray, the streets white. A great hush fell on everything. The birds didn't know what to do, or maybe they had fled. All the chatter of pets, of birds, of little children, stopped. Everything was coated in talc. Sometimes during those next days I felt we were becoming archival, the way a movie scene will freeze, lose color, turn into a silvery photograph.

We drove home from the bar through the sifting blizzard of ash, headlights arrowing through the moving gray.

The radio said to keep all windows shut; paper masks were being distributed at the fire stations, and all were advised to wear them outside. Asthmatics, old people, were advised to wear them inside too.

It was too warm inside the apartment, too hot and stale. The streetlights came on in the premature night. We turned on the television and Ren had another beer. I lay down on the couch. We went to bed, but couldn't seem to touch each other. There was a feeling of watchfulness and disaster, and of *being* watched.

Ren fell quickly to sleep, which is what he does under stress. I lay awake, then got up because I seemed to hear a shushing sound. The radiators were cool. Was it the ash? I put my ear to the window, as I would to a seashell, and heard the faint roar. The streetlight was lurid orange through the white-leaved trees. What is the opposite of photosynthesis?

In the bathroom, I saw that I was crying. Under the sink was a box the size of a cake mix. I read the instructions. I peed in a plastic cup, hot urine running over my hand. I shook half the urine with a solution in a tube, put the tube in its holder, and put the holder behind a stack of books in my little study.

The next morning Ren and I pulled all the curtains shut so we wouldn't have to look at the strange movie outside. He called the office and said he'd be in to do a few things that couldn't wait.

When he left, it was ten o'clock. I tiptoed, for some peculiar reason, to the stack of books. My coffee had turned rancid in my mouth and stomach. The tube held, as I knew it would, a perfect little Saturn ring. I was pregnant.

I guarded my secret for two days, trapped in that sweaty apartment with ash sifting into small piles in the corners of the window ledges. Outside, figures now and then walked slowly along the sidewalk in white masks. I drove to the grocery store. The town looked seared, emptied out, irreparable. It seemed sometimes that we were all peering through the ash, looking for someone to know, our bones aglow. I tasted a borderless nausea.

In the supermarket, there was none of the raucousness of an ordinary communal emergency, that sense of banding together against temporary, dramatic adversity. I don't remember it, anyway. I remember quiet. Tires making tracks through fine ash. Everything old.

Finally, I told Ren. He stood for a moment, immobile, the coffeepot hoisted. Something about our situation seemed to me make-believe, not to be credited. I remembered that first time we had made love and how I had made a drunken calculation in my head about the chances of a ready egg. Virtually nil. Virtually. Subsequent times, I'd been protected to the gills.

A hasty calculation, a fury of need, and should a child be born out of that? Well, of course they are all the time.

This is the part I wonder about now. Why did I become so crisp? So intent on a fast decision? I felt that a child would make us a couple in a way we both found impossible to accept at that point, though I look back now and wonder if I made room in the decision for Ren at all. Did I put up a screen that was impenetrable? And did that allow him to defer to my plan, which was in fact the course he wanted me to take? He could tell himself generously that it was my body and my decision. He could, with a clear conscience, then forgo the fatherhood he didn't want anyway.

I don't know. I don't know precisely what he thought. I remember standing at the window and watching his lonely back as he walked into the gray to the bus. I know now, I should have called him back. I think it would have made a big difference, even now.

A week later I sat in the waiting room of a clinic, filling out a questionnaire. I had a brief consultation with a worker, a psychological evaluation. All I could think was that she looked like a horse. Her large teeth, her forelock of bangs. I was so cool, so no-nonsense, I think I intimidated her. She seemed relieved to send me to a different room.

The young doctor draped me, stirruped me, arranged his tools. This will cramp some. You tell us if it's too much.

The white-topped trees. Ren walking under them, a little hunched. They were part of it all. The world was dead; who could want to bring a child into it?

I examined the ceiling. I watched the gloved hand picking up a shiny instrument. And then I sat up. They looked at me warily. They'd seen last-minute outbursts and they were ready. They put on that practiced, willing-to-listen look.

"Is something the matter?" the doctor said. They'd already given me a Valium IV, so I was going to have trouble caring enough to do what I had to do.

"I'm thirty years old," I said. "I'm thirty years old and I know what I want to do and not do."

Now their look was even warier, as if they might restrain me. I tried harder to push through the exquisite cloud of well-being, of unending reassurance. I sat on the edge of the table, bleery, and extended my arm. "Take out the IV," I said.

The nurse had black hair pulled back in a pretty puff, sensible cotton pants and shirt, duck-billed Birkenstocks. She consulted the doctor with her eyes. He turned to me. "It's barely there," he said. "It's a six-week embryo. You are barely pregnant. In a few minutes, you won't be."

The abrasive strain in his voice made me like him better. Something about him was tough-minded and sad. The nurse, though, was the type who gazes upon sorrow with the kind of protected pity that amounts to disdain. I sat there for a minute. We all did. There was a pile of paper masks by the door. It was warm and damp in the room. Airless. Somewhere a radio played oldies. Tiny Tim.

"What a stupid creep," I said, pointing at the intercom. The doctor shrugged. He removed the IV.

In the waiting room, I'd talked a little with a woman I knew casually. She was one of those intensely ebullient people who are great at the right kind of party but wearing in a small space. She was pregnant too, and also by herself. We had exchanged wry, what-next looks, as if we'd both discovered big holes in our socks at the laundromat. That's how many of us behaved then.

I saw her recently, talked to her in a ticket line. She stood next to her husband of seven years, a quiet engineer with a sandy mustache. They were about to go to San Francisco to pick up their baby, a three-month-old Korean girl. They'd started trying to have a baby when she was thirty-eight. No dice.

Did she remember our day in the waiting room, so many years before? I think maybe not. Or if so, we'd both put it in some compartment that really had no place in our current lives: that day of the ash, when we sat there together thumbing through magazines, tiny swimmers inside us.

"That was quick," she said when I entered the waiting room again with the straight-mouthed nurse. I shrugged. I had called a friend from work, and she was there to take me home. I hadn't let Ren stay with me. His offer had fueled my terrible crispness. No, I said. He had a big case that day — a farm worker who spoke no English had been accused of assaulting a couple of local teenagers who'd been baiting him. The friend would pick me up, take me home. He could bring me a pizza.

Now I can't believe that we did it that way. I can't believe that I pushed him so firmly away. Or that he went.

At home, I watched television and dozed while the Valium gradually wore off.

Ren walked in with the pizza and a dozen roses. He had his softball cap on. He liked to change into it in the car; it was a way to stop being a lawyer. The cap made him look too young. He had volcano dust on his wingtips. He looked relieved and solicitous. I could smell his good sweat. Everything sweated. The windows sweated. I turned the fan up higher. I said nothing about my change of mind.

"You're pale," he said. He put his arms around me and hugged me. I stood him back from me and examined him, my friend, my pal, my late-night talker. I saw what a good person he was, how guileless. I saw that I would live with him for a long time, perhaps until the grave.

"What a day!" he said. He wanted it to sound inclusive.

"You won," I guessed.

Inside me, tadpole Mack tipped forward. His fingers began to grow. The amniotic fluid lapped softly.

# 11

ONE MORNING I saw a mother slap her child in the park and heard the next instant a crow's harsh cry. They seemed absolutely connected, the slap and the crow's screech. The crow's sound was both the sound of the slap and the bird's comment on it. But that's how our minds work. Synchronicity becomes illumination. We need the safety of webbing, so we link the unalike. And are we then conspirators, paranoiacs? Or are we religious? Or do we simply have a gift for metaphor? Take your pick.

Elise Prentice walks out of my house on a morning in which she believes me to be in Greece. She gives my husband a wifely pat on the shoulder. What does this pat represent? What is the connection between what I saw and what exists? It would be in her nature to check on him before she drove him to therapy. Still, I've long thought there are tendencies in both Ren and Elise that could produce an alliance between them. A linkage. It's possible. Perhaps I sat on that park bench yesterday and glimpsed a snippet of the future.

Sixteen autumns ago, on a gusty afternoon, Elise and her husband, Roger, welcomed us to the neighborhood with two bottles of champagne. I remember the day, how the falling sun made long bars across their impeccable lawn and how they stepped across them, bottles hoisted.

Mack was ten months old. Ren and Franklin Klemenhagen defended the poor. We had bought our handsome house with a chunk of money, completely unanticipated, that Ren's wildly eccentric second cousin had left to him in his will. I worked two days a week for the environmental group but was basically being the full-time mom of a baby learning to walk, a state that seems to me now an almost pathological combination of love and idiocy. I remember pangs of jealousy that almost toppled me as I watched Elise and Roger load skis that winter for a day at the mountain with all their other childless friends. I'd watch them out there in the new day murmuring calmly, Elise with a pretty little snowflake headband in her bubble of hair. In an hour they'd be swooping down the snow, high above our sodden valley, looking as brilliant and primary as cigarette ads. At dusk I'd kick a path through Mack's toys to watch them carry ski gear and grocery sacks into their orderly home. They looked serene and oxygenated even in the near-dark.

On weekday mornings, Roger strode in his short-armed, hyperathlete's way to his Chevy pickup, carrying a plastic mug of coffee. I see his wide grin, his hearty wave. Elise scurried out a half-hour later in her suit of the day, hair fluffed, lips winy and glossed, to drive off in the opposite direction toward her office downtown. He was a building contractor. She sold real estate, as she does now. I remember them well during that time of their lives, the way they came and went, so shiny and busy.

They seemed then one of those couples who has everything already figured out. Elise mentioned early on that she and Roger planned to have no children, because they were both too selfish to be parents. She said this casually as we watched Mack in the sandbox tasting the dirt on his fingers, and what I remember is the righteousness. Everyone is selfish, she seemed to be saying, and parenthood is just a way to avoid acknowledging it.

As a couple, they did that sort of pronouncing a lot. They threw out maxims like small boulders and leaped their way from one to the other. I suppose that should have been a warning.

We met them in the fall. We got to know them better during the winter and spring. By late summer, Roger was gone. He told Elise he wanted a divorce so he could marry Joleen Worth, his former office manager, who had moved to Denver. For two years Roger and Joleen had been telephoning, meeting when they could. Recently Roger had concocted an out-of-town construction job that took him away from home for days at a time. He and Joleen had flown to St. Lucia. He'd met her Denver friends. Through all that, Elise had known nothing.

Think of a marching band; think of that pause when all sounds stop except the bass drum and the marchers begin to reconfigure themselves into a shape — a letter, an animal — that will become clear in a moment. Think of the way your eyes suddenly begin to see the sharp-chinned hag instead of the lovely young lady with the plume, the profiles instead of the vase. Elise listened to Roger, and all the data began to glide into their new place, silent and inexorable as the closing door of a big safe. And then she was living an entirely different life from the one she thought she had been living.

That first winter after Roger, Elise continued to ski with some of their group, but when they brought her home she looked sore, moved slowly. The light went on in her bathroom, then the television's blue glow and the figure of Elise in her bathrobe, moving back and forth across the woven shade.

She had been living with a stand-in. A person who has been invisible steps forth as the first, the entire person. And who, then, have you loved? And who were you when you loved the stand-in? Do you too have another entire person waiting in the wings?

About a year after Roger left — this would be 1983 — Elise began to wear an MIA bracelet. Her adopted lost soldier was one

Roland Tree from St. Louis, Missouri, missing in Cambodia since May of 1970.

Elise carried a photo of Roland in her wallet, a picture of the boy before he became frozen in time, never dead and never home.

Roland was a straw-haired, eager-eyed kid with the kind of phony solemnity that hides a big grin. He was a gunner on a helicopter that went down in a country that was not officially under American attack. To be missing in war is one thing and bad enough; to be missing in a way that officially can't happen seems some higher kind of horror.

Roland's fiancée was a teenager named Pamela Button. When he had been missing five years, she married his best friend. They had three children and lived in Seattle. Pamela corresponded secretly with Elise. She received Elise's letters at the hospital where she was a medical technician.

Elise sent Pamela everything she could find out about MIAs — congressional reports, reports from the association of the families of POW-MIAs, news stories about the endless diplomatic machinations, even an article that said the missing were alive only in the minds of those who needed them to be. Elise showed me that one. In its margin was her huge, incredulous exclamation mark.

My neighbor took on the avid, sexualized look of a convert. The world you and I inhabit becomes an amusing little play to those people. The real dramas are unfolding behind our backs, where only they can see. Their eyes seem always focused someplace just beyond you. Elise told me once that she believed the government didn't want any missing Americans to be found. This was her theory. She believed that she had, by taking on the cause, become an enemy to the powers that be, that she had become lit up like a sign. Lizard-eyed government operatives wanted her to calm down, to stop her letters and her petitions. In her mind, she lived in danger. And she loved it.

Roger went missing and now Elise had her new passion, the endlessly missing. But at least she wasn't a lone woman, reeling and needy. She had a new love and his name was Roland and he was out there someplace in the Cambodian jungle, waiting, her constancy his single best chance of coming home.

Over the years Elise's fever diminished, but she never seemed to let Roland and the others go to their graves. She simply stoppered a part of herself and turned in new directions.

Such power attaches to the ones who have disappeared. Such high power. They become anything the people left behind need them to be. They take on endless selves, endless amplifications. They become all their own possibilities, and they never become old.

That's what will happen to me if I simply disappear. Someone will pull my small rucksack from beneath a boulder on the shore of the Aegean. Someone will search my little room and find the identification for Francesca Woodbridge. But no Francesca.

To my husband and son, I will be gone but not entirely dead. Presumed drowned, but not beyond-a-doubt drowned. I will be never-old. I will resonate forever.

Elise began to date occasionally. Then she had a two-year relationship with a man named Coulee who owned an organic nursery. He had a silver ponytail and refused to drive a car (though he would, like the Amish, ride in someone else's, namely Elise's). He and Elise went clog dancing on Friday nights. Mack called him Big Cool, and we all expected the relationship to end far sooner than it did, because Elise is hardly an organic, clog-dancing sort of person. She loves artifice and enemies. When she was going with Coulee, she began to dye her hair, though he vehemently warned her that the chemicals would eat away her capillaries.

After Coulee, she joined a group for menopausal and premenopausal women — anyone who felt herself to be experiencing sputtering estrogen, as Elise put it. When she said that, I always saw a huge turbine slow, stop, grow dark. She took me as her guest once. She and the others shared tips on taking care of themselves — everything from French manicures to smart investments.

Day in and day out, Elise can seem as if she sees only trees. She find details interesting even when they don't add up to anything, and assumes that others find them interesting too. She can talk for a long time about something like the contractual language of a house sale, even when it's a perfectly routine transaction and there is no moral to the story. Or she'll tell you exactly what is going on with her body — what she weighs now, how it compares to a year ago, where the new couple of pounds have settled, and so on. But if you try to get more sweeping — try to talk about aging and its little insults, say — she looks at you as if she's waiting for the punchline.

But Elise isn't woolly and silly. Not essentially. Beneath her passing parade of enthusiasms is a competent and energetic businesswoman — she is consistently the top-selling realtor in the county — and a woman with formidable reserves of loyalty and grit.

Five years ago, she rented her house to a visiting professor and moved to Denver to help Joleen nurse Roger, who was dying of cancer. She was gone six months and came back rail-thin, her face settled into a quiet, braced look. The next morning she went off in her Saab to sell a house.

One day a few years ago, just after Coulee departed from her life, Elise returned from work to find Roberta the schnauzer in the front yard, nosing excitedly under the bushes, whining in frustration.

Elise eyed the house. The screen door was unlatched, creaking softly on its hinges. It was almost dusk.

She went straight to our house then. I was fixing dinner; Ren was on the phone with a client. He got off, and we all trooped next door.

Elise has one of those houses that smells like a gift shop. She places bowls of potpourri all over the place and lights fat scented candles in the evenings. (I think of something Mack said a few years ago, when we made him go with us to the state forest campground for a picnic. Stepping out of the car into the piny glade, he sniffed largely. "Pine Sol," he said. And I don't think it was a dig at us. Some kind of switch has occurred for his generation. Nature now evokes the imitations, instead of the other way around. I felt that Elise probably had the same sensibility. When she smelled real flowers or cedar, she thought, My house!)

The potpourri smell was there, but also something else. Something sulfurous, rank. Elise quickly checked the kitchen. The stove was off and cold. She smiled nervously at us. "Nothing cookin' here," she said brightly.

She seemed not to want to move. She put her purse on the island in the kitchen and rested her folded hands on it, gazing off, as if she were trying to think what to have for dinner.

Roberta clicked around the linoleum, sniffing. She barked. And then she barked again and kept barking. Elise looked down at her in surprise. She hushed her vigorously.

Ren suggested we walk through the rest of the house. "Of course," Elise said mildly.

We went through the living room and followed her down the hall. The door to the study was closed. We all paused there for a few seconds. The frightening smell was stronger. Ren gathered himself, turned the knob, and pushed the door away from him with both hands. The room put a long shiver down my body.

It reeked. Of smoke. Of shit. Drawers had been pulled all the way out of the desk and dumped on the floor. Papers, bills, pens, junk, mail, were scattered everywhere. The desk lamp was on its side. The television screen was fibrous with cracks. The window blinds hung wildly askew and were streaked with brown slime.

There in the middle of the rug, a lovely old dhurrie Elise had found at an estate sale, were the remains of a small obscene ceremony. Charred paper and, atop the ashes, a pile of human excrement.

"Oh Jesus," Ren said.

Elise began to cry, letting her head drop into her hands. I put my arm around her soft shoulders.

Ren strode out of the room and came back with a newspaper and a plastic sack. He scooped up the mess, marched out again, and returned with a dishcloth, which he spread over the spot, like a sheet on a corpse. Roberta barked at it frantically.

"Okay," Ren said. His face was very pale. "Elise. Call the police. I'm going to look around a little more."

I often think that this was when Ren took some final turn away from the sly and easy Ren I knew when we were young. It seemed some ultimate confirmation to him that protection was more important than exploration. He seemed to draw into himself, to reside at times in some new room where I'd never been. He brooded over crime news, went to the doctor for small ephemeral symptoms, clipped a long story in the *Times* about gated retirement towns. High walls. Pets up to a certain size only. Background checks so there could be no unpleasant surprises.

Elise became fervent about creating a fortress. She wired her house against intruders, and Ren did the same to ours. I felt sad that day, listening to the installers with their screaming little drills. Here we were on a maple-lined street in a college town, one that seems to breathe a sweet reasonableness. A town with bells, a river, handsome youngsters pedaling their bicycles across the bridge. Cops with master's degrees. Here we were, in such a town, barricading ourselves.

# 12

IN GREECE, the day before I left for home in disguise, I picked my way down the lime-washed steps to the square in the late afternoon. Four black cats with green eyes watched me from a porch so white it hurt. A large woman in a pink dress sat alone in the shade of an acanthus, a splayed hand on each large knee. The bus stopped near her and let off a young mother and two bedraggled kids before gunning off in the direction of the ferry port on the island's dry side. Shutters were closed — it was the afternoon sleeping time — but the heat felt tolerable and I was hatted and sun-blocked, so I started walking toward the sea.

I followed the same road I'd taken the day before, when I had buried my knapsack by the water. The pavement is flanked with honeysuckle bushes, and the smell of them mingles with the wiry sun-baked thyme in a heady honey-camphoric blend. And then the light, of course. Who doesn't talk about the light? What it is, is just an absence of moisture, of complexity, of interference. It comes to you weightless and straight. Hang a musty towel in that light, that herby wind, and it comes back sterilized.

The road descends gently, then climbs again. A dirt track branches off it in the direction of the cliffside and the pretty cove I had found, but I stayed on the pavement. It made a long turn around the side of a hill, and then I saw the Castro, the chalky fort town, a warren of stone on a promontory above the sea.

You approach the walled town from the back, the land-facing side, and climb a long flight of outside stairs, then duck under a low arch into the interior. It's as if you've entered a seashell or a bleached skull — a bleached skull the way it ought to look, not an empty space but with the skeleton of a brain, all corridors and hidden rooms.

Bone-chalk. Silence. Hot white corridors where everything seemed that afternoon to sleep. On a long wall, in a square of shade, a cat stretched out like something spilt.

The corridors are about as wide as a sidewalk, the archways just a few inches higher than my head. The entire town is smaller than a city block. Lidless sarcophagi, small bathtubs with blurred reliefs, sit here and there, as casual as park benches. The whole place is lidless but hidden, like an open-eyed person in a trance.

When I was twelve, I saw some paintings in a book and began to have mausoleum dreams. Tall white marble against an orchid sky — something about that terrified me and seemed to trigger thoughts that ran away with themselves.

In the Castro, there seemed to be not a single human, though from behind one set of shutters came the smell of baking cookies. A mother baking treats for her napping children to have when they woke.

The Castro a skull. My skull. I think that it may somehow contain the whole story.

I found my way to the sea side, found an opening, and became the eye, the living thing, facing the Aegean. The sea and the air were entirely without complication, like dawn from a jet. That lucid blue, like a dream of a calm death.

On that side of the stone town, a starched wind blew. Ancient enemies tried and failed to scale the walls, to enter the austere and corridored skull. I heard their falling crow-calls.

Far below, the sea rocked lightly in its big bowl.

The salt wind blew, and I felt as though I stood at the prow of a ship. I straddled the low wall and peered across the water, then down at the cliff, at the sharp slope to the rocks. The wind nudged me, rocked me a little. I held myself to the wall with both hands. I could tip. Very slowly, very carefully, I brought my outside leg back and moved away from the edge.

I thought of my clothes, my planted oar, down there by the water's edge. I felt a little shimmer of excitement, that lurch of the long-journeying train. I was about to be Jeanne Thompson, the person I had concocted. But instead of starting a life on the far side of the world, Jeanne Thompson would first go home.

Back inside the honeycomb, a door slammed somewhere. An old man coughed. I walked the white corridors toward the land side, eager now to leave. And then three things happened in a sequence that felt preordained, the way the mechanism of a clock buzzes, then chimes, then the Tyroleans pop out of the window. A large bell inside a steeple that rose from the center of the Castro chimed five o'clock. I walked a few steps. Somewhere within the walls, a man began to hum. The voice was sonorous and quickly formed itself into a chant. It had a sere Gregorian center but curled on the edges, the sound of the warbling East. It was the strong and fervent voice of a man in his maturity, a priest behind a door singing his afternoon prayers.

A door flew open a few yards ahead of me, and a young woman entered the corridor as if she had been pushed. She made a complete turn, her head craned skyward, and then she scrambled away. She was bowlegged and lank-haired. As she walked, her arms moved oddly, as if she were treading water.

She stopped quickly and turned again. Her head twisted. Her hands continued to smooth some invisible surface. She seemed the human manifestation of the priest's chant: a stern column of sound with wavering, tremulous edges. Arms like underwater plants.

*Kali méra,* I said. Good day.

Her face reached my eyes then, and it was the face of someone who has just been struck — by a fist, by lightning, by sudden knowledge; it didn't matter. It was the contorted amazement that flashes across a face when the nature and consequence of the blow are still unknown. The next look will be fear or anger or ecstasy. But this woman seemed to have no next look. She was frozen in her just-struckness.

Is that the essence of the grotesque? Frozen shock? I think of Ares and Aphrodite, caught helplessly in a web of clever chains. The gods laugh uproariously at the adulterous lovers. The glorious cripple Hephaestus, cuckolded, managed to lock them in the very throes. Frozen, they are ludicrous.

She raked me with a wild eye, then gathered herself and moved down the white tunnel into another part of the small stone town, her slippered feet silent. On her heavy ankle there was a growth like a pigeon's egg.

The bell, the chant, the demented one. Her dark skitter.

Back in my inland village, I walked along a footpath past stores that were reopening for the evening. The jeweler, blinking sleepily, placed a ring on the green velvet of his window display. Old men leaned on their tall sticks and tilted their heads at a sound from farther up the walk: Ray Charles's smoky voice drifting down to them. I followed the voice and found the Calypso.

The Calypso is a two-tiered bar. Outside, there is a veranda and some rooftop seating. Inside, there are two high-ceilinged rooms full of mirrors, flowers, and green underwater light. Old jazz floats from the loudspeakers at this hour of the day. Later the volume goes up and dance music begins.

Three people sat on the veranda in the slanted light of seven o'clock. A woman my age in a black city suit, short-sleeved with military buttons, played backgammon with a bored and beautiful waiter in his early twenties. A few feet away, a woman with long black hair, also in her twenties, sat in a straight-backed chair. She watched the young man. He spoke to her once and she smiled. Her teeth were lined with gold.

The woman in the suit got up to light the table lamps and take my order. I asked for an ouzo. She brought it to me in a tall glass garnished with a ring of cucumber. I sipped and pretended to be writing a postcard. Sweet jazz moved out of the ripply green interior and into the long evening. She sat back down at the backgammon table, crossed her legs, and made her move, her cigarette hand out for balance.

A few minutes later she sat down at my table, placing her iced coffee on a folded napkin, smoothing her skirt. Her name, she said, was Nikki.

It turned out that Nikki and her husband, George, had owned the Calypso for thirteen years. Before that they had had a very classy restaurant in Montreal, and that's where she had learned English. But George had wanted to come back to Greece. So here she was, stuck on this quiet island.

She told me there had been a big earthquake in Russia that day, then she lowered her voice. "That girl there," she said, shifting her eyes to the black-haired girl in the straight-backed chair, "she is a Russian. She is in love with my waiter. Can you tell?" The waiter leaned back in his chair, tan arms folded across his white shirt. The girl leaned forward and murmured to him, her hair a curtain across her face.

"I knew a Russian in the United States," I said. "He worked in my garden." It wasn't enough to say. Nikki raised her eyebrows, waiting for the rest. "He had so much energy," I said lamely. "He had a lot of hope."

This satisfied her. She nodded. One must have hope, she said. She herself has taught her sons to believe in God, though she does not herself practice anymore. She wants something to hearten them in this world of the Ebola, the AIDS. And had I seen the monastery down the road, the big one? It is, she said, a place to feel God. When the sun goes down, the rays? The auras? They light it all up.

Nikki's smoky voice moved off the whitewashed deck onto the rocky lane, where it met the voices of children playing in a ring of shop light and those of the old men leaning on their sticks. Her voice, her wanton city purr, was nothing like the clackety plaints of their old wives. It floated to the stiff men and made their fingers twitch the way they do before sleep.

Do you have children? she asked me.

Not even a pause. No, I said. No children.

Then I told her about the crazy-looking girl in the Castro. And the priest who chanted somewhere in the walls.

"That young lady," Nikki said, slitting her eyes against the smoke from her cigarette. "She is a famous one, that young lady." She crossed her thighs so that the black skirt of her suit pulled up the way she wanted it to. A few more customers had wandered into the bar.

"I feel" — she laced her fingers over her midriff — "as if I ate a *balloon* today! Not such a fine idea, the balloon for the food. I will maybe have a gin and tonic to see if it makes the balloon go big or go little." She scrunched her eyebrows together as if she listened to a faraway person telling her what the balloon planned to do.

"There is a story that the girl's father lives in the Castro and of course sees her every day. But she does not know, maybe, that he is her father. Her mother is an old lady with the scowl" — she demonstrated — "who works in the back of the little store. You saw the little store? The one with all the cats and they want to eat your . . . what is it? Your ankles. All your ankles! They want to eat them, but they do not, of course, because they are cats and so they have the distance." She squinted. "But in their eyes you see that they would not mind if you would fall over with a seizure of the heart, and *then* they would eat the ankles." The word sounded like a piece of heavy jewelry.

"The mother is ugly and she hunches over" — she hunched — "and she says all these years that the crazy girl only had a father for about one week and then the father, her husband, drowned in the sea. And she put on the black dress forever. That is what she says.

"Others in the Castro say the priest is the girl's father. The priest came from Thessaloniki, in the north, a year before the girl was born. And he left the Castro the day after she was born. Just left with no explanation. Did he know she was not right?" She touched her head.

"And so she was raised as the dead fisherman's daughter. When the priest left, his hair was black." She pointed to her own. "When he returned, this many, many years later? It is white. A year ago, the priest returned to the Castro with his white hair. They thought he was dead, and now here he is in that town that is like a family. He goes behind his door and chants his prayers. The mother of the crazy girl will not look him in the eyes. They do not speak. When he chants, the girl becomes excited and runs here and there, like a bug." She moved her fingertips across the table.

"It is not good," Nikki said firmly. "He must leave. The Castro is too small for their story."

# 13

THE NEXT MORNING I told Mrs. Kouki, the owner of my small room, that I would leave the island for a while. I didn't know how long. Maybe three days, maybe a week; maybe longer. I waved my hand frivolously. Who knew? But I wanted to hold my room.

Mrs. Kouki placed her hands on her large hips. She gave me a big indulgent smile. Crazy Americans. Crazy American lady all alone doing these silly things, this gallivanting as if she were a teenager.

We figured the price for two weeks and I paid her in cash. She spoke just enough English to make the transaction lengthy but not endless. She wore a black housedress and good carpet slippers. She promised me something — I couldn't decipher what — and returned with a piece of cake soaked in honey.

I told her that I was very taken with this island, that I had gone swimming in a little cove directly south of the Castro, a beautiful place reached by an overgrown trail down the side of the cliff. About half a mile south of the Castro, I specified.

I made my narrow bed, placing the identification of Francesca Woodbridge in a small purse under the pillow. It contained my passport, my wallet with all my identification, and a couple hundred dollars. I dressed in a sundress and straw hat that I had bought the day before in the village, then packed my suitcase with the rest of my clothes, my toiletries, the fax from Mack, and put it in the closet. In a colorful cotton shoulder bag that I'd bought with the sundress, I carried my eyeglasses, my packet of cash, and all my Jeanne Thompson ID. When Mrs. Kouki closed the shutters of her house against the sun, I descended the white steps to the square, just in time for the morning bus to the harbor and the boat to the mainland.

As the ferry pulled stalwartly from shore, I stood at the rail and squinted into diamonds of water. Everything seemed moving and final — the clutch of laughing teenagers on the bench behind me, the stentorious horn of the boat, the cry of the gulls — as if I had boarded a ship that was leaving the earth.

That afternoon, in Athens, I bought a stamp pad at a stationery store and a piece of molding clay, and I spent several hours at a quiet sidewalk coffee shop making a clay relief of the visa stamp I'd traced from my Francesca passport, the stamp that said I had traveled from America to Greece. I kept trying it, kept coming up with a smudged, silly replica, but eventually I got it right. Right enough. I stamped Jeanne's pristine passport.

A half hour before it closed, I found a travel agency near Syntagma and bought a round-trip ticket to Salt Lake City with a connecting flight north. I rubbed my eyes, my face, before I went through the door, and I acted quietly distraught. An emergency, I said. Did I want to go through the procedure for the bereavement discount? No. It was not a funeral, not a death. I just had to get there fast.

The clerk shrugged sympathetically and found a seat for Jeanne Thompson on a Delta flight through Frankfurt, leaving the next morning. I paid her in cash. She wished me a good day and said she hoped it all turned out all right.

At a pharmacy I bought red hair dye, scissors, brown eye pencil, and the basic toiletries. At a cheap clothing store, I bought three knit pantsuits, the wigs, knockoff Adidas, and old-lady marshmallow tie-ups. Underwear and a nightgown. A canvas hat with a brim. The kind of dark glasses that have only the faintest color. Plastic loop earrings in bright colors. A large white sweater, heavy as a jacket. At a department store I bought a cheap suitcase.

In my hotel room I sipped a beer I'd bought in the tiny lobby bar, brushed out my honey-highlighted hair, chopped it into a ragged bob, and rinsed it red.

The Frankfurt airport is like a huge hospital that is going to do quiet and terrible things to you. Booted youngsters walk on bright floors with automatic rifles in ready-to-aim position, their eyes scanning, their expressions fixed and pleasant. The bathrooms have heavy white doors that move soundlessly. They have gleaming sinks, helpful hooks. Everything is polished and hushed. Everything seems to watch. There are signs on the walls that show the figure of a running man. What does that mean? If you try anything strange, you'd better run? Even after you figure out that they mark fire exits, the runners give a tick of terror to the place.

I was edgy, yes. I sat in a black plastic seat reading a thriller that I can't remember at all. The dye in my hair made my head itch. Uniformed airport cops strolled around the balcony above the waiting area. They trained a big video camera on us, moved it slowly through the crowds. When the lens reached me, it saw a slumped woman with a strange haircut reading a fat paperback. From time to time the gigantic arrival/departure board on the wall hissed and clicked, a horde of cicadas, and all the numbers changed.

I checked in for my flight. An airline employee with a Hindu caste mark examined my passport, gazed a few seconds too long at my face, studied the passport again. She touched her own hair and examined the pulled-back, blondish hair of the passport picture. I smiled. You like the red? I asked her, woman to woman. It's a surprise for my husband. The new me. She gave me a polite twitch of a smile, asked if anyone had tried to give me anything to carry, waved me on to the ticket clerk. In a few moments my new suitcase with my costumes moved slowly through the baggage doors, bound for my home.

# 14

Mack was born with missing little toes, as if he had been pulled into the world of the living just as the big doors were slammed, lopping off his last edges. Every day for months and months I thought, Almost. The feeling has never entirely gone away.

When Mack was little, he and Ren both laughed at the missing toes. This little pig, Ren would singsong, then stop, aghast. A pig was missing! Mack squealed along happily. Only in grade school did he become ashamed of his feet, did he begin to wear shoes always, even in our house with just us, his parents. Who knows what happened in some shower room after some gym class? Who knows what betrayal Mack felt when he discovered he hadn't been equipped with self-protection, that he was a bit of a freak and no one at home had bothered to warn him?

I think of Mack when he was a baby and a small child, and I remember how amazed Ren and I were that we had produced such a creature. He had our features, but they were present in such a way that they seemed platonic. They were the ideal version, and thus so distant from ours that we could admire them unreservedly. The green of his eyes was mine, but his were tilted impeccably in a way mine only wanted to do. Ren's wry grin was there, stripped of weariness and apology. Purely canny. And the large ears too, but now they seemed like perfect tools of alertness and apprehension. And the way he scrunched up his whole face and sneezed with a scream — that was mine, but stripped of all chagrin. It seemed the way a sneeze, fully expressed, was always meant to be.

We were happy, those first few years. Everything seemed possible. With just one child, we could still entertain ideas of throwing him in a backpack and trekking through Nepal. We were a family but were not defined by our familyness, or at least we didn't feel ourselves to be. I worked part-time and did a lot of volunteer publicity for political campaigns. I was good at packaging personalities, and did it only for people I believed myself to believe in.

We were young. We hummed along.

Once or twice a year, Ren's father visited. Ever since his disabled wife's death, he had seemed to move backward in time — to become younger and more energetic even as he added years. He cut off his big white mustache, and we were amazed by the tender young man's mouth that was there. He traveled all the time, and played bridge with pretty widows, and volunteered at the soup kitchen in his town. With Mack he was respectful and attentive, as if he were talking to an old friend who had some trouble expressing himself.

I remember waking up in early summer light, the birds gurgling, the curtains aglow. Ren, half asleep, asked, "What are the funny people up to?"

"Not much," I murmured back. "One of them turned into you, but also into a mime, and he tiptoed up to me in that mime way and bit me on the chin. A nip, basically. Then a little circle of people clapped."

He nipped me on my nape. The cat draped herself across my ankles, purring, and I had the feeling that our bed had roared silently through the blue night all night, and now it was back in port.

# 15

H ERE AT THE TROCADERO, I watch the Discovery Channel. Last evening I saw a furry spider inject a cockroach with a drug, then drag him, woozy and slurring, into her lair to be feasted on by her babies. She even hauled a small rock to the door of the cave to seal him in. Yikes, I thought, and my mind made one of those wild leaps that can feel like insight.

It is a shiny autumn dawn on a quiet street on the edge of a huge campus, and I pad in my gold lamé slippers into a bright bathroom and take a shower, kneading extra conditioner into the ends of my long bleached hair. I stand before the mirror in my puffy robe with the large gold buttons and wrap pieces of my yellow hair around pink curlers the size of tomato paste cans, fastening the plastic cylinders with four-inch bobby pins. After an hour under the hair dryer, I'll brush out the hair, let it cascade over my shoulders, and watch the way it turns me, for men, from unseen to seen. The hair is the trigger.

Most of the others in my sorority house are still asleep. Faint kitchen sounds and the smells of breakfast float up the white stairs. Lotion all over my face and careful wiping-off motions, upward, to counteract the aging pull of gravity. I am eighteen. My little cake of dark charcoal eyeliner. I make the tiny lake of ink, shape the point of the brush on the edge of the container, dip it in the ink, draw the line. Staring downward, I fan with my hand so it will dry and not smudge. Then the brown shadow, brushed across the lid and out a little. Then mascara, more fanning. The pleased blinking of the furry new eyes.

Another leap: there are damp madroñas bending toward the street, leaves flickering in the night lights. We are being herded by our sisters from frat house to frat house for hazing. At the last house, in a big central courtyard, we sing for our supper. In the silence after the last note, someone whistles at us from an upper window. We look up eagerly, the whole crop of us. Pounds of icy water dumped from fifty-gallon cans fall onto us, onto our shiny, sprayed heads. One smaller girl falls to the ground, then crawls quickly upright, sheer disbelief on her face. We stand in the dark, drenched.

There was that moment before the first shriek, that moment when the heavy shock of water was falling through the air, when I thought, They fear us, and we them. You can call it youth and unease and anything else you want, but does it ever entirely disappear?

Ten years ago, at a cocktail party, one of the new hires in Ren's firm got seriously, quietly drunk and we had a talk on the piano bench. He told me he had once dumped a girl out of his car on a gravel road fifteen miles from anything because she wouldn't have sex with him. She walked home, her feet bare. He is now a tax specialist with a pretty, indefatigable wife and a couple of accelerated children. I think if I mentioned that story to him now, he would look at me as if I were crazy. He would have sealed it away, perhaps even from himself.

The year 1968 can seem, these decades later, like a single day. In the morning, the old life. A boy in a suit affixes a pin to a girl's dress, fumbling charmingly, and she, Lynette Grossweiler, aged nineteen, is engaged to be engaged. She is chloroformed with love and relief. She is pinned. In the afternoon, the ground rumbles and harlequins begin to drift across the edges of the clipped lawns. The click of our stacked heels becomes the sound of soldiers' heels, the British redcoats trying to beat down cagey rebels. But now America itself has become the stiff-booted battler, and the enemy is liquid.

A gate opens somewhere and ragged, glittering people are suddenly dancing around with their hair flying. We in our good dresses, our sheaths, are suddenly the nannies, the cops, missing history.

By the late afternoon of that long day, I was friends with a wild-haired boy with Ben Franklin glasses, a quiet prelaw student named Ren Woodbridge, the son of a widowed botany professor at a little college in the Midwest. He lived with three other students next door to the shabby Victorian where I roomed with three girlfriends. We'd boxed up our dresses and now wore pretty rags.

We sat on our porch in the sun and smoked pot and laughed so hard we hurt. Bells jingled on the ankles of a couple who passed us. Iron Butterfly floated out the window. My philosophy professor walked by in a green velvet jacket and cut-off jeans, greeting us as if he'd just stepped off a ship.

We inhabited a flickering kingdom in which all authority proceeded from ourselves, and our new sensibilities would save the world. We jumped onto the freeway, stopping traffic to stop Vietnam. Of course, we were the children of largesse. We could not easily imagine the fears of our Depression-bred parents. We could not easily imagine a black soldier waking in the jungle to the thought that he was not only Lyndon's gladiator, he was ours. All of us chanting white ones with our professors, our music, our mimeographs, our Dionysian righteous rage — he was our instigation. He, the one who crawled.

On the evening of that long day, everything bent further — the light and the music elongated and echoed through a pink Victorian and a party that was happening in many different rooms. This room was a bedroom. Eight of us sat on the floor on cushions. A young man sat cross-legged on the bed, smoking a hookah like Alice's caterpillar. He had long shiny hair, a smock shirt, drawstring pants, thin silver bracelets, a leather thong around his ankle. He was holding forth in a stoned thoughtful manner on the precise nature of his bond with his lover, a wraith who had faded off into the crowd. "No," he said exuberantly, "I *don't* trust her. I don't trust her at all. I love her, but I don't trust her. Not for a minute."

His name was Stephen Lovano. He had recently moved into Ren's house. Ren and I both were about to fall for him.

There are people in the world, a few, who seem electric, and Stephen Lovano was one of them.

He was tall and long-limbed, with a buoyant stroll that made him look both comfortable and alert in his body. He had used that body pleasurably, and it showed. His face was angled, with a beaky nose over a shapely thin-lipped mouth. His grin was ecstatic, as if it belonged to a different person from the one with the level gray eyes. But it was his kinetic quality that you noticed most. He had an almost uncontainable energy. At rest, he played a phantom piano on the arm of the chair. On the phone, he paced lightly, sweeping the cord out of his way as he turned. Quite often he burst out in a mad squeaky laugh, head back, quite beautiful.

Avidity. What does avidity look like? And do we love avid people so much because they give us faith in the richness of this world? Maybe so. They seem always to be saying that they have access to the secret sources of fuel.

When Stephen talked to you, he leaned in about an inch farther than was strictly comfortable, just enough to create that frisson of violated space. And his eyes held yours in something I later came to think of as "the gaze." Mack uses the gaze on Tamara, and it looks so sweet and foolish and transparent. But it works. It worked on me. Ethologists call it the copulatory gaze. Apes use it all the time.

And of course it is as aggressive as it is ardent, the gaze. Primates gaze at enemies to threaten them; they look deeply into the eyes of one another to reconcile after a battle, and as a prelude to sex. It works because it seems to be a request for unguardedness; it seems to say that your unguardedness will be worth it to you.

Stephen Lovano's eyes were surrounded by lines. They made him look older than he said he was. His eyes seemed, even at his giddiest, to be appraising both himself and his surroundings. There was always a twoness to him. I think about that now — how it welded doubleness and desire for me.

He was passionately articulate — valued the right word, the nuance, the audacious comparison — and this was part of the bond between him and Ren. They liked to argue politics into the night, Ren holding for subversion from within, beat them at their own game, Stephen insisting that the government, the advertising machine, would find, always, a way to coopt your best instincts, to dilute them to nothingness. That's how we talked.

He said that he was the son of a lobster fisherman in Maine, a widower; that his mother was long dead. He said his dad's sister had married well, a Boston banker, and she was footing his college bills. His many telephone calls did not include Maine or Boston numbers. He said the family was not particularly close. It all seemed plausible enough.

Stephen convinced Ren to take skydiving lessons. They practiced the jump in the back yard of their gaunt old bachelors' house, flinging themselves off a toolshed roof onto a pile of cushions, heads arched upward in the correct way.

A bunch of us gathered one bright Saturday to watch them jump out of a small plane over a small airport east of the city. Ren's face was white as he suited up, as he glanced nervously at the waiting plane. I touched his hand as they prepared to leave. It was ice.

Sun flashed off the plane's wing as it circled for the drop. And then a tiny black figure appeared, falling for those endless seconds as we caught our breath and let it out with the billowing chute. Another circle of the plane, and the second figure, the heart-sinking fall, the pretty poof of the chute.

We all cheered. They stalked across the earth toward us, the chutes bundled in their arms, laughing. I'll never forget Ren's face as he drew closer to his waiting pals. It was ignited with joy.

I had a work-study job for a young economics professor named Gregory Munro. Three evenings a week, I let myself into his office and corrected the quiz he'd given that day to his lecture class of a hundred. The answer sheet sat by the pile of quizzes in their brown rubber band. The office smelled, as they all did then, of smoke and mimeographs. The venetian blinds were closed.

I had met this professor just once, but I thought I had a sense of his life from the three photos he had on his desk. He was sandy-haired, nondescript, faded in that Scottish way. One photo showed him sitting before a white brick fireplace with his wife and three young kids. It had the relentless brightness of a fifties magazine ad, that light-flooded vulgarity. That's what I'm escaping, I thought gratefully. That's what we refuse any part of. The other photos were of an old man in a tweed hat with a fishing rod and a boy in an army uniform who had the washed-out coloring of the professor.

Stephen Lovano was interested in my economics professor. He asked me questions about him, about the books in his office, about the papers on his desk. I was puzzled. What was there to be interested in about Professor Gregory Munro? He taught Economics 101 to a huge lecture class. He had a brother in the army, probably in Vietnam. He had the three children, the fireplace, the hairsprayed wife.

"Stephen thinks there is a cabal of business and economics profs who're in the pocket of the Defense Department," Ren told me. "He thinks they're developing some kind of gain-loss model of acceptable war casualties vis-à-vis dollar expenditures for Vietnam. Something fishy they can use to keep the thing going."

"Professor *Munro?*" I laughed. "I don't think so. He's so lowly they give him all the freshmen. A war consultant? I think not."

"Well, Stephen has a theory." Ren shrugged. "That's why he wants to see the guy's office. Or he's just trying to get into your pants." He drained the last of his coffee. "Watch out," he said. "When Stephen Lovano wants to get into your pants, your pants don't have a chance."

That very evening, Stephen said he might bring me a Coke at the professor's office when he had finished studying. He said it in a tone that was sure of itself, said it with a flicker of the gaze. I said fine.

He knocked lightly, about ten o'clock, and I let him in. He brought a Coke and some cashews. I told him I had ten or so quizzes to finish correcting and he said fine, no hurry, and I didn't think to respond because I knew what waited at the end of that time. He sat in the professor's overstuffed chair, plaid, and slowly ate cashews and leafed through the faculty newsletter. Somewhere in another part of the building a vacuum cleaner whined softly. Rain tapped on the windows. I set myself to the last of the quizzes, my head down, feeling sly and high-colored behind the drape of my long hair. I made my little ticks by each good answer and I made them a little darker, a little more adamant, because my hand had a faint tremor. My breath felt shallow. The pages of the newsletter flipped slowly. The vacuum stopped and someone down the long hall had a prolonged sneezing fit, tiny little screams in succession, that gave me an excuse to look up at Stephen. He had his head cocked exaggeratedly toward the sneezes, and that made me laugh. I fell down again behind my hair. He stood up and stretched and nosed around the little room, picking up the photos to study them, examining the titles of the books in the long shelf under the window. Almost playfully, he tested the drawer of the file cabinet, which was locked.

"The professor's secrets," he said lightly.

And then I did something I never should have done. I had this scurrying eagerness to put a lit-up look on Stephen Lovano's face. I had a desperate eagerness to offer him something that wasn't — yet — me. And so I opened the middle drawer of the professor's big desk and I held up a little ring with three small keys on it.

I've always been something of a snoop. Bored one evening, I had pulled out that middle drawer to its full length, just to see what might be at the back of it, behind all the pens and stamps and so on. There was a small box with a lid, and I had of course opened that, and there were the keys. Which I held out now to Stephen Lovano, dangling from the end of my finger.

I try to think how I felt at that moment. But that is part of my problem these days. All my fiercest, wildest, most exhilarating feelings recede too often to a place where I can recall that they existed, but I can't seem to feel them again. I have knowledge of them, but it is no longer visceral knowledge. It's archival. And that scares me cold. I regard those feelings the way I regard a particularly powerful and lovely zoo animal — a lynx, a musk ox. I look at them through their bars and I think that there was a time when I was *with* them, when we all ran on the yellow grass.

Stephen took the keys and briskly opened the file drawer.

"What does Gregory Munro have that you're interested in?" I asked.

"Nothing, maybe," he said. "But Munro and half a dozen others on this campus are supposedly getting a lot of under-the-table Defense Department bucks to do a trumped-up 'study' of casualty projections in Vietnam. I'd like the rest of this campus to know what they're up to. I'd like . . ." He turned to me with a comical leer. "The goods."

I finished correcting quizzes while he went through the files of Professor Gregory Munro. What struck me was that he seemed to know exactly what he was looking for.

"What kind of label would he put on a secret government research file?" I said with a taunt in my voice. The tension of the evening had become stretched a little tight.

"Who knows?"

He pulled out a file and flipped through the papers expertly. I thought, He's done this before. He's done something like this before.

That night we went to my room together. He had some of Professor Munro's papers folded and stuffed inside a textbook. I remember that. And the rain smearing the windows, my little yellow candles, the way he linked fingers with mine and pressed the backs of my hands to the sheet. The way he turned to kiss my collarbone gently as I lay gasping, near tears.

A friend told me once about how he learned to ski jump — how you start down the steep hill on those heavy boards and reach a point, a single moment, when you either fall down, aborting the jump, or you launch yourself. A second later and it's too late. If you don't actively begin to launch — and he described a sheer forwardness, the way the body must lean out over the ski tips as the skis leave the edge of the platform, the way the body must become a wing — then you will wreck badly. There can be no guardedness, no holding back.

I jumped. I made myself into a wing; I really did. For six months, I was a wing.

# 16

IF YOU HAD TOLD ME then that Ren Woodbridge and I would grow middle-aged and perhaps old together, I would have refused the information. We knew only that we were pals, that we were companionable, that we tended to agree on situations or people who were intriguing or funny. Just that, really.

And what if either of us had simply turned to the other back then and said, I am the one who will share your bed fifteen thousand times? How could it be believed? It seems you should be granted a warning: *This is that person.* But it doesn't happen. A kid with curly hair drinks coffee with you on a sunny winter day, and you are given no clue that his smooth young hand lifting the cup could be the gnarled hand that touches your gnarled hand a half-century later. *This* person, the one with the bent smile, the little glasses. It's so ferociously whimsical.

Ren in those days was thin and knobby-wristed, slightly round-shouldered. The wild hair, the little glasses, gave him an opaque mad-scientist look that desexualized him in some way. There were a lot of costumes then, and a lot of them were — I see it now — protection.

When I first knew him, he was finishing his senior year in prelaw. He worked part-time, for pennies, for an organization that provided legal research and counsel to indigents. He had a minor in philosophy. And he had a surprising gift for mimicry. He could do anyone perfectly: Nixon, Mick Jagger, his landlady with her bizarre patois of English, French, and Basque. It was the counterpoint to his sincere and idealistic center. It was the good surprise.

Ren believed that the measure of a society was the degree of its concern for its most helpless and damaged. That sounds so bald now, so naive, I suppose. That's what a lot of us thought we believed. His plan after law school was to defend those people in their inevitable run-ins with doom.

It seems crucial to remember Ren as he was. But the memories are slim, because for me, he was basically background to Stephen Lovano. He was the roommate, the fellow admirer.

I was living that high-colored and tragic interior life you can sustain in your early twenties, that kabuki performance in which the object of love always threatens to vanish behind a new horizon; the seppuku knife is always drawn. I had, I'd discovered, an astounding capacity for obsession, for metaphor. Whatever happened or didn't happen between myself and Stephen Lovano was the measure of my life, its past, present, and future worth. There's something in that state — in its sense of terrible and ecstatic stakes, its combination of fatefulness and hope, its sense of utter infusion — that is as viscerally religious as most of us ever get. When we remember it, our mouths twist in a strange combination of nostalgia and relief. We yearn for its presence, even while we know it can't, in the end, be borne.

Stephen Lovano once peered at the collar of my shirt, then plucked from it, with the greatest finesse, a ladybug. Which he held on the flat of his hand until it zoomed away. A goofy little moment which you replay for a lifetime, wondering why it offered such sheer transport.

I remember my comfort with Ren. I remember his ecstatic face the day he and Stephen skydived from the little plane.

I remember too a gray Saturday on which we all sat around

watching a Marx Brothers movie on a secondhand television. The doorbell rang and a young guy in a bad suit stood in the doorway with a vacuum cleaner and a case full of attachments. He looked uneasy and tired, as if he'd been eating his own bad cooking for too long. He recited his speech. Someone turned down the movie and we listened to this emissary from the parentworld, like coyotes at a kill. Here was real entertainment. (That suit! That vacuum cleaner!)

Stephen uncoiled himself from his half-lotus and stretched to his full height and walked all around the salesman very slowly. He began asking him questions about the vacuum cleaner, very serious questions with a technical cast. Why this attachment for this particular job? What might be the best combination to go after dustballs on the curtain rods? (Dustballs on the curtain rods!) The salesman cleared his throat before every answer. He seemed able to look only at Stephen. Someone snickered and the salesman's face colored, but still he could not look around the room.

I'm wondering, Stephen said, if this comblike attachment could perhaps be helpful in various grooming situations. He pulled off his shirt. He sat down in the big Barcalounger and leaned back and directed the salesman to power up the vacuum. Which he did.

With the comb thing attached to the hose, Stephen lay back, eyes closed, and ran the attachment through the sparse and springy hair of his bare chest. He gazed around the room inquisitively. Did it pass muster? Was it just the ticket?

We howled. Bent over, we laughed and we laughed. And finally the salesman joined in. He jauntily vacuumed the front of his own suit and laughed. His face was bright pink. And then we all laughed again.

It seemed that we were all laughing together, at the vacuum, at Stephen and the vacuum, but also at the strange turns of life that produce a necessity to sell vacuums. It seemed inclusive, the laughter, except that it wasn't. Even with the salesman joining carefully, it was very cruel.

Stephen clapped the salesman on the back as he packed up his things and ushered him regally out the door, babbling some nonsense about contacting his Aunt Mary about a possible purchase.

This is where Ren comes in. He had been smiling during the whole show, but when it was over he said something about an errand and left with a salute. The rest of us followed, most of us to go study for a while. My roommates went to our house and I kept walking. A block or so ahead, I saw Ren. He was talking to the vacuum salesman, inclining his fuzzy head to hear the shorter man's replies. As I approached, they said goodbye and the salesman turned up the walk to a big stone house.

I asked Ren what they'd been talking about. "He's working his way through some dumb-shit junior college selling those ridiculous things," he said lightly. "Some elder in his church talked him into it."

I understood him. "He thought the chest-hair vacuum was just as funny as the rest of us did," I said lamely.

"Of course he did."

I slugged him lightly on the arm. "I suppose you bought three or four or them," I said.

"Just one." He gave a big elaborate shrug. "For my old man," he said in a perfect Groucho growl. "More than a few dustballs he has on his rods."

For a dozen years, Ren's mother had been crippled with multiple sclerosis. Ren, an only child, and his father, the botany professor, nursed her together. Everything. The lifting, the diapers, the discovery of the hoarded pills. Everything. From the time Ren was nine.

His father insisted that Ren leave home for college, and he put his wife in a nursing home for the last few years of her life. He set up a desk next to her bed and arrived every day after his classes, as if he were reporting to another job. He corrected his papers. He helped her sip juice. He read her the newspaper and the letters from Ren. He took a half-hour walk and came back with fast food for himself and finally left around ten. Every day.

She was not grateful. She was in fact furious that her body had sent her to a chair when she was twenty-nine and to a bed at thirty-six. For a dozen years she was poisoned with fury. Sometimes she wept, barking sobs. Sometimes she upended a glass of something. Toward the end, when Ren's father read her the newspaper, she tipped her head away from him in the closest gesture she could summon to utter disdain.

Ren told me all this a few months after I met him. During winter break, she died. In the spring, I ran into him one day on campus and he introduced me to Timothy, his father, a courtly white-haired man in a good tweed suit. He had a snowy mustache and looked old enough to be Ren's grandfather. The two of them talked softly, inclining their heads in a hushed, practiced way, as if the railing woman in the endless bed lay nearby. But they laughed softly too. They were easy with each other, familiar in the manner of disaster survivors. They could have worn the same hidden tattoo.

I see the two of them that day. It was a glittering day, the campus radiant with water and light and color, the fruit trees in foamy full bloom, the big fountain grabbing light and flinging it high. The white-mustached father in his old tweed suit nodded graciously and shook my hand. And Ren — Ren had a new look he'd taken on in the months since his mother's death. What was it, exactly? He had pulled the wild hair back into a ponytail. He stood straighter. He had gained some needed weight. His eyes seemed larger somehow, and very kind. Both father and son looked newly emerged.

We had a party for Ren's father, and Stephan Lovano was at his most charming. He told several long stories that set up gales of glee. He ran his fingers lightly across the back of my neck in a way I can feel today. I was temporarily sure again that he wanted only me. He conducted an intense and flattering conversation with a homely grad student who, it would turn out, was about to go to South America and join Marxist guerrillas and disappear.

His fingers waved through the air, summoning Ren. Do it, he urged him. Ren shook his head shyly, laughed, tried to throw him off. But Stephen was incandescent and Stephen was powerful. Ren looked at him and wanted quite simply to *be* him. And so he offered what he could. While his silvery father watched, puzzled, Ren mimicked the vacuum salesman as he explained his attachments, clearing his throat before each sentence, twisting the phantom hose. His face was flushed. It was vicious and it was perfect.

So there it was, a clue to a later Ren. And Stephen too; his future was evident in him, if you looked.

Every day Stephen went to his classes, then took the bus to his job downtown, which he described vaguely as some sort of work with a left-leaning polling organization. One day Ren and I happened to take the bus downtown together and we decided to have coffee at an outdoor café. It was a sunny afternoon, Mount Rainier floated grandly on the horizon, and everyone on the street looked happy and eccentric. It was a great day to watch the walkers go by.

We'd been there for perhaps fifteen minutes when a dark car pulled to the curb. It had government plates. The driver wore a business suit. The passenger was Stephen. He got out, gave a severe flat-handed wave to the driver, and walked toward us, a distant, almost sad look on his face. He wore his usual faded denims, ragged fisherman's sweater, sandals with socks, and did an exaggerated double take when he caught sight of us at our sidewalk table. I thought it was mock surprise, but now I know it wasn't. He was just that quick.

And why was a federal employee in a dark-blue sedan driving Stephen around? Who was that driver? Peculiar as it seems, neither Ren nor I asked. I see now that neither of us wanted any information that would work in even the smallest way against our idea of Stephen Lovano.

One day he was simply gone. Vanished. And a week later a letter arrived with a Washington, D.C., postmark. It was addressed to Ren. It apologized for the rapid departure and said that he, Stephen, was engaged in work that he couldn't talk about and that had taken him somewhere else. That he was likely to be there a good long while. At the bottom was a sentence for me: "Please tell Francesca she is terrific and I won't forget her, and I'm sorry I can't tell her that in person at this time."

Terrific. The comic wanness of that word should have told me what he was, essentially. He couldn't summon up anything better than that? But here's the strange thing. Not even that feeble little greeting and goodbye could help me detach myself from him, chalk him up to experience. I thought angry thoughts, I articulated the anger to myself, but I didn't really feel it. What I felt was sheer grief, and a kind of madness that made me think I could summon him back if I could just come up with the right incantation, the right words.

The man had lied to me. To all of us. We didn't know how he had lied, only that he had. He probably worked for the government. And what he had done was to get something on Professor Gregory Munro that hurt him badly, in what precise way I was never to know. All I know is that Munro resigned from the university a couple months later and left the city with his family.

And yet I only wanted Stephen Lovano back. For years, *years,* I wanted him back. I imagined him yearning to contact me but refraining because he wanted to protect me from his dangerous life. I imagined him a double agent, living undercover in the company of ruthless and wrong-minded people. I wrote letters, stark and pleading, and sent them to the phony home address he'd given in the school directory. Many were sent and none came back. Who read them? I wonder. What went on in their minds when they did?

# 17

WHEN REN WAS SHOT, my father arrived alone to stay with Mack and me for a few days. He sat in the kitchen a lot, and he and I didn't know quite what to say, though I felt his steadiness and appreciated it. He wore a solid, almost set look on his face, as if bracing himself for the next shock.

What will it do to him and my mother and brother if I disappear? What will it do to Ren, to Mack, to Siobhan? It will do damage. I know that. That's a given. I have to think, though, that they would all, over time, find a certain comfort in the idea of my death by drowning in a beautiful sea. Never would I grow sick or bent, reduced by the cruelties of time.

My parents live two states away in a little prairie town surrounded by underground missiles still aimed at Russia. They are busy, kind people who worked hard to send their two kids to college, and didn't seem surprised when I stayed away and my brother returned home. Their little town is so far out there on the plains that I only see them once or twice a year. They don't travel much.

My great-grandfather came to this country as a Basque sheepherder, and I am named for a favorite daughter he lost. It has often seemed to me that my parents set out to become the antithesis of that wandering Basque. They celebrate plantedness, routine, coherence, and are utterly mystified that anyone would want to leave their little town, aside from a youthful foray or two. They talk about permanent departures in a way that gives the departed a sheen of scrutability. He's always had an itchy foot, they'll say. She's a city girl at heart.

Gratuitous emotion dismays them. When we were kids, Siobhan and I would sometimes press pillows to our faces and scream as loudly as we could, shrieks that would have gone a long way if left to themselves. Once, she sat on a pillow over my face and I shrieked, and my mother knocked at the door, *rap, rap.* We scrambled up, my face purple from suffocation and excitement. She gave us a long look. We were panting. It seemed to me that a very large thing in a corner had stirred a little, something my mother was noticing apprehensively out of the corner of her eye. She shooed us out of the house, told us to go ride our bikes, breathe some fresh air. She sounded disgusted.

When Mack was little, I sent him, twice, to stay with his grandparents for a week. He came back a little subdued, and I suspected that my brother's boisterous kids had made him feel his only-child singularity. My brother, Michael — Skip — is my parents' perfect child, in the sense that he embraces what they do and so does his wife, who was his high school girlfriend, and so do his four kids. So far. He runs the drugstore he took over from my dad, and Cheryl runs a day-care center in their home. Their children, three girls and a boy aged eight through fourteen, are athletic and pretty and directed.

The family has a boat that they haul to lakes in the mountains, and season tickets to the football games at the small college down the road. Skip calls once a month and rigorously updates me on everything he and his family and my parents are up to, and laughs a genuine big engaging laugh. I feel when I hang up like someone with a handicap who's been encouraged to do just a little more.

Siobhan had parents who were interesting. That was the careful word that was generally attached to them. They had college educations and read books and had children by previous marriages. Siobhan was their only child together. Her mother was the principal of the grade school, her father a geologist for an oil company. They were dramatically good-looking people, tense and long-limbed.

They didn't scrutinize Siobhan. That's what I envied the most. They seemed to think that she was someone apart from them, interesting in a way they didn't have to understand. There was, too, a kind of dark humor that seemed to move around the edges of that household, a sense of rue. Ruefulness toward themselves, somehow — a nod to the ultimate futility of sincere striving, combined with the willingness to do it anyway. I loved that.

Both of them, cruelly, have Alzheimer's disease. Their personalities are not greatly changed, but they have forgotten their lives. At roughly the same rate, they have forgotten why they held to their dark wit, what brought them together at the cost of two marriages, who their children are. That emptying before death is a terror, and Siobhan feels it. I think sometimes that she has pared down her own needs in order to preempt the possible processes of her genes, to dramatize reduction, make it artful. I think too that she has invested her intelligence in computers because they will carry her thinking forward, even if her own brain someday can't.

The last time I talked to Siobhan, she told me she had looked up from her coffee at a little shop in Seattle to gaze upon the virtually unchanged face of Ronnene Haberchat, whom we'd known as a child. We talked about Ronnene and then, quite naturally, about a teacher named Will Stephens, whom we count as our first love.

Ronnene, in fourth grade, had a ring that was a pearl with two tiny diamonds on either side, a gift from a grandmother who had married a man who struck oil. No one had a ring like Ronnene's.

If we had rings, we had inconsequential little sparkles, or tinny little bands, or flowers of Black Hills gold. Mine was blue glass, shaped like a heart. My mother gave it to me to get rid of my warts. It couldn't hurt, she said. It was a very deep blue, deep-water blue, and the day I put it on, my warts began to go away. For two months, three months, they melted. And then I buried the ring with all the wartiness gathered into it, because I had read a fairy tale along those lines and it seemed a sensible, almost instinctive thing to do. Scapegoat that ring.

Ronnene was quite plump, and so her pearl-and-diamond ring seemed to nestle into her finger comfortably, like a cat. She sometimes got a meditative look on her face when she was bored in class, and then she'd lick a forefinger and dolefully clean her pearl.

There was a bomb drill one day. We were told to imagine a Russian bomber droning overhead, cranking open the big doors, smashing us all with a huge ball of fire. Having imagined that, we were asked to respond by crawling under our desks and waiting for some kind of all-clear. Thousands, millions of American children in those years huddled periodically under their desks, noses right down on the scuffed floor, the feet of their teachers passing slowly, an occasional hand descending to bunch the child up further under her tiny piece of furniture.

Ronnene will always remember the drills as the occasion of specific loss. After one of the all-clears, she began to cry. One of the minuscule diamonds that flanked her pearl was missing. It was there when she went under the desk. It was gone after she'd worked her way out. For the heavy children, those self-extractions were sometimes complicated. All of us sneezed a lot and clapped the dust off our hands.

"My diamond," she cried, holding her ring finger at eye level, crooked pathetically. "It got lost during the bomb."

Our teacher, a spectrally thin woman with hair so gauzy her

scalp showed through, clapped her hands rapidly. She was eternally exasperated and distracted, an unnerving combination because you could never place the source of the trouble.

"Hurry, children," she said, clapping, her gaze somewhere over our heads and to the side. "Find Ronnene's diamond. Quick, now."

We crawled around on our hands and knees, squinting at tan squares and brown squares, all scuffed and filmed with old wax. Up close, the floor was more interesting. There were little maps on it, little roads that led to huge cliffs which turned out to be the leg of a desk, or stacked books, or the teacher's foot. Ronnene sniffed and didn't help. She held herself apart so that nothing else would be taken from her.

We searched and searched. Someone went to the janitor's closet and fetched a big broom. We moved all the desks. Our teacher solemnly swept every inch of the dismal linoleum, and we poked our noses down to the line of dust and probed it with our fingers, spread it out. Nothing.

Ronnene eventually went home early, inconsolable, and the rest of us shrieked onto the playground. Our teacher, Mrs. Flickinger, stayed inside to hunt quietly by herself.

For quite a while after that, the diamond came up in classroom conversation. A child might pounce randomly on some tiny bit of glitter, only to find that it was a bit of foil, a shiny snippet of pencil lead, the sequin from a Halloween mask. It gave a little waver of hope, of oddity, to a long day in that room. The sun would arrow onto the floor at a certain time of the afternoon and our eyes would follow it, searching for the tiny wink. But by the time Mr. Stephens discovered the diamond, most of us had forgotten to think about it except during bomb drills, when Ronnene would recall the whole trauma in lugubrious detail.

Mr. Stephens was the new fifth-grade teacher, and carried a certain excitement with him simply by the fact that he was a tall, broad-shouldered, suited man in a building full of women and children. He knocked on the door of our classroom one day, in that careful way large people do, and then he walked in with a folder of some kind for Mrs. Flickinger. He handed it to her and bowed his head in a mock courtly way, and when he did that, he squinted at the floor. He squatted in his suit and pressed his finger to the linoleum and came up with a diamond on the end of it.

Mrs. Flickinger explained to him what he had found. He tipped back his head and laughed. Ronnene trudged up to pluck it off the tip of his finger, and there was something sad in that walk, because, of course, now the story was over.

In Mr. Stephens's class the next year, I watched him do math on the board with different colors of chalk, so wild and careful at the same time. To be brilliant, you do not refuse the ordinary, you infuse it. That's what he taught us. The band of his white cuff widened, narrowed, as he reached and wrote and dropped his arm to face us, sardonic and kind, eager for us to rise up out of our no-fault *lumpen*ness, confident that we would come to love those numbers as cosmic signposts, the way he did.

He gave us names that had the effect of taking our mockable qualities and turning them powerful, or at least interesting. Hey, Hair-on-fire. You, Quiet-as-rain. Yes, Math-is-my-middle-name? Again please, Jester-to-the-kings. He was the first teacher any of us had who singled out those parts of us that didn't blend and said, Well, take a look at that!

Someone asked him one day what the iron curtain was. It seemed so odd an idea that adults were subscribing to, as if it could be true. It made me embarrassed for them. We asked Mr. Stephens, What exactly is the iron curtain? I saw a metal wall hanging from space to ground somewhere far away, its invisible joints chinging in a high wind. He said it was an imaginary curtain that divided half of the world's idiots from the other half and gave each half a reason to hate the other. He said that hatred made many people feel alive and upright. I remember his words. I remember the old look on his face when he said them.

One day there was a vase of flowers on his desk. Big showy carnations, and a little card taped to the green foil. He backed off from the bouquet, mockingly shot in the heart, pleased, curious, mystified. I remember his shoes that day, how shiny they were, as if he had risen in the night to buff them to glass. He spread his eloquent hands over his heart, and the grin on his face said he'd die happy. Then a sideways glance, the readiness for the joke, the squirt of water in the eye.

He opened the card. His face turned two shades lighter, as if the plug had been pulled. He tore it up and clapped his hands once, then extended them and pretended to patiently pluck something clinging and stringlike from his fingers. He placed the bouquet in the wastebasket, gently. He got out the colored chalk and began to do math. His back I see. The white cuff widening, shrinking.

He never said what the note said, never mentioned the flowers or the note again, but he seemed after that to become smaller in his suit.

He took my hands one day, held them, examined my fingers. (Was there something untoward in this, something transgressive? We would think so now. Has any sane male teacher held a little girl's hands in the past decade?) You have the hands of an artist, he said. A pianist, a painter, a writer. Someone who captures the emanations with her fingers. And old eyes, too, he said kindly, even admiringly. Hey, Old-eyes.

I wore my Brownie outfit that day, my beanie. I wanted to cry for reasons I couldn't begin to understand. I feel the same way at this moment.

He had us draw the world news. A boy named Artie drew a mushroom cloud in a desert and then, in a burst of inspired madness, drew the Alice caterpillar on top, with his big hookah. Oh,

Gift-of-the-gods, Mr. Stephens praised him. Oh, Eye-of-Ra. He showed us Egyptian hieroglyphics and had us make up the stories they told.

He came to class once smelling like stale medicine. He looked scooped out. A few weeks later he was brought before the school board and asked to defend himself against the charge of entertaining communist sympathies. It seems he had been fired from a North Dakota school on similar suspicions. He laughed out loud, our parents said, and his contract was not renewed. He went away forever, and we, his students, mourned.

In the middle of all this, I had a dream that began in a living room, warmly lit, with a Christmas tree at one end. There are other children in the room. It is winter and night, and we are warm on the russet-colored rug. Adults are nearby who are taking care of things. We wear flannel pajamas with feet. The night is suffused with the kind of silence that went away a few years later with the presence of freeways, the electric hum you don't even hear until the switch is off. The sounds in the dream — the owl in the cottonwood, gravel under tires, a barking dog — popped up out of nothing.

And then, in the middle of the dim warm room, a prince on a modest throne. He is high and kind, like a young and friendly pope. He wears the signet ring, the cape edged in ermine. His round and burnished face is framed with cropped blond hair. The crown is modest, almost casual. A prince! A prince! We gather round his feet, the way children in storybooks gather round the feet of storytellers in chairs. Invisible adults mill around, out of sight, happy with it all. A bonus to the evening. A prince.

In a tenor voice, he begins to tell us a story. His mouth shapes itself into his first words. He draws an anticipatory breath.

We hear new sounds. A flutter of leathery wings up in the shadows of the ceiling. Whispers that say, He looks like a prince, but he is something other. And you should have known that. And no, he's not going to attack. But you will be harmed in some way if you do not do exactly this thing: bend over, curl into yourself, the way you do under the desks, and expose the back of your neck.

And we do. And a wind passes over our necks, raising the hairs. Standing them on end. A breath that might also be the trailing tips of skeletal fingers. Another whisper: He is a Russian. The word is the sound of black wind.

# 18

A SICKLY, Y-shaped inscription written in smoke hangs above the year 1986 — hangs above all those horrified faces that watch the Challenger fling its cargo, the astronauts and the schoolteacher, across space and down to the sea.

In 1986, this is what happened to Yuri Petrov, my Russian. One day in April, three years after they arrived from a farm collective outside of Moscow, he sat with his mother on the steps of their new house in Pripyat, the town of the nuclear future. The little city was growing by the day. It was full of babies; babies in prams. Two kilometers away, the Chernobyl nuclear plant gleamed in the warm light. It was one of those days when everything looks freshly watered, full of incipient green. Summer waits just beneath the surface, and what you get for that one day or five is a fizziness to the trees, a fragile incandescence. The weather held and it all burst forth in a way that was extraordinarily beautiful that year. The cherry and apple trees turned into clouds of white and pink, making canopies over the masses of tiny yellow flowers below. Yuri's mother had a little plot in a nearby forest where she cultivated mushrooms, which she sold in town on Saturday mornings.

He told me this as we slowly dressed each other, taking our time. A fan in the window fluttered the curtains, cooled our skin. We talked as we often did afterward, in the hushed, intent manner of those who have lived through a recent large storm.

Yuri said that on the Saturday morning of April 26, he could sense some sort of agitation in the air, though everything looked as usual and it was in fact another deliriously sunny spring day. Everyone was out and about. But there was, he said, an odd glitter to the day — to the buildings, the streets, the sky, even the eyes of the people. He would remember that later, and others would too. That manic sparkle. He would remember a peculiar acid taste on his teeth, as if he had licked a weak battery to test it.

So he didn't know what was wrong, exactly, until he noticed that people kept glancing shyly in the direction of Chernobyl. There were rumors of a fire, an explosion. They looked but said nothing, kept moving about their business, laughed too loudly.

At the Chernobyl plant, one of the big blocks had a hole in it. A wall had split open and a column of smoke was rising from the gap.

Yuri asked a policeman what had happened. A fire, the cop said. But the fire is out. He lit a cigarette and offered Yuri one, which made him know that something very bad had happened.

Well, said Yuri, and what about the reactor? What about the radiation? He looked around him at the city going about its business — at mothers wheeling prams, at children playing in the dirt, at a big banner near the grade school that announced the Health Day races that afternoon. The banner snapped in the breeze. A big-bellied man stretched out on a lawn chair on a rooftop to tan himself.

Don't worry about anything, the policeman said. The authorities have the matter in hand. Go about your business, he said, tossing his cigarette into the street.

And so for twenty-four hours Pripyat went about its business, bathed in radiation. Saturated with radiation. With not a word from anyone who knew what had actually happened, not even the suggestion that children stay indoors that day. Or that everyone stay away from the forest where Yuri's mother had her mushrooms, because that is where the debris from the exploded reactor had been dumped.

There was a road through the forest, and it was a popular walk. All day, women wheeled babies along the road through the forest, which literally began to glow and then turn from green to a color that was something like rust. Later they called it the red forest. The birds sang among their radioactive leaves.

Yuri's mother, picking her mushrooms, took in many roentgens of radiation and suffered terrible burns to her legs. A third of the babies later developed thyroid cancer. Yuri himself stayed inside most of those first few days, but he suffered for years from aches and shivers that were fierce, episodic, almost malarial. And I suspect that if he is still alive, he grows more sickly over time.

Firemen who were summoned to the plant in the black early morning hours after the explosion extinguished most of the blaze at the cost of their own lives, and arguably saved much of the world from poisoning. No one had taught them radiation protection. No protective garb was available. They couldn't even locate functioning dosimeters to measure the full presence, the speed, of their impending death.

Already firemen and plant workers lay in the hospital with their "nuclear tans," full-body browning, a very bad joke. The man who had been sunning himself on the roof was vomiting, raving.

But for twenty-four hours, no one in the Zone — the thirty-kilometer radius of the plant — was told a thing.

Eleven years later, Yuri arrived in my yard, on a spring day exactly like the one in the sweet Ukraine before the reactor blew. That tenderest time.

They finally evacuated the Zone. Hundreds of buses moved in a slow line away from the towns as frantic dogs barked to be let on with their owners. The pets were left; their coats were perfect traps for irradiated dust, and they roamed in packs until they were dead.

Yuri and his mother moved to Kiev, where the radiation was only one hundred times higher than it should be and machines were available to wash, wash the streets. Everyone washed — for months, it seemed.

Yuri's cousin Andrej was a policeman in Kiev. He had a lot of power and, it seemed to Yuri, money to burn. Andrej was also an ethnic Russian who had migrated south for the opportunities, said Yuri.

Yuri once saw a street vendor paying money to Andrej, and another time he heard some men in a café talking in low tones about how certain vendors had disappeared because they hadn't performed their payoff obligations. Yuri heard this and wished he hadn't. He'd always been afraid of Andrej. And then he became more afraid.

Five months after the explosion, residents of Pripyat were allowed to go back to their homes to salvage valuables that were not unacceptably irradiated. Many people were by now far, far away, placed in new villages and relocation centers, without the means to travel. So they never did return. They had been told the evacuation was for three days only. Three days and they would be back home.

But Yuri went back. Pripyat, once home to 40,000 people, stood suspended and empty, all of it behind a wire fence now, to stop looters. Everything was irradiated, fixed. The old life. The first life. Laundry on lines. Dishes on tables. Beds unmade. Money and documents and photos and mementos waiting in drawers, maybe forever. Yuri saw nothing alive except two ravenous pigs devouring the remains of a Great Dane.

Yuri left a beautiful old rug, his grandmother's, which would never pass the dosimeter test, and took only two small boxes of photos, heartbreaking in their ordinariness. A man in a field.

Some uncles, arms around each other, toasting something. A baby in a huge white dress.

In Kiev, Andrej had a post-Chernobyl business. He brokered train tickets out of the city. Beneath Kiev's shiny calm and the constant washing of the streets, there was a quiet panic to leave the area. Some people managed to get train tickets, but they could not enter the station for departure unless a policeman let them through. Policemen could be persuaded.

Andrej made a killing off Chernobyl. He charged Yuri, his own cousin, almost all the money he had to get out of Kiev and onto a plane for America, a trip sponsored by a pentecostal organization in California.

I see Yuri's face as I remember this, see again how old it became whenever he mentioned Andrej. I see the small sad boxes holding images of vanished ordinariness, of lives on the brink of ashes.

My silver box of ashes sits near my bed, here at the Trocadero. When I grabbed it in haste from my kitchen shelf, I thought only of something I could use to deflect police attention from Jimster Reece. I would plant it somehow on Andrej, and that would be the proof that he had entered our house.

I peer into it now, press my finger to the plastic bag around the volcano ashes, and think about that May day in 1980. How my first thought as we watched the ash coat our town was nuclear disaster. How the volcano is for me forever linked with the beginning of Mack and the beginning of my marriage, and how my first urge, faced with both, was to run.

In 1986 — the year of the Challenger, the year of Chernobyl — Ren's mother had been dead for seventeen years. His father, Timothy, in that time had grown into a new version of himself. He had refused to look at his wife's ravaging illness as a cruel joke on them both and spoke of her in a respectful, almost awed manner, as he would speak of a genius in his field. He went dancing with widows. He signed on for a cruise to Turkey. He bought a hot tub, took Spanish lessons, coedited a guide to the state's roadside flowers. He joined a charismatic Catholic church. Hired indigents to work in his yard. And one day, in 1986, he picked up a hitchhiker.

The hitchhiker swore later on the Bible that he simply had not wanted to chat. But Timothy Woodbridge kept asking him questions about himself. There was a long silence. They drove along. Timothy asked one more genial question, and after that the screen went dark.

In the police photo, Timothy is tied to a tree with his feet burned black. His head falls toward his bony rib cage. His snowy hair veils his eyes.

The man who burned and shot Ren's father was represented by a public defender, and he fit the profile of any number of Ren's early clients: born drunk, brutalized as a child, addicted as an adult — a trapped rat gnawing its own leg off, then lifting its head to appraise the rest of us.

During the trial, Ren developed allergies that put him in the hospital for a couple of days and have never fully left him. His eyes became chronically irritated-looking, chronically red. Since 1986, his eyes have looked sore.

Not too long after Timothy Woodbridge's death, Ren's law partner, Franklin Klemenhagen, said he felt ready to move on. He'd decided he could do more for the unfortunate as a minister than as a public defender. He'd decided that spiritual counseling coincided better with his own evolutionary situation, as he put it, than the mundane and exhausting details of defenses and appeals did.

Now here is a part of the story that turns out, in terms of both Ren's life and mine, to be pivotal.

Shortly after his father's death, Ren began to take on personal injury cases, representing mostly workers who had been injured at the mill or on the railroad. Certainly at that point I was on his side. He simply felt that most large companies will make do with the legal minimum in terms of safety equipment, their prime concern being the bottom line. I couldn't know then that he was developing an obsession with safety. It would grow fiercer in the following years and culminate in the installation of our elaborate security system after Elise's house was ransacked.

In his personal-injury work, Ren occasionally went head-to-head in court with an attorney named Warren Evinrude, a senior partner in a firm that provided local counsel for the company that owned the mill. Evinrude is a blocky man with a short crewcut, hyperthyroidal eyes, a delicate shapely nose. He's smart, cynical, almost genial in the way you can be if nothing about other people's needs or feelings really affects you. You just turn on the button, genial, and leave it there until another mode is called for — courtroom outrage, say — but the brain, the heart, are reptilian. His wife was on the symphony board with me, and we saw them occasionally at parties or a fundraiser.

I always felt there was something a little too vehement in Ren's disdain for Warren, as if he were insisting to himself how much he hated the guy, how weasely he thought he was, because something about Warren was attractive to him. Warren's absence of doubt, perhaps, or his matter-of-fact cruelty. His imperviousness to any consideration but winning. So perhaps I shouldn't have been as surprised as I was when Ren came home one day to say he had taken a job with Warren Evinrude's firm.

I was shocked. Shocked and angry, too, that he'd made the decision without so much as running it by me. I argued with him. I begged for some kind of explanation that made any sense. And what I remember are his raw-looking eyes and the way he simply smiled and shrugged, as if he were almost as surprised as I was. He seemed at that moment as strange to me as if he'd suddenly put on a woman's dress and declared the emergence of a squelched part of himself. For years he'd been fueled with disdain for that firm; he'd crowed when they lost; he'd done perfect imitations of Evinrude, of his bullying little belly-out walk, of his imperious whine. And now he was one of them, claiming that he needed to know the enemy from the inside out. He said it, "the enemy," in a way that seemed to mock his previous naive and hopeful self.

There is one more bit of bad news from 1986, the bad year. One night Ren and I watched a television report about the dismissal of the most recent ambassador to Honduras. It seemed he had cared more about Honduras the country, its feeble economy and fledgling democracy, than he had about Honduras as a staging area for the contras and their CIA runners. The ambassador had not summoned the proper fervor for all-out military action against Nicaragua. Our man in Tegucigalpa was history.

What we saw on the television was a correspondent in the capital, explaining the dismissal as he stood before the American embassy. A man in a suit walked out of the embassy, carrying a briefcase, looking very governmental. He passed very briefly by the camera, casually turning away from it when he noticed its presence. He had graying hair, a fast and lanky stride.

He was Stephen Lovano.

Ren and I both recognized him at once. He was there and then he wasn't. And then they moved to sports.

What was he? An attaché? CIA? Consultant? A good guy? A bad guy? I felt sure we would never know. And we looked then at each other, Ren and I did, and I thought about Ren and Stephen dropping one by one from a small plane so long ago. How I couldn't tell who was whom as they leaped. How it took them so long to reach the ground.

# 19

I CAME HOME from work one day last summer to find Yuri talking to a man with yellow-white hair. There is a low stone wall at the back of our lot. Yuri stood on one side of it. The man stood on the other, in the alley, next to a silver BMW. I greeted them.

The visitor was strongly built but with a rancid little mouth, an infantile mouth. He nodded but said nothing. Yuri didn't either, so I gave them both my big hostess smile and went into the house. They resumed their conversation in low voices.

I put away groceries and watched. The man was Yuri's height and wore khakis and heavy boots, a windbreaker with some kind of logo on it. I would later see a certain faint resemblance between them, but everything that was liquid in Yuri was clotted in the visitor. He was claylike, opaque, and his hair was the color of dirty smoke.

They talked intensely, the visitor occasionally chopping the air, and then he patted Yuri on the face in that cuffing way that is the opposite of affection. He retrieved a pair of round, very blue sunglasses from his jacket pocket, put them on, stared at the back of the house for a few long seconds. And then he drove away.

He began to show up once or twice a week. Each time he left Yuri pale and furious. After one visit Yuri planted his shovel in the ground and turned on the hose, letting the cold water run over his head and shaking himself like a dog.

Who was the man?

"He is a Mister Big-shot," Yuri said bitterly.

It was Andrej, the cousin from Kiev. The cop. He had taken the graft money he'd made from Chernobyl escapees and his many scams since then, and he'd come to our town because Yuri and the others were here and he'd heard about some opportunities. Within a few weeks, he had a job as a security officer at a parts warehouse that had been looted a number of times. In return for a certain fervor in carrying out his job, they paid him in cash and didn't get curious about working papers.

In the light-blind moth knocking against the globe of the lamp, in the cockroach, in the bat, there is a skittering sideways movement that resists prediction and therefore frightens us. They don't travel in the manner of most things that are alive. Andrej belongs to them.

"It is temporary," Yuri continued wearily. "He is a Mister Big-shot and he has big ideas about the money, but he will move on." His fingers rubbed imaginary cash.

Andrej wanted to get Yuri on at the warehouse, but Yuri didn't want that. He wanted to work in people's yards, with dirt, with plants. I thought of the earth he'd tended in the Zone. Of the crippled animals that wandered across it after all the humans had left. Of plows left standing in the middle of fields. Of that bitter, bitter silence. No birds. A tangled, charred tower.

Yuri bent and patted the good soil around a pretty little ornamental cherry tree we'd chosen, and I wondered, how could he ever look at a tree now without seeing its poisoned ghost?

Andrej too was some kind of poisoned presence, and it seemed impossible that he was related to Yuri, whose very skin, the suppleness and tawniness of it, was the expression of grace in all its meanings. As simple as that. The lovely V to his belt line. The way he seemed to glide downward when he squatted, smooth as a cat — all of it was grace.

.   .   .

For days at a time, Yuri worked in the yard alone and at peace. He did beautiful, meticulous work — the edging, the mounding, the planting and replanting, the moving of old plants. He broke up the grim concrete walk with a sledgehammer — a week-long, backbreaking project — and replaced it with a lazy S of flagstones. This was our best idea, and it changed the entire space. It gentled it. It carried the eye in a curve.

He drew diagrams, and we sat on the deck and talked about the diagrams, our plans. We toured the yard, talking plant talk to each other, which became at some point an elegant code.

There would be days of this, as I say. And then the gray BMW would glide into the alleyway. Andrej would get out and hook the air with his finger, and Yuri would walk slowly to him. I see Andrej still, waiting at that distance. The booted feet, the windbreaker, the blue glasses. He built some kind of rage in Yuri, the lid-on kind that is so fierce it actually gives off a smell.

Andrej once killed a dog for the fun of it, Yuri told me one day. He hunted it down, and he did not kill it quickly.

On one of Andrej's visits, I made myself feel bold and I went out of the house to ask Yuri a question. Something unimportant. Was the new cayenne spray working on the aphids? Something like that. What I wanted, really, was to force Andrej to acknowledge me. I don't know why, exactly. It seemed important. I had on a yellow linen dress, I remember. I was buoyant. I was feeling a kind of steady exuberance that I didn't want to examine too closely.

Yuri introduced me to his cousin. Andrej extended his hand in an elaborate, almost mocking way, and I shook it. There was nothing there. He had one of those handshakes that has no skeleton, that is dead. I pulled my hand away. I thought of a dog dying slowly. Andrej watched me calmly. His neck was deeply pockmarked. The little mouth chewed gum; chewed, chewed. I wished he were behind glass.

·   ·   ·

The yard took a new shape. The big square of grass bordered by disconsolate shrubbery and a few perennials had become a garden. A beautiful room. There were curving beds and raised beds, planted to bloom white and deep blue, shades of lavender, brilliant yellow. There was the lovely snaking path. There was a half-circle of herbs, and a separate patch in the shape of a figure eight that would be planted entirely with basil. There was a circulating pond. It was eccentric and vivid and full of surprises. It was ours.

I think now about Andrej's physical presence, the way the components of his physical self war against each other, and how that may be some key to the way he seems to skitter even as he stands in place.

There is the mean little mouth that is by itself simply a baby's mouth. But it's at the bottom of a coarse block of a face. And the face is topped with old man's hair the color of sulfur. His body has the trussed bulk of a powerful man, but his robust build is undermined by a faint limp. He heaves his shoulders around when he walks, compensating for it or distracting the eye from it, but it is there. It's the result of a compound fracture he got when he was shot off a motorcycle in Kiev. I know that from Yuri. I know too much about Andrej.

Andrej drives his BMW around town and looks, from a distance, not so different from Warren Evinrude, whose bulk is similar if his hair is not, and whose BMW is also an ashen gray.

One day Yuri brought me a trellis he'd made out of willow branches. We'd decided to use a trellis, and I was shopping here and there, looking through the catalogues. Then he simply brought his own, unloaded it from the back of his noisy red pickup. The branches were a burnt red and were twisted into a design of ovals atop ovals. It was put together with tiny nails, branches curved and bent.

He said, "You do not have to have this trellis." He smiled. "I found the branches in the forest and I made it, but you do not have to have this for your own. I can find a customer, I think." But he was watching my face and he knew what I thought, and he knew how beautiful it was, apart from what I thought. So the offer, the words, fell away to nothing. I thanked him and he put it where we had wanted it.

I thought of him making it, bending the branches with his slim fingers, knocking the nails into place. Did he draw out the design beforehand? The legs of the trellis were long. He set it deep into the ground. He walked through it. Curved shadows ran across his head and face as he did. Then I walked through it. And we did it again, so gratuitously that we both laughed.

After he left, after he was long gone, I examined that trellis with no idea what I was looking for. I found his initials, YP, carved in small letters on one leg, near the base. What was he thinking when he did that? Was it the simple gesture of a crafts-man who knew he had made a fine thing? Or was it a way to place himself in a strange place? To say, I was there in that little American city in the mountains. I was there. This is my sign.

It may have been the day he brought the trellis. A story ran in the paper and I told Yuri about it just to entertain him — a bit of quirky news from the larger world. It was about a new wave of global life insurance scams. An immigrant to America buys a life insurance policy and names a brother or a friend who is also in America as the beneficiary. The purchaser then goes back to Haiti, to Mexico, to the former Soviet states for a visit. Calamity befalls him. Word is received in America that his car overturned, he was taken to the hospital, he was pronounced dead. This in-formation is accompanied by the kind of documentation that a "dead" person is able to purchase in a country in turmoil — a place where the shenanigans of minor officials are the least of anyone's worries. An official death is purchased and the documentation is sent to America, where the beneficiary cashes in. What company will go through the trouble of subpoenaing an official from, say, Ukraine?

The problem, of course, is that the purchaser cannot reappear or he might be identified. The purchaser cannot resume a life in America without significant risk. The purchaser must basically stay gone.

"Stay gone, yes," said Yuri. "The person who gets the money will want the purchaser to stay gone." He said this sardonically. "That is easy enough," he said.

One day I saw Andrej take a letter out of his leather jacket pocket and dangle it in front of Yuri. Yuri reached for it. Andrej snatched it back, the little mouth pulled into a grin. He put a flat hand on Yuri's chest and pushed him very slowly until he had him standing where he wanted him, and then he dropped the hand and moved back. Yuri's clenched fists rested on his thighs. He stood cocked and cocky, but he didn't move from the place where Andrej had put him.

Andrej removed the letter from its envelope and held it by a corner, as if it were something soiled, and farsightedly read from it. Yuri didn't move. A breeze lifted the hair from the crown of his head.

Andrej held the letter, read it, dangled it, dropped it in the dirt, and ground it with his boot as if he were stubbing out a cigarette. Then he saluted and climbed back into the BMW and glided away. Yuri retrieved the matted and torn paper and put it in his pocket without reading it.

Sometime later he told me that the letter contained details from one of Andrej's "colleagues" about the old people who were returning to Chernobyl and Pripyat. Yuri's mother was one of them. She had lived more than a decade in the settlement camp where she had been sent after Chernobyl. She had recovered from the deep burns on her legs. She had refused to travel with Yuri to America because she felt too old to start a new life. And now she was going back to the Zone, where she had been poisoned with radiation. She and dozens of other elderly ones had decided to reoccupy abandoned houses, to grow contaminated food in hot dirt. What difference, when there were only a few years remaining to them?

Officially, these old people would not exist. They would take themselves off the map when they moved back. This interested Andrej. They needed protection, yes? Bad people could come along and do terrible things to them, and who could help them, if they lived in a place that didn't officially exist? Who would they go to? Andrej had friends. Andrej's friends were in a position to offer protection for a price. He thought Yuri should know this.

I saw Yuri's mother as a ghost in a kerchief, tending a gray garden.

She and the other old ones would reinhabit houses that had been freeze-framed, because no one had thought they were leaving for long. They would go back to houses interrupted, houses with unwashed dishes, desiccated curtains, children's clothes, a half-finished jigsaw puzzle, photographs, letters, marriage certificates, a grandmother's icon of the Virgin. Houses like dioramas of sudden abandonment. The bones of pets on the step. That is where Yuri's mother would go to live.

Yuri told me this, not long before I would never see him again. My head rested in the warm crook of his arm. By this time he spoke English with few stumbles. He said it was a very small world in the end. He said Andrej had his ways of getting what he wanted.

And what does he want from you? I asked.

All he can get, Yuri said acridly. All.

What in particular does he want from you? I asked, trying with my tone of voice to make Andrej a faraway trouble needing no immediate response. A thundercloud a day away.

What can you offer him? I said too lightly. Money? You are so wealthy, Yuri, that he hangs around waiting for you to pay him a share? A guy with a BMW? He can get something from you?

And then there was a moment. I remember the slam of a neighbor's door, the rumbling of the dishwasher downstairs. I thought, Well, Yuri does have the inside of this house. He does have me.

It was a thought I didn't want to have. Are you here because you want to be? I could have asked that, as he closed his eyes and kissed the hollow of my hand.

But a question like that is an accusation. There seemed to be no way to ask it and still have him, and I chose to have him.

At this point, it was as if Andrej stepped into the room. Stepped at least into the hall outside the room, and stood there smoking, a little smile coming and going, and I couldn't make him go away.

In Kiev, Andrej had had a girlfriend for a while. She was very quiet and seemed not to have anyone who cared much about where she went or who she went with. A sick old grandmother was her guardian, Yuri thought. Or maybe the girl had just left home. She didn't speak much. She and Andrej were together all the time, but he always spoke as if he were alone.

Then she was seen less often with him. When she did show up, she looked very thin and suddenly old. No one could understand what he saw in her. One day she was found in a ditch, fully clothed, with a crushed temple.

Andrej paid for a funeral and bought a huge wreath of blue flowers. Two or three other people were there. Someone said, very matter-of-factly, that she was a prostitute. That Andrej had run her; that she had disappeared; that he had hunted her down with a patience that was terrifying.

# 20

LATE THIS AFTERNOON, as I surveyed the Trocadero parking lot, I saw the Reverend Franklin Klemenhagen's shiny head emerge from a parked car in front of the restaurant next door. He didn't go into the restaurant but walked rather carefully across that lot, onto the Trocadero lot. Yes, it was Franklin Klemenhagen. The palms of my hands began to prickle.

He had a cloth hat tucked into the pocket of his Bermuda shorts and binoculars hanging from his neck. He turned toward the river, then looked quickly around and knocked on the door of the last ground-floor room. It opened. He disappeared.

I was so amazed I couldn't stay put. I walked around my room, did some stretches, peeked out the window to make sure his car was still parked. I tried to find something calming on television — a documentary on photosynthesis, a biography of an inventor — but caught only the end of an interview about the fantasies of young females versus those of young males. "A girl might pretend that a banana is a telephone," a scientist said gravely. "But in the hands of a boy, it becomes a magic wand."

I watched someone on the shopping channel give a little speech about seed pearls, and wanted to hit her. I turned to the weather channel, then started thinking about Jimster's father passed out in front of the weather, the endless weather. The weather channel reminds me of the ocean, of the way humans will watch for hours its lulling, rhythmic waves. A long swoop of weather spirals gracefully out of the Pacific to move across the country, left to right, dipping playfully into the South, bringing moisture, precip, and sometimes a big unseasonable cooling front.

Unseasonable. That's about as dramatic as it gets on the weather channel. The announcers avoid all hyperbole and anecdote, the stuff of real-life weather. The weather person would never tell you the story my cousin in Tuscaloosa told me about a maid at the Super 8 getting sucked off a second-story balcony by a tornado. She was lost entirely to existence. Blipped off the earth. Not even a dropped shoe. That's a story you won't hear about on the weather channel.

I kept checking the lot. In a couple of hours, Franklin emerged from the room. He looked around like a cartoon adulterer and sauntered studiously toward the river. In a few minutes a second person emerged from the room and threw a light sweater around her shoulders and took the gravel path toward the river, following Franklin at a respectable distance. Her auburn hair seemed iridescent in the early evening light. Her step was springy.

I watched her amble carefully toward the river and I thought, What do I know about anything, actually?

She stopped, turned slightly, as if someone had called her name. It was indeed Elise Prentice. My neighbor of many years. Elise. She caught up with Franklin and they walked together to a bench. They sat down, looking small before the pink-streaked sky. I thought of the call I made to my great-uncle Ben a few years ago on his ninety-second birthday. I asked him what he was doing. "Sitting in an armchair," he cried. "Watching the end of the world!" Franklin and Elise on their little bench in front of the huge inflamed sky made me remember that.

I examined myself in the mirror and thought with a lacy little trickle of excitement, I could walk past them, and they would never know. I think I could do it. I think I could pass.

I began to go through the motions of preparing, just to see if the idea would stay or go. I put on my pale pink pantsuit, my gray wig, my face-shading hat. My sunglasses. I had been practicing an old woman's gait and had improved it.

Again I entertained the idea of walking out the door, passing their bench, greeting them. But what if Franklin or Elise turned to me and said incredulously, "Francesca! What are you doing? Why are you dressed like that? When did you get back?" After all, I'd altered only the superficial details of myself: the appearance of my hair, the level of my taste. What if they knew me?

Gerrald was working the last half of the day person's shift for her. She hadn't been able to get a babysitter, so Gerrald was going to work fourteen hours straight. He told me this and looked quizzically at me, but said nothing about my appearance. I walked slowly out the door, grateful for the hat brim that shaded my flaming face, and approached Franklin and Elise.

As they heard my steps on the gravel, they moved apart, because who ever knew, in a town of sixty thousand? If he happened to be recognized, he could pretend to be counseling her, but not if he ran his fingertips up and down the inside of her freckled arm, as he had been doing a few moments ago.

"She goes around looking like an old lady," Franklin said. "And there's something about it that makes me incredibly sad. Why can't she simply be what she is?"

I stopped, startled.

"What is she, Frank?" Elise said.

I examined my feet. They couldn't be talking about me. It made no sense. I thought of the little crack that begins to seep into so many voices after sixty-five or so, how I would make it present in my own greeting. I had to focus on something small like that or I couldn't move on. I drew up to them. They both turned their heads, too quickly, eager to be reassured that it was a stranger. And here's the little miracle: they were.

I turned my face only slightly in greeting, as if my neck were too stiff for anything more. I nodded and made a little sound that wasn't a word, and kept going.

"Pretty evening!" said Franklin, relieved that it was only an elderly stranger. And also out of a kind of rote imposition of his presence on the unfortunate, I thought. Now I was expected to respond. "Very," I said, the little crackle quite successful. I limped on.

"I just worry about her," Franklin said. I bet you do, I thought. Your wife the Montessori teacher, cooks some heart-friendly something for your dinner while you screw Elise Prentice at the Trocadero. Do it or don't do it, I thought. Sin or don't sin. But don't insist on divvying up your guilt.

"I worry that she's sad somehow," Franklin said. How far was he going to take this? And why was Elise murmuring sympathetically? It was ghoulish.

"She's a kid," Franklin said. "A kid who is acting out some kind of complicated rebellion with a kid who is even angrier and more desperate than she is."

"Mack?" said Elise. "Mack is so desperate?"

I stopped dead in the path and pretended to search in my purse for something. Their voices were almost out of earshot.

"I don't know," Franklin said. "Despite their little mom-and-pop act, I worry that they have some kind of totally precarious hold on reality. That they're hanging by their fingernails." His voice had real heaviness in it. "And that if I even speak to her..." I lost the rest of it.

Not so long ago, Franklin's photo was in the newspaper. When I saw it, I thought he had been ill. All his hair was gone, and he wore a white shirt that looked like a movie doctor's smock. Tamara explained that he had shaved his head because he thought all bald looked more virile than part bald, and that the smock was a new hemp shirt that he liked because it looked South American. "He's the same old Frankie, though," she assured me. The way she said it made him sound like a big dim pet.

Franklin was in the newspaper because his church was co-sponsoring an appearance in town of some sort of drumming group. "I think they're those sensitive guys who are trying to get back in touch with their *really* sensitive guys," Tamara said. She picked at her fingernail polish. "Frankie thinks he might get to drum with them." She smiled sweetly. "Let's all keep our fingers crossed."

Someone was coming up the path from the river toward me. I was eager to pass close to him, confident that I'd passed one test and could now pass all. He looked at a distance like an old man bent under the weight of some kind of bundle on his shoulder. As he drew closer, I saw that he was young, his face creased with dirt. He seemed to be spitting words at me.

"Don't you just *know* it," he said acidly, stopping to stare straight at me. He was smoke and urine and venom. I turned around and began to walk slowly back toward the motel. Franklin was on his feet.

"I'm talking to *you*," the man with the bundle warned. I walked a little faster, losing my limp, wanting only to get into my room, where it was dark and quiet. His footfalls picked up speed. I ducked my head for some reason, just watching my own moving feet. I looked up and bumped right into Franklin. Smack into his chest. He steadied me. I could smell his aftershave, his stale breath. I was an aged lady in the arms of a man I'd known for years, who didn't know he held me. I turned my head aside and shielded my face with my hand.

Franklin rested a hand on my upper arm and lifted Elise up from the bench by an elbow — all of this quite brisk — and instructed both of us to go to the motel lobby while he talked to the venomous drifter advancing on us.

Elise now scurried down the path to the motel with me, urging me along, glancing anxiously over her shoulder at Franklin. "A little faster," she murmured. "Oh God," she said under her breath. "What if he has a knife, a gun?" She broke into a little trot, still grabbing my arm, and I ran too. She seemed not to notice my new elasticity.

When we got to the motel lobby, she parked me on a plastic bench outside the door. She sat down next to me. "Now I want you to listen very carefully, dear," she said. "I'm going to leave you and drive away in a car. What I want you to do is this — you go inside to the clerk, and you tell him to call 911." I nodded. "He needs to tell 911 to send someone to help."

Franklin and the drifter were still talking, or rather, Franklin was talking and the drifter was yelling at him, his face twisted. Elise grabbed my arm. She shook it a little, the way she would rouse a dreamy child. "Do you hear me?" she hissed. I nodded. "Okay. Now do it. And do it fast."

She disappeared around the corner. Her Saab appeared from behind the building and pulled onto the frontage road.

"Gerrald," I said. He looked up, a little disoriented. "Call 911 and tell them a guy is about to assault another guy out there on the river walk." He looked at me, eyebrows raised, and went to the door to have a look.

Franklin had bent his head, as if trying to listen harder to the screaming man. A priest in confession. He was standing too close. The man was shifting back and forth on his feet, chopping at the air with the flat of his hand. Franklin looked incredibly frail. I noticed for the first time how rounded his shoulders had become. His shorts and his sandals made his legs too spindly, too thin for his top half.

"Call them, Gerrald," I said. "This guy isn't fooling around."

"He hasn't done anything," Gerrald said patiently. "What do I tell them? A goofball bum is shouting at a guy who apparently likes to listen? There's no law that says all the parties in a conversation have to be polite."

The man had begun to bark at Franklin. He'd unloaded his big pack from his back and placed it by the side of the walk, and now he had his thin hands on his hips and was literally barking.

"Call them," I said again. Then I saw a glint of light near the belt of the ragged man. "Call them!" I shouted.

He saw what I did, and ran for the phone.

Franklin toppled sideways. The tattered man grabbed his bundle and ran toward the bushes by the river. I ran out of the motel, really ran. Franklin was curled on the walk like a baby, groaning. There was a smear of blood on his shirt near his waist. He was groaning softly. He looked very confused.

"It's all right," I said, my hand on his shoulder. "It's all right. People are coming. You got a cut, but it's not serious." I hoped I was right.

Franklin examined my face, squinting as if I were a long way away. "Francesca?" he said, sounding as if he were about to cry. "Why are you here? Why do you look like this?" He closed his eyes and opened them again.

"I'm going to leave now," I said. "A man from the motel will be here in a few seconds. And the medical people are on their way. Do you hear the sirens?" He nodded wearily. He groaned.

I ran back to the motel. Gerrald was coming out of the door. I put both hands on his shoulders. "I'm not here, Gerrald, and I never was," I said. I shook him a little. "I was never here, Gerrald, and that's what you're going to say."

I heard, ummistakably, the imperious tones I would have used in my waiting life. Directions to a servant. I sounded horrible.

He looked at me warily. "Right," he said. "What about the victim out there?"

"He's raving," I said softly, trying to apologize with the tone of my voice. "He's in shock, I think. He's saying anything that comes into his mind."

Gerrald gave the empty front desk a worried look. I thought about offering to answer the phone, then saw that it would be impossible. Whoever was driving those sirens would want to talk to me.

"Scamper off," he said, flicking his hand at me. I watched him move at a slow trot down the walk to the fallen Franklin, and I did what he said.

My room. My cave.

Voices outside now; the sirens moaning to a stop. That pause before the urgent footsteps on the concrete. "Stand back," someone called eagerly. "Don't touch him." I moved the curtain an inch. A huge yellow fire engine was arriving. Why do they send a fire engine? What could be the use of a fire engine except in the case of self-immolations?

They did their busy things to Franklin. The wound had looked superficial to me, but maybe it wasn't. Maybe Franklin was out there dying. Tamara's father, Krystal's husband, Elise's lover — a pudgy do-gooder in happy-camper clothes who, whatever else he did wrong or right, had dealt with that madman as if he were a human being.

I tried to hold to my idea of Franklin as a bully altruist who enjoys the power he wields over the desperate, but I was having trouble with that. There had been something valiant in his solitary engagement with that raver. He had acted with no idea of an audience, and he had to have been terrified.

Those stupid white socks in sandals. His fanny pack and binoculars. His knock-knees and pear shape. That shaved head, like a little kid trying to be tough.

Now they will come for me, I thought. Gerrald won't be able to contradict Franklin, who is probably right now sitting up on the stretcher and calmly describing his encounter with a person he's known for years who was, inexplicably, dressed up like an old woman.

I felt as if I'd slipped behind enemy lines, done what I was supposed to do, and slipped back. Now I waited.

Late that night I woke from a short, sweaty sleep. Gerrald had not even rung my room to talk about Franklin. He was leaving me alone. I'd heard some people unload their car around nine, and some others around ten. All I heard now was a television, maybe two, in the far distance.

Gerrald sat at the desk, head in arms, catnapping. I approached quietly and murmured his name. If he didn't answer, I'd let him be. I'd never seen him napping before. He raised his head and looked at me. "Hello, dear," he said. He looked very tired.

"Sleeping at the wheel?"

"That's the size of it. I'm wiped out." He looked wiped out. Very pale. Hair out of place for the first time I could recall. Tie flung over the back of a chair.

"What's wrong?" I said.

He looked at me mildly. "Well, I've been here eight hours already. And I spent at least an hour lying for you. It took a lot out of me."

"What did they ask?"

"Well, I hardly know where to start." He yawned widely. There was something different about him. Not antagonism toward me, not that I could identify, but a self-protective nonchalance that I hadn't noticed before. A studied casualness. The day, I sensed, had reintroduced Gerrald to some specters that had shaken him badly. The man with the knife? The police and their questions? My snapped orders? All of it together seemed somehow to have damaged him a little. Hurt him.

"How bad was the wound?" I asked.

"Not bad." He looked at me, his gaze not quite on my eyes. "At least, they didn't seem all up in arms about it. Someone said something about blood loss that wasn't profound."

"Profound?" I said, trying to stress it in a way that would forge a tiny alliance of disdain for such big-shot talk. He didn't react.

"So the owner happened to call when I was outside with that guy, and he called back and chewed me out for leaving the phone unattended," Gerrald said.

"What were you supposed to *do*?" I cried, sounding outraged. "Let a stabbed man lie bleeding while you took calls for reservations?"

Gerrald shrugged.

"I couldn't stay out there," I said, trying to make his eyes look at me. "And I couldn't stay in here with the phone. They would have questioned me."

"I'm not saying this or that about what you should have done," Gerrald said. "You have your reasons and I'm not going to ask what they are, and I can't say I'm really surprised." He raised his head and I saw how truly bruised and angry he was. "It's just that it was no party trying to answer all this and that kind of question, like how did I notice the stabbed guy, and why was he saying there was someone else, a lady, talking to him after he got stabbed, and he knew her. For almost twenty years, he says!"

"Strange."

"That's when they kind of figured that he was out of it, I guess."

"Well, I'd guess so," I said. "He was hurt. He wouldn't have been himself."

# 21

WHEN WARREN EVINRUDE SMILES, he simply bares his teeth. He cultivates a year-round tan and wears English suits, Italian loafers. But they look like a costume on him. He made his early money from a sophisticated and untouchable real estate scam, then went somewhat straighter. He owns half a dozen shabby buildings in town that he rents out to groups of students for criminal prices. As a lawyer, he represents the Recon Corporation, which ignored its own accident probability data and put the flawed pipeline through a big valley west of town — the pipeline that broke and forced all those people, including Jimster and his father, to find new homes. He owns, with some hidden partners, golf courses in Arizona, and in Florida an amusement park where all the employees have to sign loyalty oaths and accident waivers.

Evinrude, Terwilliger, Dennehy, and Fleet, the senior four, have wives who are of a kind: clotheshorses with great hair, teeth, nails, and a bizarre steady-state effervescence. They are now in their mid-fifties, just that cultural jump ahead of Ren and me. They married young, when the central idea was that they'd be the cultured adjunct of a moneymaker, and a mother, and the locus of virtue and constancy in the marriage. Their kids are mostly grown and gone, and the wives are expected now to stay looking good and performing in an unlayered, spirited, consoling manner around their men. I imagine one or the other of them from time to time becomes cranky, perverse, testing. *How* much room do I have? But they quickly find out that if they cause trouble, they have no value.

Warren's wife, Tricia, is the paragon. She has well-cut, well-dyed hair that frames her lifted face, and she likes to wear expensive short-skirted suits in fabrics like silk and satin and colors like mauve and white. They almost work, but not quite. Her legs are too undistinguished.

There is no swiftness in her. I suspect she was a semipopular high school girl, the slightly heavy one who was always with the pretty, sexy one and who scanned for her cue before she rendered an opinion of anybody; who believed in the osmotic effect of confidence, verve, magnetism, and money. You stay by them, and they will seep into you.

The problem with being married to Warren Evinrude is this: nothing he gets is ever quite enough. He needs another affair, a new pair of Italian loafers, flown-in smoked salmon. He needs for everyone to know the salmon is flown in. He needs a driver mower, Cuban cigars, a personal trainer.

He needs for Tricia to have more clothes and more expensive clothes, whatever it takes to keep herself polished, buffed. He sent her to California to have her teeth capped and her cesarean scar lasered. Someone said he inquired about an operation — too dangerous — that could make legs longer. He wanted hers longer.

Their deal, as I read it, is this: they agree to despise each other but to practice a kind of loyalty. In return for all the money she wants for herself and the kids and the house, she is expected to project an air of opulence and verve and to ask no questions about his life outside their home.

Tricia laughs on cue, pats her husband with fake affection on the knee, poses with the other wives for party photos, all of them smiling forever. The Four Graces, I call them. Ren is only half amused.

They scare me silly, because I am clearly expected to become one of them. For a long time I was, at any rate.

Ren has always pretended to be amused by Warren Evinrude, but the truth is, he loves to be in the glow of power. It makes him feel alert and engaged in a way that little else can. He hates that need in himself, and is finally helpless before it.

A year ago, just days after Yuri came to work in our yard, Ren and I celebrated our seventeenth anniversary. We smoked a joint, the first in years, given to him by a silver-haired hipster he played squash with. Its potency surprised us. We walked hand in hand to a little Italian place downtown. I noticed that Ren, stoned as he was, looked carefully around the restaurant before we sat, satisfying himself that no one he knew was there.

Four months had gone by since Ren had banned Jimster from our house, and I was beginning to rationalize both my behavior with Jimster and the fact that he was no longer in our lives. My sadness was lifting, I hoped. As Ren and I ordered our meal, I felt drifty from the pot, but also as if I had been granted the temporary ability to slow down and see my husband in his discrete parts. The good hands, the halo of graying curly hair, the sideways smile — I could see it all with restored clarity.

We walked home. A three-quarter moon. The May lilacs, those clumps of faint, fragrant luminescence in the dark, so pretty. The smell of lilacs is the final smell of winter's end. After lilacs, it's full summer. They are verge flowers. Maybe they were the reason we checked the house to see if Mack happened to be there — he wasn't, so we knew he was overnighting at Tamara's — and went out again into the soft darkness. We strolled around the park across from our house, laughing and chattering at first, then lapsing into hushed attention — to the night, to the way the other physically displaced the dark.

I glanced behind us at some point. Ragamuffin, the cat, was

following us through the moonlight. This was strange, as she is a cranky, sedentary little beast, not given to adventure in any form. But there she was at our heels, scurrying from patch of light to patch of light. A flicker of calico, swallowed by shadow, the flicker again.

"Rags!" Ren said when he caught sight of her. "What are you doing out here in the wide and precarious world?" She meowed and sat down, then leaped up to follow us as we moved away. All around the big park, until we got home again. It was so odd and heartening.

In the living room, I lit a couple of candles and got out the brandy. Ren unhitched his suspenders (he'd taken to wearing suspenders in imitation or mockery of Evinrude's recent adoption of them; I feared it was sincere). He put a Moody Blues album on the old turntable. We laughed dismissively at the lush, grandiose naivité of the songs and sang along mockingly for a few minutes — knights in white satin, doo doo doo doo doo doo doo...

Then we swayed together, almost dancing, and I went into this funny split state — it seems the defining emotion of our time — in which I both scoffed at that silly tune and wanted not to. I wanted to ingest it unfiltered, to drift off into its corniness, but I couldn't. Or only a little — only when I closed my eyes for a few seconds, rested my cheek on Ren's starched shoulder. When I opened them, Mack was leaning against the doorjamb, watching us, a funny little half-smile on his face.

I jumped a little, the sight of him was so unexpected. Ren's back was to him and he looked at me quizzically, then whirled around. The record seemed to increase in volume. It was very scratched.

Mack, as usual, wore his business suit and his tipped-back fedora. He stood like an extra in *Guys and Dolls,* arms folded in a cocky, self-referential kind of way. But his face . . .

What was that look?

It was a look of both real and pretended surprise. And something else, too. Some kind of startling receptivity to what we'd do next. I sensed that he was ready, for once, to withhold any laughter, simply to let us be his parents in a moment of absolute sentimentality. I think if either Ren or I had done something other than what we did next, we might have kept our son closer to us. We might have remained more allied.

What I did was this: I held out my hands, inviting him into our twosome, but in the exaggerated way of someone stoned. The dope made me suddenly feel waterlogged and odd, muffled, fat-fingered, sheepish. So there was, I know, nothing charming or generous in the gesture.

"Christ!" Ren snapped. And he marched over to the turntable and stopped the record.

Ragamuffin rubbed against Mack's leg, and he reached down to scratch her head. He has always been gentle with animals. When he looked up, his face had settled into something harder. I wanted to put my arms around him, but the moment had turned.

"What a sight," he said.

"What are *you* doing here?" Ren said. "Have you been ejected from the connubial bower?"

Mack jammed his hands into the pockets of his floppy pants. "Hardly," he said coldly.

I saw at that moment, in a way I hadn't before, the length and breadth of the anger between them. Something about it went beyond rebellion, mutual irritation. Something about it was torturous.

Mack tipped his hat mockingly and sauntered off to his bedroom. Ren snapped his suspenders over his shoulders, put on his shoes, and started his rounds of the house, his nightly safety inspection.

I went upstairs and ran a bath and stayed in it until I knew both suited men were asleep. And that was our seventeenth wedding anniversary.

During the next five months before Ren was shot, he got a series of strange phone messages. A muffled voice would come on and say things like "Hey, bud, what does it feel like to poison people?" Or, "Hey, Toxic Man, how would you like some bad fumes in your own house, that big white house of yours on the park?"

The voice wasn't just muffled. It sounded as if the person were on nitrous oxide — that high, quacking sound. So I began to think it was kids. Jimster maybe, because his father had been evacuated from their shabby trailer and Jimster himself had been banned from our house.

Or — and I don't know why I kept coming back to this — Mack. Could the voice be Mack's? I wondered. Mack, trying to get back at his father for whatever it was that had gone on over a period of years. I didn't know what it was. I knew only that it was not small.

# 22

I KNOW THAT GUY," Gerrald said. "The stabbed guy. It was scratching at my mind, and now I know." He was working the crossword puzzle, something I'd never seen him do before.

Gerrald had made one friend, sort of, at AA: a truck driver who had been involved in an endless suit with Tri-State Trucking Company over his back injury. Ren's firm represents Tri-State. Something had fallen on Gerrald's friend, something that another employee hadn't fastened tight enough because he was new and no one had taught him the ropes. So the friend of Gerrald's, Frisco, ended up with a dragging leg and new, bad habits, and then a wife who filed for divorce and threatened to go after a big chunk of any settlement money he got from the company. All of it together plunged Frisco into the abyss.

"He told me, 'I'd be better off financially and every other way if I was dead,'" Gerrald said.

Frisco had been beaten down by lawyers, Gerrald said. Even the ones on his own side. They'd come into the meeting rooms for those depositions, and they'd have their racketball cases and their gym bags and their two-hundred-dollar sunglasses hanging off them with straps like some old lady would. And now Frisco's at AA talking faster than you can think, and divorced with a little daughter he cries over every day in some southern state.

Gerrald's big eyes swam around the room, looking for some sense in all this.

One day Frisco heard about a concert down by the river that was free and dry and put on by a local preacher and his wife, who were going to perform some kind of skit and then put forth a band that was only drummers, the point being the food. There was supposed to be a lot of it — Polish sausages and potato salads, all you could eat.

Frisco convinced Gerrald to go with him. There were a lot of people milling around, including some real dregs, and a couple of big buses from the rest homes. And tons of food, as promised. Frisco took his own bottle of hot sauce, the hottest you can get, and dumped it all over everything. He said the peppers were a painkiller and made you high.

The preacher doing the skit was the guy who got stabbed outside the Trocadero. He had introduced himself as Franklin and his wife as Krystal, and they had talked for a while about using your creative outlet. Then Krystal recited some of her own poems and Franklin strummed chords on a guitar. Gerrald thought the poems were so short it was hard to catch the drift. But Frisco said he liked them just for that reason, and he thought Krystal was a piece of work. She had that sorrowful and patient look that is 100 percent the opposite of Frisco's ex-wife, a tiny brunette named Edie Tripp. Frisco calls her ET.

The drummers were a bunch of white guys with dreadlocks. Gerrald didn't know where the preacher and his wife had dug them up. They looked like rich college kids with wigs on, and the preacher played with them.

Then Gerrald had to go to work, so he left Frisco shifting back and forth on a bench, because of his bad back, listening to that weird drumming and waiting for some kind of dessert table that was supposedly in the works. Krystal was drifting around in her white dress, smiling at senile people like there was no tomorrow.

She and Franklin were people you didn't forget, Gerrald said. That bald head — shaved, actually.

Gerrald said Franklin struck him as a totally social kind of guy, that day with Frisco. So that's why it was hard to match him with the guy he'd seen by the river, alone, with a knife wound that would probably cost about three thousand dollars to get stitched up. And he'd probably have to fight some insurance company for every penny of it and end up with about as much as Frisco, which was exactly nothing.

# 23

F<small>ROM THE TROCADERO</small>, the houses up there on the sides of the mountains look solitary but unremarkable, because there is nothing near them to offer a sense of scale. Up close, they are enormous. I took a short walk early this morning and studied those houses from below — studied them as my adopted self, Jeanne Thompson, might. The one highest up is Warren and Tricia Evinrude's. It is a strange rounded affair, very white, with columns along the curved front and a bizarre turret that doesn't reach above the roofline but squats flush with it. The house has its own long road, cut across the flank of the mountain. The last time Ren and I drove down that road together, we were so angry we were ice.

It was a Fourth of July party, and the evening had begun in a predictable sort of way. Tricia gave us big scented hugs, as if it had been weeks and weeks, and called liltingly to a server who passed a silver tray of asparagus wrapped with prosciutto. Tricia makes her own party food and has entire menus, with recipes and shopping lists, filed in her computer under various themes.

She wore a red sundress with red-white-and-blue star earrings. I wore Chinese pajamas and felt a little reckless. I had that urging-me-on voice in my head that passes itself off as celebratory, as what-the-heck. Not that I'd disgrace myself. In my waiting life, as Francesca Woodbridge, I tend not to embarrass myself in company. I just become more and more surface-shiny, a little wittier if I'm lucky, then a little poisonous, or too chatty, and then I stop drinking. And it's water for the rest of the evening, and a sincere hope that the evening is short.

I wandered around with my martini, smiling. Warren and three other men greeted us out on the deck. Ren stayed with them. I passed on, into the many-windowed room that hangs off the house like a large bombardier's bubble, an anchorite's perch. Tricia calls it the sun-and-fun room. There's a device in there to practice putting golf balls. There's an old-fashioned pinball machine, an antique she found at an auction. There's a huge black television set like the entrance to a mineshaft. A marble bar. Leather chairs, men's-club chairs. Wrestling trophies won by Warren and Tricia's son, Brant.

From the big windows, the rooftops of the houses lower on the hill melted and shone in the late-day light. The blue mountains across the valley began to etch themselves cleanly onto the sky. A kite climbed toward me, red, quavery, trailing blue streamers. It stiffened and climbed, looped madly, plunged, then shakily climbed again. I cheered it on.

On the large flagstone deck at the rear of the house, shrimp and scallops were piled on platters, about to be quickly seared on the barbecue. More martinis were passed. Dixieland floated out of hidden speakers. We would wait out the light on the deck, then wander inside to the U-shaped alcove before the cyclopean stone fireplace, cold for the summer, fronted with a huge arrangement of dried flowers. Or mill around on the sloping front lawn, waiting for the fireworks to erupt in fountains from the fairgrounds far below.

I talked with Tricia about something I can't remember now. She had just had her teeth resurfaced to a blazing whiteness, and she smiled constantly. I talked with a young woman who was engaged to an accountant, both of them new to town. She was very young, full of plans to get an MBA and a job on the coast. Very assured, very pretty, and she wore an AIDS ribbon on the lapel of her linen jacket, which I found interesting.

But the only real surprise at this gathering was the couple whose vacation house down the valley I had visited a few months earlier — the hedge investment guy from San Francisco whom I had interviewed for the speakers' bureau. It turned out he had roomed with one of Warren Evinrude's partners, Jim Dennehy, in college. He'd flown in for a long weekend. He was tall, tanned, hatchet-chinned in a way that kept him from conventional handsomeness but intensified his dense energy. He seemed to crowd even himself. His name was Jason Rademacher.

He and Jim had spent the past few days fishing a blue-ribbon stream and had not done so well fishwise, Moira Dennehy told me sotto voce. This had plunged Jason Rademacher into some kind of terminal gloom, which made Jim's ulcer flare up. As far as Rademacher was concerned, the trip had been a complete and utter bust. Watching him, I saw that he said virtually nothing. He simply tolerated the person who spoke.

"But isn't that part of it?" I asked Moira. "The bad days, maybe some bad weather, an element of inexplicable unforthcomingness? Isn't that why it's called fishing instead of catching?" My voice was a little too fervent.

"Tell that to Jason the Inconsolable," Moira said, making him sound like an idiot king.

"I think I might do that."

She gave me an odd consolatory pat on the arm and called out to someone she pretended to have just noticed, moving off helplessly as if the new person were reeling her in.

Jason Rademacher stood with Ren and Jim Dennehy and Jim's miserable-looking son, a skinny seventeen-year-old who, it turned out, had been commandeered to go along on the disastrous fishing trip. My husband smiled at me cautiously and introduced me to

Rademacher, who stepped forward to shake my hand, bending two inches too close.

"We've met," I said. "I was in your house." A startled look passed over him. "I interviewed you for the speakers' bureau."

He leaned back and examined me.

"Right," he said, vaguely remembering.

"So," I said. "How was the fishing trip?" I could feel Ren warning me off the topic with his eyes, which I wouldn't meet. Those kinds of vehement silent conversations happen when you've been married a long time.

Rademacher shrugged stoically. Jim clapped his poor son heartily on his thin shoulders. "They're there," he said in a tough-guy detective voice. "We know they're there. They know we know they're there."

"It stunk," said Rademacher.

"What stunk?" My voice was high and bright. "Two, three days on a beautiful river with your best buddy from college, just tromping around in perfect summer weather in one of the grandest places on earth?" I thought, Is anyone over twenty-five really named Jason?

"The fishing stunk," he said grimly.

"How so?"

"We caught no fish," he said, as if he were trying to buy something from a foreign street vendor.

"Well, maybe you should pay six hundred dollars a day for a guide who could steer you right to those waiting fish, tell you just when to cast, create, shall we say, a fishing experience for you."

He simply looked at me. Then he looked at Ren. Then he looked at me again.

"Let's see." I knew I should stop, but I couldn't seem to. "If your guide steered you into the laps of, say, six fish, and you snagged them, mangled them a little, put them back into the water, well, that would be just a hundred dollars a fish! Why stint? If that's what you came for, go for it!"

The server appeared with a plate of sliced salmon on toast, and they all turned to her gratefully. Ren's neck was red. Rademacher excused himself. Ren and Jim and Jim's son — I can never remember his name — nibbled their salmon toasts.

"As a matter of fact," said Jim, "we did hire a guide. We're going out tomorrow."

The son piped up in a cracked voice, "Jason won't eat stuff like this." He pointed to his salmon. "He's a vegetarian."

I laughed. "No!" I said to the kid. He nodded solemnly, one corner of his mouth slyly curling in a smile. Ren and Jim were gone. They'd simply walked away. I saluted the kid with my own salmon toast. We said nothing, then both snorted at the same time.

The car hummed down the long road to the valley floor.

"You're embarrassing, Francesca," Ren said in a mild, let's-talk-about-it voice. "You bounce around at these things like a, like a . . . Ping-Pong ball. No one knows where you're going to land, what you're going to do."

"A Ping-Pong ball."

"You know what I'm talking about." He fiddled with the air-conditioning button in an aimless, irritating way. Intense and purposeless. We didn't need the air conditioning on. My window was open to the summer night.

"You make me seem unreliable," he added.

"What about me makes *you* seem unreliable?"

"You do. The way you, I don't know, come out with these barbed, off-the-wall comments. Like the fishing. If Jason Rademacher wants to catch fish, let him catch fish."

"No one is stopping Jason Rademacher from catching fish." It was turning into one of those conversations that are difficult to believe in later on. "How do my views about Jason vis-à-vis fishing make you seem unreliable?" I forged on.

"It's not about fish," Ren said, spreading his patience like a shawl on the ground. "It's about your attitude. The way you get half lit, then start basically insulting people. Especially people who just happen to have some say over whether I — actually, you and I, in effect — stay okay with Warren and the rest."

"Did I take the bar exam in my sleep?"

"You know what I mean, and I don't want to fight about it. I'm just trying to explain that your behavior sometimes isn't quite as casual and charming as you think it is."

"I have no charm goals."

He turned the AC fan on high. Its whir sounded labored. I turned it off.

"Well, Francesca, maybe you should get some."

"And I wasn't half lit."

I was thinking then that we all, all of us at that party, would be old or gone in thirty years. Prostate cancer, hip replacements, the skin cranked back another notch. I was seeing Tricia's new white teeth, glowing in the dark.

# 24

A BURNISHED DAY under a blue-china sky is essentially disarming, or so I felt the day I met some of the lawyers' wives to celebrate a birthday. I arrived in a state of excitation that had nothing to do with any of the people present. Yuri was coming the next day to begin work on a flagstone sitting area in a corner of the yard, and my body already felt switched on, like the lights of a small airport when the night plane is coming in.

I had some idea, certainly, of running away with him. I had all my Jeanne Thompson ID by then, and I thought sometimes of the two of us in some new life.

"Your skin looks great," Tricia Evinrude exclaimed as I sat down. "Did you get a wrap?"

Tricia, Moira Dennehy, Kathie Fleet, and I had invited Laura Terwilliger, the widow of the founder of the firm, to a birthday lunch. Sally Terwilliger, Laura's daughter-in-law, had begged off at the last minute with a migraine.

Laura was eighty-one and was a calm, constitutionally gracious sort. Her large, rather regal face contained weathered, intelligent eyes. Her children liked her. She had her interests — the arts-and-crafts museum, heart association fundraisers, genealogy — and she was basically just lively and sweet and, since she was a rather recent widow, someone to be somewhat solicitous about. Her only oddity was that she had been a pilot during the war. She had flown planes. Her heart now was said not to be so good.

There is loveliness in a good lunch with a white tablecloth in a place with big windows that look upon a green lawn. Everything that day seemed freshly washed, ungrimed. It's a frantic world and we need these islands, I thought.

We had scheduled a late lunch, so there was only a scattering of customers in the restaurant. Driving there, it had occurred to me that I could be more intentional in my relations with people I didn't particularly like — that I could simply pay closer attention, and if I was bored, I could change the direction of a conversation instead of letting it wash over me. I didn't have to listen to Tricia talking about clothes or trips or parties. I could find out from Laura what it had been like to be a pilot during the war — how she learned, where she flew, if she was scared, when she stopped, whether she missed it. I could try to bend the conversation in a direction that seemed promising.

Laura arrived looking a little disheveled, as if she had had a small accident with her car, embarrassing but not serious. That look. Usually she carried with her the faint scent of Chanel. On this day there was a neutral skin smell to her, like the damp nape of the boy at the grocery store as he lifts the sacks into your summer-heated car.

She sat down with a long sigh and gave us her familiar wide smile. She had handsome yellow teeth. Moira told her she loved her jacket, the flecks of lavender in the linen. Laura examined the jacket, raised her eyebrows as if to say, Well, that's true, there are flecks of lavender in it. She smiled in a way I couldn't quite decipher. Appreciatively, because she hadn't noticed the flecks before? Tolerantly, because she'd heard so many *pro forma* compliments during her life? Affectionately, because it really was a golden high-skyed day, and she was at a table with friends who had gathered for her birthday? What was there not to like about this day, this place?

She seemed calm and self-contained, and I had a flash of envy. She seemed more comfortable with herself than I could imagine being, ever.

"Laura," I said after we made small talk for a few minutes, "this is sort of out of the blue, but I wonder, how did you decide to become a pilot during the war? Weren't you terrified to learn?"

The waitress had arrived at our table with menus and was pouring water. She was dark and high-colored, quite young, and she did everything with the self-consciousness of a novice. She looked curiously at Laura, waiting with us for her answer.

"Well, I'll tell you a little secret," Laura said. "Terror is never a reason not to do something. The higher the terror, the better the ride!" Her voice was a notch louder than we were used to. It occurred to me that she might be taking a new arthritis medicine — she'd tried many — and that it had affected her hearing slightly.

"One of my college boyfriends took flying lessons," Moira said. "The day after he got his license, he made me go up with him. Every minute up there, I felt as if I were going to be sick. Every second. When we finally landed, I broke up with him on the spot."

"Naturally," Laura said buoyantly. We all laughed. "Give him the boot because he took you for a good ride," Laura insisted, pounding her fist gently on the arm of her chair. We all laughed again, because we didn't know how else to react.

The waitress asked us if we wanted anything to drink. Everyone wanted a celebratory glass of wine except Laura, who wanted Campari and soda with lime.

"Roses' Lime Juice?" asked the new young waitress.

"No, dear, a lime from a tree," Laura said. "What you must do is *verify* that it has been removed from a tree, slice it, and put one of the slices in my drink. Can you do that?"

Tricia smiled conspiratorially at the waitress to soften the sharpness of the remark.

"No problem," the waitress said cautiously.

We waited for Laura to ameliorate the remark herself, to acknowledge that it was out of character. She simply smoothed her napkin on her lap and looked around the table mildly. I was beginning to feel the way I do when I see standup comedy, even if it's televised. I get desperate to usher the performer offstage, desperate to keep the next thing unsaid, because it can never be funny enough to compensate for such public vulnerability.

"Well, speaking of airplanes," Tricia said, "Warren is threatening to buy a little jet. Can you believe it? Or do some long-term lease thing or something, some arrangement that includes some kind of on-call pilot. So he can go where he wants when he wants." She sounded as disingenuously dismissive as a mother who'd just bought her teenager a Porsche.

"Where do you actually buy a jet?" Kathie Fleet asked.

Tricia brushed away something in the air. Her shiny bob swung prettily. "I don't know. The *jet* store?"

We all laughed.

"It's a bore," Laura said pleasantly, almost to herself. I thought I had misheard her, and leaned in closer.

"Jet store," I said helpfully.

"What a bore," Laura said. She smiled at us.

"Laura," said Tricia, jumping into the silence, "did you have trouble getting here? Car trouble?"

"No, Tricia," Laura said gently. "I'm just bored with all of you. You bore me to tears." She smiled helpfully. "Really," she said.

She leaned back in her chair and folded her arms like a man and moved her eyes slowly around the table. Kathie Fleet had a gift-wrapped box in front of her, all done up with an elaborate silver bow. It was our gift for Laura, a Waterford pitcher. Kathie cupped her hand around the corner of the box as if it were going to run away.

"Well, what are we talking about here!" Laura said, a teacher trying to coax a tired class.

Getting no answer, she answered herself.

"We're talking about Tricia, who happens to be miserably married to one of the most distasteful men on the fair earth but hangs in there because the thought of paying for her own face surgery and little tart-suits and capped teeth is . . . what is the word? Daunting. I think the word is daunting." She seemed to be trying to think of a better word, then gave up and swiveled her eyes to Moira.

Tricia started to speak. She opened her slapped-looking mouth, then simply stopped.

Moira Dennehy is a tall athletic blonde who co-owns a store that sells top-of-the-line bathroom fixtures. She and Jim have four freckled offspring, rangy like their parents. Moira seems always to be running to the next energetic event. She was a champion golfer in high school. She has a strange, small voice that doesn't belong with the rest of her.

"And Moira," said Laura. "Moira who is a hornets' nest beneath that big show of volunteer stuff, store stuff, run, run, run." She leaned forward on her elbows. "Make that a vipers' nest! Because sweet Moira likes to bite, bite away at her so-called friends" — she swept us all again with her eyes — "when the so-called friends aren't, shall we say, watching." We were all watching Moira now. She blinked rapidly.

"Such as," Laura went on. "Well, for instance." She thought, her eyes on the ceiling. "Well, let's say that sweet Moira has been known to make certain intimate facts known to her husband, intimate facts about her so-called friends, that the husband then passes on to the powers that be in order to further his own gain at the expense of the husbands of the so-called friends." She flipped her bony hand dismissively. "Abortions. Affairs. Debts. Psychiatric consultations. You name it."

No one had anything to say. Now we just waited. Kathie studied the huge silver bow on the present, her head tilted as if she saw some kind of code in the wrapping paper. The waitress, her good spirits restored, came around to ask if we wanted to order, if anyone wanted another drink.

"No," said Tricia stonily. The waitress registered this and moved off without a word.

I thought about simply getting up, simply leaving, before it was my turn. But I felt Laura would be more vicious if I left than if I stayed.

"And Kathie, the bearer of gifts," Laura went on. Her voice was becoming a little gravelly, but great good humor still radiated from her face. She had more sheer energy than I ever had seen in her. She was enjoying herself.

"Well, Kathie, I'm afraid, just isn't very bright. Kathie, I'm afraid, does not know how to *be* in the world because, well, she just doesn't have the . . . wattage. And so Kathie is the buyer of presents, the helpful person, the dim-bulb maid for all the rest of you." Another frank swift circle of the table. "And you let her do it. And then you laugh at her for it. Don't you!" She clapped her hands excitedly. Rings slid sideways on the gnarled old fingers.

A pause now. We sat at our empty plates. Two couples in the far corner of the dining room toasted each other. They laughed. Their happy noises reached our table and slid down a glass wall.

Something about Laura's face was not quite right. I noticed that now, as I waited. She smiled, and then she stopped smiling, and then she smiled again. But one corner of her mouth didn't move the same way the other did. It lagged.

She sat for a moment, gazing meditatively out the big window, hands folded on her lap. She farted quietly. She opened her eyes wider, and now they were for me.

"And Francesca," she said in a sorrowful voice. "Francesca is a snob. Francesca concocts grand adventures for herself in her head and uses them as proof that she is better than anyone around her. Except the problem is this: her visions stay in Francesca's head. They fuel her. They console her. They are her fine lies. But they don't take her anyplace, do they? She tells herself stories. She is the heroine, we are the villains. But she's too timid to slay us. Yes? She is — what is the term? Chickenshit." She came down hard on the last word, and her smile mostly went away.

And then she folded the big napkin slowly with her bent old fingers, and she rose and gave us all a small bow and said she truly must be on her way. She left a ten-dollar tip for the waitress. She took the lime slice from the rim of her glass, bit off a corner, walked out to the parking lot.

"Should someone go with her?" Kathie said. "I think she's drunk."

"Oh Christ, let her run herself up a telephone pole," Tricia said, tight and tough. A street kid.

We all got up. Kathie didn't seem to know what to do with the birthday present. No one helped her. She gave us a go-to-hell look and marched over to the waitress, who was glancing at us as she set up a long table. She thrust the present into the waitress's hands, said something, wouldn't take it back. And marched out the door ahead of the rest of us.

None of us spoke to each other for a week. I saw Moira at a stoplight a few days later but pretended I hadn't. Tricia, who had wanted my help on a fundraiser, left a clipped message saying she'd handed the job over to someone else and we were both off the hook. Then I got another call from her. Her voice had a doleful eagerness in it that was both affected and genuine. She was very happy about something but knew she had to pretend otherwise.

"Laura's in the hospital," she said. "It's bad."

Laura had something wrong with her brain. She was being tested for a stroke, maybe a small series of strokes, a tumor. Her cleaning lady had found her on the floor in her kitchen on her hands and knees, laughing helplessly. Calls went around. Her daughter and son-in-law flew in. It was a tumor and it moved fast.

She became incoherent, she lost consciousness. In a month she was dead.

But that isn't the story. The story is that her disease made us glad. It endowed her frankness with pathology.

For weeks after her death, people — and not just the four of us at that luncheon — never spoke her name without mentioning an oddity, now attributable to her disease, that had been politely ignored by her many friends. A lack of inhibition that was entirely at odds with the healthy Laura and that carried with it, we all agreed, an undeniable element of aggression. When we couldn't supply our own examples, we drew on secondhand information, on rumors. How her cleaning woman had said Laura spent hours on the telephone insulting her children, even her grandchildren. How Laura had told her dentist that her dear departed husband was a big old fraud. How she had put to sleep an old cat, just because she was tired of it. Peculiarities everywhere, when you looked for them.

Tricia said there was a place in the brain that concocted lies, and this was where the tumor had been pressing. The person could seem coherent, logical, in control of her faculties, but an organic disturbance was creating the capacity for elaborate lies and the urge to hurt.

"Look at the cat," she cried. "That cat wasn't a bit sick. She just decided she hated it."

These kinds of discussions occurred. But what never occurred was any mention of that particular lunch. That lunch with Laura was wiped out, off the map, though it sits there at the edges of our days like something lethal that can't be moved.

When poor Laura went kaflooey. That's the phrase that survived the strong old horse-faced woman who had flown planes, who had lived a half-century as a mild wife, a calm and tweedy paragon.

When poor old Laura went kaflooey, and the waitress got the Waterford.

# 25

IN AUGUST, two months before Ren was shot, Yuri Petrov
went away and didn't come back. I called his house and learned
that the phone had been disconnected. I called information, and
there was nothing. I had a dream of his face at the window of a
locked room. His eyes behind the glass were alert and unsur-
prised.

After Ren came home from the hospital, he began to add to his
account of the intruder. He told the police that the bandanna
covering the man's face was dark blue. The man was slim, strong,
springy. His voice, his grunts, when the two of them struggled,
were the voice of a young man. Everything happened so fast that
he remembered no actual words, if they were spoken. Or perhaps, he said, the words were not in English. He was not sure.
He couldn't be sure. He was trying to recall.

There was a story in the newspaper. Captain Maynard
McDean, who was in charge of the investigation, said that he
had every confidence the intruder would be apprehended; the
apparent motive was robbery, and the intruder had perhaps been
taken by surprise, since the absence of both vehicles might have
suggested to the perpetrator that the occupants were away from
the home. The home was equipped with a security system, he
said, and the intruder had some knowledge of that system. That

was key. There were a number of possibilities to follow, and members of the family were being interviewed to determine whether some outside person had been told, or could have learned, the entry procedure. The story ended with a vague little homily from Captain McDean about the need for vigilance as our town hovered on the brink of urban woes. Most particularly, he stressed the need to monitor the growing presence of teenage and immigrant gangs. "Nip them in the bud" was the phrase he used.

When someone looks as brittle, as whipped as Ren did, the source of the injury can seem almost beside the point. There is, foremost, the bald fact of the damage, and uncertainty about its extent and its permanence. You simply wait and work and tend, and put everything else on hold. I made him as comfortable as possible in the big chair where he wanted to sit, propping pillows, wrapping his legs in a blanket. He thanked me. At that moment I would have offered myself in exchange, to spare him.

His spinal cord had been winged, as the jovial young doctor put it, and the extent of the nerve damage wouldn't be known for a while. He might suffer permanent impairment; he might not. Time, plus extensive physical therapy, held the answer.

There was an evening several weeks after Ren got home when the two of us ate dinner together alone. Mack had appeared briefly, then gone to Tamara's. I helped Ren into his study and brought us tea and dessert so we could watch a movie. He had eaten more at that meal than he had since getting home; he hadn't yet taken his evening painkillers. He was more alert, more present, than he'd been so far. A sleety rain was falling. It made ticking sounds on the windows.

Ren's eyes had been sliding off mine ever since his injury. Sometimes his sight seemed to be turned inward, to the travesty of his damaged body, to the greedy presence of real pain; other times he seemed, because of the drugs or his own exhaustion or inclinations, simply not to see much. But especially not to see me.

The afternoon before this particular evening, Captain McDean had returned to interview Ren further about the night in question. McDean is a portly, fiftyish man with a single black eyebrow across his eyes that gives him a dogged, beetling look. He conveys the kind of tenacity that may or may not have real intelligence in it. It's hard to tell. Sometimes I think he is hard-wired only to keep pushing.

The detective came; they had their talk. Ren told McDean that the intruder may have worn white socks. He remembered too that he had heard the receding sound of a loud muffler some minutes after he was shot, after the man ran away.

So, I thought, he remembers Yuri's pickup. He knows about Yuri and me.

After the detective left, I made dinner and we ate it and placed ourselves in front of the television. The almost-snow fell with a sandy sound.

"You're making things up, Ren," I said. "Why are you doing that? You keep adding details. It's becoming a game with you."

A long time ago, I took a beginners' class in fiction writing, and the teacher asked us all to make three statements to the class about something odd that had happened at some point in our lives. One of the statements was to be a lie. The class got to quiz the speaker, then voted on the veracity of the statements. The idea was to make the lie work — to fool everyone. And the way to do that, of course, was to supply the small details that embedded it in something that sounded like a real life. That's what Ren was doing. I could see that he was enjoying it and was doing it quite well.

"You've been making things up since the beginning," I said.

"Why are you doing this? Let's say they arrest someone. Let's say your embellishments steer them toward someone who didn't do it."

"I'm doing this for us," Ren said, looking straight at me. "For us."

"I don't happen to agree that you are doing it for us," I said.

"Well, I'm the one who was shot, wasn't I? I'm the one who was clearly there. When it comes right down to it, you can't have that much to say about it, you know." And then he shook out his pills, swallowed them, and switched TV channels.

In our town, winter can be very quiet. The snow comes without storms or wind and eventually lies around in an archeological state: layered, crusted, grimed. This is the season of inversion. On too many days, our big lake bottom fills with cold soiled air, sealed to the ground by warmer air above. The worst of it isn't the grayness itself. It's the knowledge that not far away, perhaps a few miles out of town, through the canyon, down the valley, life is bright and blue. The grayness then becomes not a season to wait out but a localized infliction. You feel targeted.

This past winter the snow muffled everything. Mr. Puermutter, the raker, got out his snow blower and blew the whole block. He was in heaven.

The blower screamed past our house at dawn, but how could we complain? The alternative was shoveling it ourselves, hiring someone, I don't know what. Mack wouldn't do it. Or rather, he made one attempt when I asked him, but managed to clear only a straggling path, and he came in complaining of the cold, and I got so angry I couldn't speak. That was the worst of those long months in some ways — the way all the sorrow, all the necessary patience and slowness of life with an invalid, would get chan-neled suddenly, fiercely, into something like a sidewalk that wasn't shoveled right. And the shoveler. Frustration can feel like hatred. There's such exhausted grabbing for some kind of organizing principle. The way Mack shoveled the walk became the way he would live his life. Or the way I would live my life.

I fell asleep one morning just an hour or so before light. All night Ren had had back spasms, terrible charley horses that didn't go away with the muscle relaxants or my massaging hands or heat, until finally they did, just as we were going to try to bundle him up and get him to the emergency room. He finally nodded off. I fell like a stone into my own sleep, and then the snow blower was there and the night was over. I stood at the front window in my bathrobe, almost swaying with exhaustion, and looked out upon the gray morning. The temperature had risen. The snow looked like concrete. Mr. Puermutter, in his red hat, was vanquishing it. I tried to curse him, to put some kind of stymieing hex on him, and couldn't even manage that.

By February, I lived constantly with the glassy exhaustion that comes from a long emergency. Ren was beginning to respond to therapy. There was no reason not to hope for a full recovery. How long it would take was anyone's guess. "Motivation" was a word that had started to come up a lot.

At night I listened to him breathe and thought about the imperiousness of pain, the way it points you at your physical existence, makes everything deliberate, makes everything an obstacle, strips the world, your body, everything, of all that is unpremeditated. I would watch his white hands grip the walker and I'd be washed with remorse, ready to offer him anything. Anything that could help.

I couldn't think about Yuri without a leaden combination of loss and guilt, without that cause-and-effect feeling: you transgressed and this is what comes of it. Disaster, like a crow's cry and a slap. I went to a counselor, who told me there were drugs that helped evaporate obsessions, doom thoughts, but the idea that such emotional power could wilt at the touch of a pill was at that point more dismaying to me than the thoughts themselves.

Andrej knew where Yuri was, I felt certain. And I knew where Andrej lived. By chance, returning from a graveside service for the father of a friend, I'd seen the BMW with his plates parked incongruously in front of a rundown house on the north side. The address was 194 Olive. I thought to check the current city directory, which matched the address with the name but listed no phone. Neither did telephone information.

I wanted to believe that Andrej had everything to do with the sudden absence of Yuri, that he had exercised some kind of hold on him. Perhaps he had sent Yuri to some small town in Russia to stage a phony car wreck, so the proceeds of Yuri's new life insurance policy could go to his esteemed cousin Andrej. Perhaps Andrej had made sure the accident victim was truly dead. How could I ever know?

I couldn't. I couldn't know if he was in danger, if he was dead, or even if he had simply come to know that we could not fit in each other's lives. That when the garden was done, so were we.

I mourned. I mourn to this day.

This past March, five months after Ren's injury, I went for a long drive. It was a balmy day, extravagant with newness. All the old snow was almost gone, and the blue-eyed sky was filled with the improbable cumulus towers of an illustration in a children's book. I rolled down the windows. There was a tinge of green to those hillsides that got the day's longest sun. The rivers glinted. Everything seemed to have relaxed. A kind of untrussing had occurred. Spikes were twigs, glass was water.

A man passed me on a midnight-blue motorcycle that seemed the distillation of the idea of motorcycle — low and loud and fast — and he waved and I waved back.

I thought of the brown sack in the basement of our house, stashed in a storeroom behind piles of junk, containing all the

Jeanne Thompson identification I had accumulated, including the passport in her name.

It's the inconceivable thing, in theory — to leave your flesh and blood. But people do it all the time. Fathers do it all the time. But do mothers? There you have the unforgivable sin.

Mack and I had bickered constantly through the long winter. It grew worse after Ren told McDean that the intruder may have been a foreigner, that he may have been driving a vehicle with a loud muffler, then repeated the gist of the interview to Mack.

Now Mack thought he knew. And what he thought he knew was that Yuri had learned the security code from me, and that he had used it to break into our house, and that he had grievously wounded Ren. That's what he thought he knew.

He began to address me, when he did, with a furious combination of politeness and pity. I knew that he wanted me gone, removed. That is what I told myself.

I could leave. I could become Jeanne Thompson for a while or forever.

"Clinical exhaustion," Mack said to Tamara on the phone. "That's what they call it." A pause. "Hang up, Mom," he said.

When I began to talk about Greece, everyone acted as if I'd discovered a lost kingdom. A few weeks, I reminded them. A tour group, a few weeks — all very ordinary. Ren urged me to the point of insistence. We'll be fine, he said. Mack or Elise can get me to therapy and back. Go. You've had a long siege here too. You've been great. Now go. We'll be fine.

He had been watching me in a way I don't like. Examining me, my face, every time we talked. We hired a woman to come in half a day to clean, to help with the meals and with Ren, and she too kept shining her eyes all over my face, and so I avoided her as much as I could. I slept a lot. I had the mausoleum dreams again — white blank buildings, something frighteningly blank-eyed, impervious, and perfect, a white windowless building against an India-ink sky. The terror of white stone.

I tried to put myself inside Ren's mind, to see the scenario he had begun to create for Captain McDean in bits and pieces. It comes out as a familiar story.

He could have done it. Yuri and Ren and that particular night — it could all fit.

Let's say that Yuri Petrov parked that old beater pickup in a pool of halogen light at Towne Square, a few blocks from our house. He parks the truck and walks briskly toward our hushed and leafy street. He wears running clothes and thin gloves and a watch cap, and now he jogs gently, a young businessman or a lawyer getting some oxygen after a day of deals. He has a bandanna around his neck. His feet slap the sidewalk quietly. A police car passes, and he puts his head down to look hard at his luminous watch, logging his progress.

Near our house he slows to a walk, cooling down, it would seem. He stretches. He looks casually around. Small warm lights glow in our windows, but he knows they are on a timer. He ambles up to the garage and checks the small side window. The cars are gone. No one is home. He doglegs around the side deck and ducks through the trellis into the back yard. It is raining lightly. The rain will freeze by morning. He hears the faint mumble of the television, some tiny cheers of a tiny crowd, and smiles, unfooled. He's done all this before, but not at this particular house, so familiar even in the dark. He finds the key under its rock and lets himself in and walks straight to the wall panel and punches the numbers. And all the little eyes turn from red to green. The house is breached. His shoe squeaks on the tiles.

What does he think at this point? That he is in a kitchen where he has sat so many times in the daylight, talking? Does he smell the coffee, my basil plants, and think, How did I come to be here in the night, my fingertips electric?

The television sound disappears. He exhales slowly.

And then, like an echo of his long breath, the light in the recesses of the house grows dimmer. A bolt of adrenaline shoots through him. He freezes. This is all wrong. This is not how it works. The lights go on, they go off; the television murmurs, then doesn't murmur. But not this. This is a human presence, this slow muffling of the light.

The creak of a floorboard. The slow sound of a drawer. His blood begins a frantic thumping in his ears. He pulls the bandanna over his lower face. And why does he not then simply leave? Go away? Leave the kitchen, the yard? Sprint down the alley and onto the street, bandanna down around his neck again?

Why does he not run lightly in the dark, back to his little truck? Is it because he is filled with hatred, the kind that can only advance?

He begins to move toward the person who has dimmed the light, who has opened the drawer. He slides along the wall of the dark dining room and peers across the foyer, and he sees Ren's back. Ren in his old gray cashmere, his slacks, his stocking feet, facing the direction from which he thought he heard the sound. The light from the television flickers across him.

Ren turns, the gun extended chest high. Yuri leaps toward him, and Ren is now toppled. The gun clatters off the coffee table, and they are both scrambling for it. And they both reach it, and it fires.

Red panic. Now Ren is no one he has ever seen. Ren is the groaning, bleeding stranger on the floor.

He runs, he fades into the dark, a huffing jogger again. Back in the battered truck, he tears out of the lot, cursing the loud muffler.

And where does Yuri go then? Does he drive west of town on

the frontage road, watching the speedometer, hearing tiny sirens on the edges of everything? Does he think, I have slept in that house? And does he then remember how he woke up disoriented and pulled the sheet up over his nose and it smelled good, like rich people's clothes dryers? And he thought, for just a moment, I am here where I belong. Then the next thought always came: This is not my home. And that was the one that always felled him, because he realized he lived the flip-side existence of the way a lucky person woke up. The lucky person's first thought: What awful place have I been? Then relief: I'm home. I'm safe.

For him, it was reversed. Waking produced fear.

And now there was a man on the carpet, bleeding.

# 26

O N   T H E   N O R T H   S I D E of our town is an old neighborhood that lies between the railroad tracks and the freeway. The houses are modest and ungroomed; the roots of the gnarled trees push up through the walks. On one edge of this neighborhood is a shady cemetery, and next to the cemetery is the field where Ren played his softball game the day that Mount St. Helens erupted.

Trains traverse the south end of the area. The freeway skims the north and is higher than the rest because it runs along the flank of the hills. In this neighborhood, you look up at the moving cars from below. Which seems right, because freeways are essentially air routes. You enter freeway existence and you are traveling the way you do in a jet, smoothly, quickly, on a corridor that looks the same wherever you are and that exits to the same restaurants, the same motels, the same unobtrusive, efficient predictability, wherever you happen to be. No one on a freeway thinks about the bumpy streets and the people who exist along them.

This north-side neighborhood is bordered by periodic movement and noise — the clanks and calls of trains, the swish of the freeway cars — and when there is not noise, the streets hold the kind of quiet that seems to exist most profoundly next to the memory of noise. This morning, during one of those quiet times, I paid my visit.

·   ·   ·

It is raining, a very light misting rain that mixes with the smell of young leaves to seem like nourishment — the kind of rain that makes quiet quieter.

I've borrowed an umbrella from the girl at the motel desk. They have a small stash of them that have been left behind by guests. Mine's travel-sized and shows a map of the world. Continents and oceans hover over my head.

I've fixed a scarf over my dark wig, a double cover, and I carry my bright shoulder bag. Dark glasses too. As I walk along the damp sidewalk, I talk quietly to myself, trying to remember whether Olive Street is two blocks or three blocks from the cemetery side of the neighborhood.

Most of the houses are old and low to the ground, though there is the occasional grander specimen, like the two-story brick that holds in a window an oversized statue of the Virgin. Paint is faded here. Flowers grow tall and rangy — hollyhocks and sunflowers mostly, and weeds. Trikes lie tipped; motorcycles sit amid their parts. One tiny shabby house has low Corinthian columns and curtains imprinted with ducks.

I've managed to put what I'm about to do into some part of my mind that isn't thinking about it yet, except to make me highly alert. I notice everything. And I'm struck by the quiet, tangled loveliness of this part of town, which I've never before looked at closely.

A woman on a bicycle swishes past, her white hair flying. She reaches down and rings her bike bell. I wave. I catch a whiff of cookies baking, and that smell, coming to me through the flowery rain, seems like one that could shape a person's entire life. The memory of it or the need for it.

There's a black object in the street. It looks odd — too small to be a dead squirrel or bird, too sinister for a toy. I study it from twenty yards away and then I scan my surroundings, and that's when I see the street sign that says "Olive." I'm near.

The thing in the street is a bat. A bat with its wings spread and head flattened. I can look at it only in quick darting glances — the sharp leathery wings with points to scrape across your head, tangle in your hair; the shrieking look of the thing and its blood in a smear.

Sounds start up now. My blood in my head. A train, screeching, coupling. The heavy hum of a truck on the freeway above. And the day has warmed, too, making my clothes stick damply. Birds exchange frank hopeful whistles. I wish I had not seen that bat.

Olive Street is a neighborhood of what we call the working poor. And some grizzled hippies too, I suppose. And retired people. The rain seems to have pushed everyone inside for the morning. No one gardens. No kids play in the street.

Andrej's house, 194 Olive, is an army-colored bungalow with an open porch. The blinds are pulled. A spool table sits in the long grass with some kind of machine part on it. What's missing is his car, the silver BMW. This is good; he's gone. I've prepared for the thought of Andrej inside that little house, but he is somewhere that is not here. There is a small oil spot on the street where the car might have been.

Does Andrej have a wife? Children? Is anyone else likely to be about? I have no idea. Somehow, I think not. I can't imagine him in a situation that holds the slightest tenderness.

I walk slowly past his house to the corner, keeping my umbrella open though the rain has stopped. It hides my face. The alley is lined with small detached garages. There they are, just what I expected, low wooden paint-peeled structures built for the cars of a half-century ago. They slump sleepily. My feet on the gravel are thunderous. I collapse my umbrella and bend my head, and walk as wearily as I can manage.

There is a space between Andrej's garage and the neighbor's, and it's not empty. It holds the BMW, backed in and shiny in the sun. A Playboy bunny air freshener hangs from the rearview mirror. He is home. I stop. I breathe thinly, and listen very hard. I should have waited for a weekday and can think of no reason now why I didn't. Perhaps I simply didn't imagine him to be home much of the time. Or some part of me wanted this kind of proximity, this potential confrontation.

Every small sound seems to belong. I hear nothing inside his garage or in the weedy little patch of back yard that says he is near. Maybe he is on the phone or making a sandwich, and this is only the pause before he bursts out the door. This is the moment to move on. To come back another day. I listen. I don't move.

In my white room on my Greek island, Francesca Woodbridge's passport hides beneath a pillow; her clothes wait in a closet. Mrs. Kouki, the landlady, waits for Francesca to return from an island-hopping jaunt. When will she grow curious, irritated, apprehensive? When will she let herself into my white room with her key because she has people who want to rent it? I am paid up for another week. How long will she give me after that? When will she alert the island police?

Tourists will be there in greater numbers quite soon. A few will be adventurous enough to wind their way down the long cliff to my little beach. Eventually someone will find my rucksack in the darkness under the big rock. My airline stub, my change of clothes. Eventually they will say I apparently went for a swim before leaving for the other islands and I drowned. They will put it all together, and that is what they will decide.

I lean casually against the door of the old garage, as if resting. The doors are the old-fashioned kind that open outward. You lift a bar and pull. Inside, small windows transfer feeble, grimy light. The garage is empty of vehicles but cluttered with steel drums, crates, tools, strands of wire, some shapes under a big tarp. It smells of cat piss and gasoline. I look for a place to put what I have brought with me.

Under the tarp are half a dozen boxes made of stiff cardboard, with numbers stamped on the top and labels that say they are the property of the United States government. I lift a corner. They are filled with something heavy. It seems important to know what is in the boxes. An awl, lying among a haphazard batch of tools, works on the staples. With a little groan, the lid comes loose. I close my eyes and listen. Then I open the box.

It's filled with binoculars, heavy ones, in foamy packing material. When I press a button and look through a pair at the dimness of the shed, there are glowing places in the room, the largest in a far corner. A cat darts from that corner and scurries behind another pile of boxes. Infrared. Our Andrej is a busy man.

I rearrange the packing materials, close the lid, and try to fix the staples so they won't look pried.

Behind an ancient-looking row of paint cans under one filthy window, I place the small silver casket I took from my house. The little box filled with the ashes of Mount St. Helens.

I slip out and walk as slowly as I can make myself walk. Down the alley. My umbrella shields my eyes. And then I do something I don't understand. I circle the block and walk once more past the front of Andrej's house. I think I want to make sure that it is as sleepy as it seems. The sun has come out fully, and the side-walk sends up ribbons of steam. Only when I draw even with the house do I see the dim figure on the porch, in a corner, in a chair. A man in a sleeveless white T-shirt, smoking.

I feel myself curl in like a turtle whose head is touched. I feel myself tightening, becoming old. I limp a little. I hum a crackly little tune. I tip my umbrella so my face is hidden, but I seem to see his eyes through it. They are sullen, slow. He makes not a sound. His eyes raise the hairs on the back of my neck.

.   .   .

I nod to the day girl at the desk and go quickly to my room. My heart won't stop hammering. I think of Andrej's thick arms; of Andrej and the vendors in Kiev who would not pay; of the girlfriend's murder. And the disappearance of Yuri.

It has begun to rain again, a murmurous rain. I stretch my arms over my head and spread my legs wide and run the palm of my hand up the inside of my thigh. It's possible that I am only halfway through my life. On the other hand, I'm two thirds of the way through the three score and ten. And again on the other hand, an artery in my head could burst before I leave this bed.

My life has been accelerating. Or maybe it just feels like acceleration because I've applied a drag. I don't want to reach the end, so I pull back and therefore feel the speed in a way I wouldn't if I were leaning into it, scanning eagerly from the open boxcar.

The rain is millennial. A gushing, endless rain. My son and my husband sit together in our house, their heads tipped together, talking, hidden by curtains of rain.

# 27

THERE IS, of course, the possibility that Ren will tell the truth about what happened on the night he was shot. There is the possibility that I will return as Francesca Woodbridge and we will go together to the police and tell them what we know.

There is also the possibility that I won't return as Francesca, or that if I do, Ren still won't tell what he knows. His own ideas of survival will preclude it. What then? Then the investigating officer, Captain Maynard McDean, receives a letter. If I have come home, it will be followed by a visit from me. If I have not come home, it will have to persuade in itself.

The letter will go something like this.

*Dear Captain McDean:*

*As the chief investigator of last October's assault on my husband, Renton Woodbridge, you probably have some sense by now that some of us are holding pieces of the puzzle behind our backs.*

*I've recently learned that Jimster Reece is now the prime suspect; that he doesn't have an alibi; that his behavior in recent months has not encouraged the confidence of those in law enforcement. He has "gang" friends. He is full of anger. He will therefore be charged by a process of elimination, yes? And of course your own weariness with this case has some bearing on developments as well. I understand and sympathize. It is a deeply wearying case.*

You no doubt know that Jimster and his father conceivably have reason to be furious with my husband because he represents the Recon Corp., and it was the Recon spill that forced the evacuation of the mobile home village where the Reeces lived. People under that kind of stress can behave in a bizarre and vindictive manner, you may be thinking.

This letter is to tell you that Jimster Reece is not guilty of breaking into our house and assaulting my husband. I can say that with full conviction.

I can say it flatly because I know Jimster very well — as a son, in some respects. He comes from a troubled home and has been basically on his own since he was very young. Technically, his father was often at home when Jimster returned from school, but never in much shape to take responsibility for him. Jimster was welcome at our house, and he spent many days and nights with us as a child. I calmed Jimster when he woke up screaming with nightmares; I helped him with his homework; he practiced his jokes, his riddles on me; I bought him vitamins; I called his mother in Idaho to try to persuade her to care about him more than she does. I loved that child. I loved him as a young adult. I love him still.

During the past few years, Jimster has branched out on his own. He is old beyond his years and is an independent personality, so it hasn't surprised me that he has struck his own course and that we, his foster family, if you will, have seen much less of him than we did when he was young. He and my son, Mack, no longer have as many interests in common as they once did, though there is no bad feeling on either of their parts, I can assure you. Life goes on. We seek out the company of those who most enliven us.

Jimster and Ren, my husband, have had their differences and disagreements in recent years, but they are the kinds of disagreements that occur between parent and teenager — that are, I think, inevitable. The most serious of them involved some boundaries Jimster failed to respect with regard to Ren's private property. Ren let his anger be known. He is angry still, and has therefore been slower than he should be to insist on the physical discrepancies between Jimster Reece and the intruder he saw.

As regards the Recon spill, Jimster once told me that he holds no particular grudge against Ren because of his work with Recon. Jimster is astute enough to know that an attorney's job is to make the best possible case for a client, not to decide issues of justice. He would, I believe, think less of Ren if Ren did not wage the best fight he could on behalf of his client. Jimster has no particular love for his father or for the shabby trailer they called home. I know Jimster has been resourceful enough to find better lodgings while this long and complicated legal action goes forward, and I hope his father has as well.

So as you see, I don't think it is remotely in Jimster's character to break into our house and engage in a struggle that ends in the near death of my husband. I realize also that my word about Jimster's character may not persuade you to disregard him as a suspect, particularly in light of his recent scrapes with the law, so I would ask you to consider the following facts:

For a number of months before Ren was shot, I employed a Russian immigrant with landscaping skills to work in my yard. I have nothing but good things to say about him. I trusted him implicitly and saw no reason, ever, to change that opinion. However, a disturbing thing happened one day that involved this person, Yuri Petrov.

One morning while Yuri was working in the yard, a silver BMW pulled up and a man of perhaps thirty-five got out and signaled to Yuri. Yuri seemed shocked to see him — shocked and scared, I now believe. The man signaled to Yuri, as I say, and he put a hand on Yuri's forearm and spoke very intently to him for what seemed like a long time. I observed all this from my kitchen window.

The man had strangely white hair, a sort of yellow-white, and a tanned face. He looked our house over carefully. I noticed that. He said something more to Yuri, who turned his back on him. The other man shouted something and stomped to his car and roared off. I found some excuse to go out into the yard. Yuri was yanking out weeds, and he looked very pale. For the first time since I'd met him, his movements looked tired. I asked him if the man with the smoky hair was a friend. He replied that the man was his cousin, and that he was, in effect, bad news.

Over the next few weeks, the man returned once or twice a week— perhaps more often when I was not there. Each time he seemed to upset Yuri. "Oh, Andrej," he said once, wearily. "Andrej is a real operator."

I began to imagine things: blackmail, gang pressure, all the kinds of things you hear about. I wrote down the license plate number of the man's car. And then he quit coming by. At least, I never saw him the last month that Yuri worked for us. I did, however, see the car. One day I returned from the burial of a friend's father at the north-side cemetery and I drove around the block to get back onto Spruce, and there was the car, the BMW, parked in front of 194 Olive.

I had the distinct sense that Yuri was being threatened by this man. I had too the distinct sense that this man, this Andrej, was very interested in our house. He kept scanning the windows and doors, it seemed to me. Once I think I saw him point toward the back door and ask Yuri a question.

Several months before Ren was shot, I cut myself quite badly on a kitchen knife. Yuri, who was working in the yard that day, took me to the hospital to get stitched and bandaged. When we returned, I unthinkingly pressed the numbers on our alarm system in such a way that he could have taken note of them if he were interested. I did not mention that occurrence to the initial investigators because the truth of the matter is, I had forgotten about it. I know that sounds unlikely, but very often what's unlikely turns out to be the truth. Only when I heard that Jimster Reece was the prime suspect, on the basis of his knowledge of the alarm system, did I remember that there was another person who also knew, or could have known, those numbers: my gardener.

So is Yuri Petrov the person who broke into the house? No, he is not. I would find that impossible to believe, knowing him as I did. He was a *kind man and an honest one. Two months before my husband was shot, Yuri Petrov stopped coming to our house. I tried unsuccessfully to reach him. He seemed to have disappeared. I suspect Andrej had a hand in that development. I don't think Yuri was anywhere near our town when Ren confronted the intruder. But Andrej was.*

*Andrej, as I mentioned, lives at 194 Olive and drives a silver BMW. His last name is Kuglov. He is, I am convinced, the person who broke into our house. I suspect that he threatened harm to Yuri if he didn't obtain the security code to our home, and that he was the person who ultimately used that code to gain access with the intent of burglarizing our house. He was surprised by the presence of my husband and didn't therefore have the opportunity to take anything obvious that was of value.*

*However, I believe he did take something. Not long ago I noticed for the first time that a silver box was missing from a shelf in our kitchen. It's a cluttered shelf, one I don't take much notice of, so the disappearance of that box wasn't evident to me until very recently. It is small enough to fit in a large pocket, has scrollwork on the lid, and contains a plastic bag filled with ashes from the Mount St. Helens volcano.*

*I suggest that you put some questions to Andrej. I suggest that you search his property. I urge you to take a close look at this man and that you question any alibi he offers. He is a violent person with much power over others, including the power to encourage a lie on his behalf. When you investigate this man, I trust that you will find him a far more viable suspect than Jimster Reece.*

*I will be happy to talk to you about these matters in more detail, at your convenience.*

*Sincerely,*
*Francesca Woodbridge*

# 28

AROUND THE TIME that Mack and Tamara began to see each other, he brought her to the house to show her a new computer game and in that offhand way to introduce them to us as a pair. Ren and I had seen the Klemenhagens hardly at all since Ren joined Warren Evinrude's firm. When the Recon spill happened, Franklin and Krystal Klemenhagen and members of their church picketed the Recon office, accusing the company of buying off those who might sue for relocation and medical expenses in the future. The company would pay everything that was needed at the moment, but the recipient had to sign away any future claims. Franklin and Krystal thought this was bribery.

Ren began to call them the Quakerpuffs, although they were Quakers for only a couple of years and then moved on to a more flamboyant denomination with a name I can never remember. Ren claimed that for all their peace-and-tolerance talk, the Quakerpuffs had to have an enemy in order to muster themselves, to apprehend their own righteousness. If they didn't have an enemy, one must be created. And Recon was handy. That was Ren's line.

Mack and Tamara sat at our breakfast counter drinking coffee before they went wherever it was they went in the evenings. They seemed oblivious to any strain between the Klemenhagens and Ren. Somehow the subject of a christening came up. Tamara sat there with her schoolgirl hair in its little clip, her housewife dress, and her little cat's-eye glasses and complained to us all in her pale voice that her parents had dragged her to a hippie christening the day before.

"It was in some *meadow*," she said, "and it was like wall-to-wall tie-dye?" She and Mack exchanged tiny smiles. "And the mom and dad or whatever consulted, like, four *goddesses*?"

"Yikes," Ren said.

"And then they tossed grain and water and some flowers, I think, to all these various points of the universe. And lit up these sweet-grass things and wafted the smoke all over the place." She moved her boneless little hand through the air in a pretty gesture. "It was hot too, so I was, like, passing out." She smiled serenely at Mack. He gave her a look that said, Pass out, Tamara! I'll catch you!

"Well, you know," Ren said, almost apologetically, "that's not so different from some ceremonies that went on before you were born, Tamara."

I tried to think what he was talking about but could summon up only the vaguest recollection of some kind of gathering that had amused Ren a lot at the time. Mack is ten months older than Tamara, so I would have been in a baby haze when she was born. A lot of things passed me by.

"I know, I know," Tamara said. "I know the whole story." Krystal had known exactly when she must become pregnant in order to bear the child that would be a perfect complement to the child's parents and older sister, Ariel — who would have the characteristics that would balance those of the others and make them a karmically vital family. And so there were circles of joined hands and then potions and positions and charts and calendars. And Tamara was conceived, with deliberation and joy, at the very moment that was most opportune, and when the news became known, their friends gave them a huge party that was, yes, in a meadow and involved chanting and the flinging of grain.

"Mom changed her name from Christine to Krystal because of me," Tamara said. "She said I was an amazing and beautiful lens on the future that she and Franklin had created, and so she didn't want to be Christine anymore." She shrugged tolerantly.

"Why didn't they name *you* Krystal?" Mack asked.

"Because Tamara is my grandma's name, and she would have pitched a fit."

"Cool," Mack said sternly.

A few days, maybe a week later, Mack and Ren and I ate one of our rare breakfasts together. No one was listening to NPR. No one was reading the newspaper. No one was ready to dash. We simply sat at the table together and peaceably crunched our cereal. Mack may have been in his pajamas. I'm not sure. What I remember is that his hair was still rumpled from sleep, and he had a sad little spray of acne across his forehead and a faint new loamy smell to him.

"Krystal and Franklin," Mack said, as if he wouldn't believe they existed if he hadn't seen them with his own eyes. We all smiled.

"So did you guys do ceremonies and stuff to beam me down from the universe?" he said.

I saw an ash-covered street, Ren's lonely back, the brusque doctor. I saw a decision reversed and marriage in its wake, as skittish and breathless as a late guest.

"No ceremonies," Ren said lightly.

I got up to make some toast, and I stood by the toaster, waiting.

"Did you want a boy or a girl?" Now he looked at me. "You can tell me. I won't be insulted."

"Either was just fine," I said. I tried a smile, but I knew it looked wrong. He sat up straighter in his chair.

"I realize you were sinners," he said jovially. "Bun in the oven, and it's off to tie the knot!"

"That sounds a tad crude," I said. "I mean, we wanted each other and we wanted you, and our timing and arrangements just weren't the best in the world." I looked to Ren for some help. He was examining a tiny stain on his cuff.

"So when you found out you were pregnant, what did you do?" There were spots of color on Mack's cheeks now. He looked almost eager.

"We decided to get married!" Ren said heartily, looking up from his cuff with a big phony smile, as if that finished the conversation.

"Before that," Mack persisted. "The day you found out. Did you go, Hey, here comes a beautiful lens on the future! Or did you go, Oh shit! How do we get out of *this*?"

He looked carefully at each of us. Coolly, I'd be tempted to say. My whole head seemed to burn.

His eyes closed down a notch.

# 29

WHAT DID ANDREJ WATCH as he sat smoking on his Olive Street porch? He watched a woman behind an umbrella when there was no rain. And was there something about the woman that caused a little ripple of recognition? Something that tied her to the woman in the handsome house who could not get enough of Yuri and his projects? To the suave Francesca in her house?

It seems impossible. The contexts are so different. But if you are, as Andrej is, so new to a place that context doesn't obscure what you see, then perhaps I looked exactly like Francesca Woodbridge.

It's evening and the Trocadero feels very empty. It's Gerrald's night off. There are footsteps and murmurs in the hall. They pass my door, they fade away.

Let's say he did somehow recognize me. Let's say he became curious and he followed me. Is that entirely unlikely? He followed me and he saw me enter this motel. He wondered who I really was and what I had been doing near his home. He has taken it into his mind to decide that I have threatened him, and he waits now to make his move. And if he decides to harm me here, he will destroy my Jeanne Thompson ID and take my cash. And what would they find in my room? Three changes of clothes, fake hair, two pair of shoes, the remains of fast food. And what could Gerrald tell them? That her name was Jeanne? That she seemed lonely?

Yesterday there was a dusting of snow on the tops of the mountains. It can happen here, even in late May. A motel guest left some items of clothing in a dresser drawer a month or so ago, and Gerrald gave them to me for early morning warmth. He had them in a large brown sack: a big sweater with reindeer on the front and back and a stocking cap. If the guest called about them after all this time, well, too bad. When he said that, I knew that Gerrald expected me to stay indefinitely, and that the prospect was a comforting one to him.

*The Exorcist* plays on the old-movie channel, and young Regan is beginning to look curdled. The shopping channel is conducting a seminar on dinner rings. Didn't television used to end? Wasn't there an end to the television day? Of course. A long, long time ago, there was. The test pattern appeared and television, for a few hours, just went away.

My heart is galloping. I fear Andrej. I fear that he has already begun to retaliate. The idea doesn't seem as crazy to me as I would like it to seem.

The reindeer sweater has a sour damp-basement smell. With my nail clipper, I unravel the yarn at the wrists and make some small holes in other places. I've let my hair go for a couple of days. It hangs lankly. I mess up my bangs as if I've slept face down, passed out. With the cap on, I pull some random strands of red hair onto my pale-lipped face. Shoes with no socks. The eyeglasses Jeanne Thompson likes to wear.

A motor outside stops. A door closes. And now I'm running out of my room, down the too-bright hall, down the back stairs of the Trocadero, the ones that avoid the lobby.

Running almost always makes you feel as if you should have started running earlier.

The walkway that parallels the river has lights along it nearer to town, but it is dark here. The river seems to sigh at my heels. The barking man who assaulted Franklin — where is he at this moment? Does he sleep beneath a bridge, damp and exhausted?

Once in college I sat up all night in the cold, on a cold sidewalk, waiting for a ticket office to open. I had company. We had whiskey and coffee. We laughed and played cards and it was a big lark. Ren was there. He was the funniest one of all.

I walk briskly, as if I'm late for work.

At home, Gerrald will be awake, reading his new thing: L. Ron Hubbard. Gerrald is now investigating scientology, and more power to him, but how can you believe someone named L. Ron?

On the river walkway below the main bridge, several benches are bolted to the walk. Metal stairs ascend to the street. A distant bell chimes five. I sit on a bench and listen to the grand old slide of the river and pull my big unraveled sleeves down over my hands. An occasional car rumbles across the bridge, chasing an arrow of warm light. The smell of roasting coffee floats from the coffee-roasting place a couple of blocks away. Cottonwood brush, the astringent fragrance of it, roasted coffee, the river — those are the smells, and they produce in me a kind of fateful calmness. A dog, a Labrador, clicks along the sidewalk, smells my oddness, does a funny sideways trot to face me more directly, then reorients himself and proceeds.

The sky begins to drain itself of darkness, to move toward a pale greenish blue. And now, between me and the river, a calligraphy of trees, stern downstrokes with wiry embellishments of branches and crowns and reverberating leaves, rehearsing their daylight blaze.

Two people emerge from the tunnel under the bridge. They have blankets over their heads and shoulders. The taller one carries a guitar case. Their cigarettes are tiny penlights in the dark. They slow down just a shade when they see me, then keep walking. I slump, my arms tight around me. They walk right up to me, bend down, and examine my face.

"Hey, Rosa," one of them says from the depths of his blanket. I give him an irritated, uncomprehending look.

"Hey Rosadoza!" He's boisterous. The other shape is a woman, I think. Even when she or he mutters, I can't be sure. Neither person is the raver who attacked Franklin, that's clear.

"That's not Rosa," the gravelly voice murmurs. "You ain't Rosa." It's as if I've shown her false ID. I shrug elaborately, watching myself in my mind's eye, the sweatered shabby frightened me. I have no energy or time to convince you I am not Rosa, my shrug says.

"It's Rosa," the man says briskly to the other blanket person. "Tri-Cities. That stinkin' wind. Pasco and whatever."

"Kennewick." The blanket shrugs. "And whatever. Where they make that Hanford A-bomb."

"Richland," I say.

He claps me on the knee. "Fuckin' Rosa!"

He has only bottom teeth. From inside his blanket, he extracts a narrow bundle of rags and unwraps them to produce a rusty fishing rod in two parts. He fits them together, shakes himself out of the blanket, strides rigorously toward the bank, and casts out upon the flickering corridor of water.

"There's metal in the fish," I murmur. The woman has her blanket off her shoulders now. Her colorless hair is pulled into a Mickey Mouse clip.

"I found a fortune cookie once and it said, 'Your luck has completely changed today,'" she tells me. "He *likes* 'em with metal," she adds. "That's his favorite way." She takes a last drag of her damp-looking cigarette and bends over in a prolonged and unexcited bout of coughing, as if that's the way she kickstarts the day.

"From the big mines upstream. Old tailings," I say. "The fish are . . . You shouldn't eat them. They're dangerous."

She looks at me and laughs. It's a barking dry laugh, but clearly her real laugh. As if I've just told a good one. There are tears in her eyes from the coughing fit.

"That's the way he likes 'em, Rosa," she says patiently, patting my arm. "Rosa. He likes 'em glowin' in the dark." She pulls a pint from somewhere in the depths of her clothes, takes a reverential swig, and hands the bottle to me.

"What do you think about a fortune like that? 'Your luck has completely changed today.' Is that good or bad?"

"It depends upon where you're starting from," I say.

"Depends upon," she mocks. "Depends. Upon."

A yip from the bank. A curse.

"Hey, Bunny!" she calls. "Rosa says them fish are glow-in-the-dark." She laughs again, shaking her head. She extends her flattened hand toward him and ushers his response to the two of us.

"That's the kind I like!"

She smiles, satisfied. "Maybe if he eats a couple, he'll glow hisself in the dark," she says. "There's a terrible thought." She yawns mightily.

I swish the whiskey around, trying to run the liquid up on the rim to kill some germs. "Hey," she says gently. "Quit playin' with your food."

I think now, Did I dream it? But then I feel that particular edge-of-the-day coldness, the nakedness of my sockless feet. There was the ragged couple and their reek, and the salt smell of the cottonwood brush along the riverbank. And fear. The fast beat in my throat and clarity racing through my veins. Would they give me a long and terrible disease? Would they pull knives and stab me because they had smelled something about me that said clean blankets, and food, and toothpaste, and fakery?

Bunny returns fishless. The sky is now huge streamers of gold and pink flung raucously across its new blue, and the traffic on the bridge above is steady with the early-to-work.

We all sit on the bench for a while. The woman — he calls her

Ruthie — begins to cry. Bunny absently pats her knee. "She's been looking all over for her girl," he says to me. "The state took her and wouldn't give her back, then they handed her off to some foster parents, and the foster parents didn't treat her right. And then they took off. With the kid." He bent his head to peer at Ruthie's wet, puckered face. "It's killin' her."

"The state knows where she is," Ruthie says in a tiny voice. "But they won't say."

I begin to see that there is a sense of schedule with Bunny and Ruthie. This brief ceremony of grief probably has a slot of the beginning of each day, though it's no less sincere for being ritualized. It's simply part of the way Bunny and Ruthie pace themselves. That's my sense of it. We're quiet together for a while.

"Over by the Tri-Cities," I say, "where you think you saw me?" A little grunt of assent from Bunny. "There's the Columbia River over there. That's basically where I dropped off the earth, so to speak." Ruthie gives me a brief, alert-bird glance.

"My husband at the time, L. Ron Ronaldson, was running with freaks, and I feared for my life. He was pretty much a psycho case when it got right down to it. I knew he'd hunt me down if I left. He was that type. Put your life in danger. Track you down so he can do it some more." I pause to tweak their interest. In the growing light they look stunned with exhaustion. "One afternoon I hitched a ride down there to the Columbia to think over my next plan. I had this old purse with my wallet in it and so on and so forth. My plan was to watch the water for a while to cool off, slow down, gather my thoughts."

Neither Bunny nor Ruthie is paying much attention. He's examining a hole on the bottom of his ancient sneakers, worrying the edges with a pocketknife in what seems to be the preliminaries of some kind of patching operation. Ruthie's head is tipped back; she is studying a flock of ducks, check marks drifting across the sky.

"So I found this bench by the river," I say. Bunny grunts. "So I put my wallet and purse under that bench, but first I wrote a little message to L. Ron. 'This is it, L. Ron,' I wrote. No goodbye, no nothing. Then I made footprints to the water and walked in the water along the bank for quite a ways upstream. Then I went back to the freeway and watched for some out-of-state plates coming down the road, and finally some stoned kids took me as far as South Dakota. Then I caught a lift with a trucker, then another one, and ended up in Ithaca, New York, where I spent most of the winter at a shelter and my part-time job at St. Vincent de Paul." I stop to remember the shelter.

"I assume they found my ID and gave the word to L. Ron, so he can move on to other concerns and let me rest in peace." It seems time to wind it up. They're both so bored they're yawning with clenched teeth, and Ruthie also has hiccoughs that are interfering with any mood that might be trying to gain a foothold.

They fold up their blanket capes and we all have another gulp, then the bottle gets stowed inside Bunny's clothes somewhere and we begin to climb the metal stairs to the street.

"You were good people, over there in the Tri-Cities," Ruthie says stoutly.

"Thank you," I say.

Up in the land of the living, we move in a little cloud of ammonia and grime. We make ourselves look purposeful and march wordlessly to a corner downtown. Ruthie spreads a blanket in a silent businesslike way and digs into her big sack to produce a dozen or so pairs of beaded earrings, vaguely Navajo, which she places on the blanket. Bunny takes out his guitar and nods for me to sit against the wall, which I do, head bent.

He begins to sing. He wails, actually. Folk songs. "John Henry." "Green, Green." His voice is so loud and extended and bad that most of the people who pass us smile slyly to themselves. They offer no money, just smile to themselves, as if something funny had come on the radio. And Ruthie sits by her earrings, eyes half closed, hands folded, a putrid little Buddha. She seems to have gone into some kind of state that isn't sleep but an energy conservation measure, like a stove turned down, like a machine on idle. Her hands are very small and brown.

I can't begin to guess her story, except that there were undoubtedly two times, or three, when what happened to her was grievously at odds with what she had expected — so grievously at odds that any return to the faith or the patterns of the time before the event became impossible.

A young kid with droopy pants throws a dollar into Bunny's guitar case. "Bless you!" Bunny calls out, and breaks into a chorus of "Kumbaya." The kid walks on as if he's paid a toll, and I think, He didn't have to do that. What made him want to do that?

It's warming up. I sit on a sidewalk in my town. Legs. Legs and shoes. Raincoats, running shoes. No one looks familiar, then everyone does. Over there, yes, our accountant waits at the corner for the walking man to light up. Next to him, a young clerk from the health-food store fiddles with his horsehair bracelet. And now a mother of one of Mack's grade school friends passes by, inches from my feet, oblivious to us all. Something shimmering runs along my skin to quaver at the tips of my fingers. This is the most amazing thing I've ever done.

This may be what it feels like to be dying. You inhabit a completely different realm, a different state of existence, from anyone around you, and yet those people can go about their business like nurses, chattering in the hallway about their mothers-in-law, a recipe for no-flour chocolate cake. While you begin to die.

Do I have that aghast look in my eyes that I've seen in the eyes of the very old? An old man, once powerful, once leonine, now gets hauled around in a chair. You ask him how he's doing, and the discrepancy between the inquiry and the honest answer is such an amazing gulf that he can only stare at it, at the question, so terminally inane.

I see her from a block away. Some kind of antenna goes up and I straighten against the wall, my disguise suddenly a collection of transparent furbelows. Beneath them, Francesca Woodbridge sits on a downtown sidewalk, homeless.

I've never before noticed that Elise is knock-kneed, but I've never observed her from street level either; haven't noticed how girlish her legs are, how coltish. She grows larger and my eyes fix on my own folded legs. She didn't know me, the day she and Franklin Klemenhagen met at the motel, but he must have told her afterward that he recognized me. Or thought he did. She will surely know me now. I don't have a second chance. She will know me, and I will lose the option of reassuming my old life. That fact rings loud. She can make me forever strange to those in my waiting life.

She passes us. I watch her knees. She trails a little cloud of White Shoulders — not Elise's scent. This woman has the whole Elise uniform: the short-skirted suit, the shiny bob, the briefcase. But she is knock-kneed and younger and no, she is not Elise. And no, I am not found out. The false papers have worked. The guards gravely wave me on.

That first autumn we knew Roger and Elise, Roger brought out his guitar one day and we sat in the back yard with the yellow leaves falling like rain, the way they do one day a year. One windless day, all remaining leaves drift off the trees in utter capitulation. Mack crawled around in them. Ren and I threw them high, to make him laugh. Roger played "Green, Green."

I bury my head in my arms, as if I've fallen asleep. "Don't," hisses Ruthie. "They'll bust you." She's trying to look busy selling earrings. A girl with torn white jeans and a spider tattoo on her hand has squatted down to examine them. "They're genuine," Ruthie assures her.

The Chrysalis is a combination gift shop and coffee bar. In my waiting life, I sometimes stop there for some small gift for a friend. A packet of sea salts, maybe. Ladybug earrings. In my waiting life, I dash into the store, make a quick decision, dash out, vaguely grateful for the advent of boutiques in our town — scaled-down, fragrant little emporiums where everything is smaller than a breadbox. The Chrysalis hires nice smart kids and forgoes the most obvious kinds of preciousness. Street people sometimes hang out in the alcove near the front door, and if they are quiet and undemanding, no one tells them to move on.

There, in the recessed entrance, I stand in my frayed sweater, my pulled-down hat. Bunny gave me a couple of dollars to fetch coffee for them. He sent me on this mission. The wooden floor of the Chrysalis is soft and scuffed, like suede. I seem to feel it, a small warmth, through my shoes. The tall, dim, long room holds the smells of sandalwood, lily of the valley, tea. Formosa, oolong, starfire licorice — jars and jars of tea. Henna. Candles. Silver bangles and deco frames. The ceiling is hammered tin, painted a hopeful yellow. The espresso machine hisses somewhere at the back of the room. Customers in booths hunch over their newspapers.

The girl behind the jewelry counter has a shaved head and brilliant turquoise contact lenses. She smiles at me, which allows me to move to the back of the long room to order the coffee, the fresh huge muffins filled with berries. A young guy with a long ponytail puts my coffee cups in a box so that I can carry them. I feel the long looks of some of the readers in the booths, feel their careful eyes on my back, but no matter, I'm on my way. They won't be bothered.

Suddenly I'm exhausted. It's ten in the morning, and I am

completely depleted. My eyes are gritty. My joints ache. Bunny and Ruthie seem to be a long way away, too far away. I watch them from the Chrysalis alcove, gauging the distance I must walk. Bunny sits next to Ruthie now, his guitar at his side. Ruthie has her knees drawn up to her chest, her head bent. He leans his head toward her. He listens. He places his hand very gently on top of her small foot.

Five hours ago, just before I saw Bunny and Ruthie trudging toward me behind the red embers of their cigarettes, I stood by the river and felt as if I were the astronaut who'd left the ship on a tether. There he was, drifting in the stars, and what if the tether should break?

I heard river rustles and behind them something very faint that sounded like a child humming behind a closed door. I thought of Gerrald at his 4 A.M. desk, Mack asleep in his suit, Yuri in flight. I seemed to feel the outlines of myself, Braille-like, from the inside: the tension I carry in my neck, the heavy chill in my fingers as they swing along, the mechanisms of my breath, the set of my good teeth. All of us seemed gorgeous, seemed valiant to me.

Now Bunny and Ruthie do too. He places his dirty fingers across the instep of Ruthie's exhausted foot. She shifts slightly, like a cat. They will wait. And then they won't wait anymore, and when they go, they will fall into a step that doesn't match exactly but is essentially the same. A kind of sturdy, elegant swing. The way horses can look elegant even when they are pulling something heavy — a barge, say, or a metal sleigh.

The two of them together, as wrecked and uneven as they are, make something coherent. Apart, they would be plateaued, cul-de-sacked, cropped off, misshapen. So what does it mean to be, or not be, in love?

# 30

In the week I've spent at the Trocadero, Gerrald has changed. The day I arrived, he was natty. The slick black hair, the pressed shirt, the golf-club cufflinks, the polished shoes — they made him seem carefully put together. Now he has blue smudges under his eyes, almost pretty, like plum-colored powder applied with the tip of a thumb. His rather regal impassivity has turned brittle. His smile is a bad replica of a smile. His voice on the phone is an imitation of how he thinks a voice on the phone should be. His eyes move around the room too quickly. I know that look. It's the look of someone having to pay attention to rather shocking pain. I saw a version of it in Ren for a long time after his father's murder.

"What's wrong?" I say. "You look a little green around the gills."

He bends to wipe a spot off the top of his shoe. He flicks his tie, trying to make it lie flatter. His hair makes wide brushmarks across the pale flesh of his skull.

"I've been having some woman trouble," he says, not joking in the least.

He'd been running an ad in the personals of the weekly newspaper, he told me. Two days ago he finally received a serious reply. She sounded like exactly what he had asked for: a slim, sincere person between twenty-five and forty-five who was looking for friendship and maybe more. She provided a phone number, and he mustered the nerve to call her. Her voice was as sincere as she'd promised. It sounded like a friend's voice.

They agreed to meet for coffee at the Red Robin Café yesterday after Gerrald got off work and went to AA. He didn't tell her the AA part, just said 10:30 A.M., as if that were a reasonable, what-the-heck idea, though he knew he'd be stuporous with lack of sleep. Later in the day was impossible for her, for reasons she didn't go into. Her name was Terry Ann Rideout.

So he went to the Red Robin at 10:25 and took a seat in a booth where he could face the door. He looked around at the other customers to see if there was anyone between twenty-five and forty-five wearing a black cardigan sweater, as she'd said she would be, and saw no one. The restaurant was fairly empty. He felt weird in the big booth and thought about moving to the counter, but he didn't want to join the man and woman who were sitting there, an empty seat between them. They were bent toward an open newspaper and were laughing. They seemed to Gerrald to be strangers who had struck up a casual flirtation.

At one point the woman twirled her seat all the way around and passed her smile across the room. Then she did it again, this time smiling straight at Gerrald. She settled back into some kind of banter with the guy next to her. He was a big guy. Gerrald thought he might be a custodian of some kind, because he had one of those things on his belt that holds dozens and dozens of keys.

Gerrald waited. He scanned the room again, then became convinced that the woman who had answered the ad had entered the restaurant, looked around, maybe looked right at him, and he'd been too foggy, too beat, to recognize the look. And she'd left. He started to feel sure that this had happened. He'd missed his one chance, because he knew he wouldn't be so bold again.

Some people left. A family with some fat kids. Two creaky ladies and a teenage girl in overalls. And then the couple at the counter. Still laughing, they went to the register and paid. They ambled out the door. As the woman stood out on the sidewalk, she pulled a black cardigan from her big woven straw bag — she looked distant and wavery through the restaurant glass, but there was no mistaking the sweater — and she put it on and walked away with the guy with the keys.

Gerrald got up and paid for his cool coffee. He drove home and then he sat down and just looked at the whole situation head-on. She'd been waiting, the woman from the ad. She'd been waiting right there at the counter, and the minute he walked in she'd struck up a conversation with the guy two seats down. Why? Because she hadn't liked what she'd seen. From clear across the room, she hadn't liked what she'd seen. So she just let Gerrald sit there in that immense booth. Then, to top it off, she'd taken a couple more looks — those cute little whirls on the counter stool — and made her decision and marched out, not even waiting until she was decently out of sight to put on the sweater.

He felt such humiliation, such fury, that he couldn't even remember what she looked like. Some kind of blond puffy hair on top of an ordinary person. What did it matter? As he sat at home, his hungry cats yowling, he thought he was going to have to have a drink, or he was going to have to get back at her somehow. Maybe both. He looks defiant when he tells me that.

"So. I take it you've done neither."

"Not yet," he says. His eyes look as if he's been hit in the face.

"There could be more than one woman in the Red Robin with..." I think better of it. "You're probably right," I accede. "It was probably the ad woman, completely different in person than she sounded on the phone. I mean, Christ. You really wonder what rock some people live under."

I'm trying to whip him into a state of cathartic indignation, but it isn't working. He just looks at me mildly.

"What is it?" His voice is very quiet. "What is it about me that would make a person look once and want to go away?" He tucks his shirt in tighter. "What is it about me ... per se?"

That "per se." So on-the-mark in its sorrow. There is nothing I can say.

It's almost time for Gerrald to go home for the day. Long strands of the rising sun stretch across the mauve carpet.

"I'm going to take a wakeup shower. Why don't we buy ourselves breakfast after that?"

He looks at me, puzzled, as if there are several voices on the line and he's trying to decide which one is talking to him.

"You can skip your meeting one time," I say. "You aren't going to fall off the wagon."

Gerrald shrugs.

"Twenty minutes," I say over my shoulder. I shower, dress, recomb my black wig, and pin it on. We climb into Gerrald's red Colt and drive to a pancake house a few blocks away. Several people are setting up markers for something that a big banner calls the Fun Run. They're tanned and muscled and intent. They wear running shorts and fleece jackets in stained-glass colors. The Colt's muffler has a hole in it and the car is burning a little oil. The passenger door is sprung and doesn't fully close. As we rumble fumily past one of the race monitors, he swivels his etched bronzed face and looks at us as if we're dragging a string of corpses.

I tap Gerrald's knee. "I'm quite desperate for pancakes," I tell him. He looks at me warily. "I'm serious. It came upon me as we were talking—I get pancakes or I do something ugly." He smiles as much as Gerrald ever smiles and speeds through a yellow light.

When the waiter comes around for our orders, I nod at Gerrald. "Your call."

He runs his finger slowly down the right side of the menu and stops. "Two of those Dutch Babies," he says sternly. The teenage waiter, a hormonal mess, scratches on his pad and retrieves the menus with a disheveled sigh.

"You look like you did something to your hair, hon," Gerrald says to me, with the faintest note of shyness in his voice.

"Which hair would that be? As you may have noticed, I have a few different heads of hair."

"Well, this one looks better than the others."

His color has returned somewhat. He looks more awake than he did an hour ago.

"Those people from the Southwest are back," he says. "Checked in just after midnight. Ed and Mary-Doris something. Taffelmeyer."

"The GM guy and his wife? The ones who were here a week ago?"

"They asked after you," he says. "She wanted to know about your divorce. I said I couldn't say much about that." I feel as if I've somehow betrayed Gerrald by sharing a confidence with someone who means so much less to me than he does. Even if the confidence was a lie. "Some big long story they had, about getting most of the way back home and here comes an emergency call from their daughter who lives here in town."

"Who got a restraining order on her husband, Toby Hennepin." I make my voice bored with the Taffelmeyers.

"Sounds like a helluva mess of some kind," he says. "That's all they need in their peaceful old age. A big ol' batshit daughter." I laugh, and he does too. A dry little laugh, like an old hinge.

"Well, I'm sure the daughter doesn't mean to shorten their lives with her messes," I say. "Some people are just completely clueless about their effect on others." I speak emphatically. Gerrald picks at a spot of leathery ketchup on the table.

"Some people just don't get it," I say. "We should perform citizen's arrests on them all. Make them perform disgusting tasks."

"Something," Gerrald says, signaling briskly for the check. "Something they might remember."

．　．　．

· 215 ·

I call my home and get my voice inviting me to leave myself a message. I hang up and dial again. When Tamara wants to talk to Mack, she does that and he picks up. It works.

"Where are you?" he says.

"Still roaming," I answer lightly. "But not for too much longer. I'm just touching base to tell you I'm about to fax a letter to the police about Jimster. They're barking up the wrong tree."

"How do you know?"

"Because I know. It's complicated. I'll talk with you about it when I see you, okay?"

I didn't know how to say the next thing. So I just let the silence grow for a few seconds.

"It wasn't the *florist,* as you like to call him," I say, as gently as I can. "I also know that."

"Well, since he doesn't seem to be around, we'll never really know, will we?" Mack says carefully. Another wait.

"How's your father?"

"My father seems to be quite upset that no one from the office has bothered to drop by or call since just after he had his run-in with the burglar who isn't the florist and who isn't Jimster. All these months later, it has registered with him that they do not seem to be overflowing with compassion or interest."

We both think about that for a few seconds. It's worth thinking about.

"Well, Mack," I say. "This is costing a fortune. And I really just wanted to hear your voice. The rest can wait."

He says nothing. I can hear him breathe.

"And Mack. You know, there's nothing you could do that would make me not glad that you're my son. That would make me not love you, just for yourself. Just per se." I catch my breath. "Got that?"

"Check," he mumbles.

·  ·  ·

At the airport, I pay cash for a ticket on the commuter to Salt Lake, which leaves in an hour. I show the clerk my Jeanne Thompson driver's license.

I buy a card and stamps in the gift shop and write a note to Gerrald, thanking him for his company and insight during "my stressful time." I include ten one-hundred-dollar bills, address it to the motel, and mail it. Keep the change, Gerrald.

No one I know is on the plane except a receptionist from my dentist's office, who smiles vaguely, trying to place me. All she really knows are my teeth. At Salt Lake, I check in for my flight to Athens via Atlanta, again showing Jeanne's license and passport. And three hours later I'm in the air.

# 31

A MAN SAT next to me on the plane, writing in that pulling left-hander's way, his wedding band bright and heavy on his hand. He'd pause to think, like a parody of someone pausing to think, and then bend again over his work. The clouds floated away from his head as we climbed.

He scribbled furiously, crossed things out. Now and then he paused to consult a manuscript of some sort, something that looked reproduced too many times. He was in his thirties, it seemed, but had already settled into the soft-cornered, short-sleeved look he'd carry to his death, given a little shrinkage toward the end.

This was a weekday flight, and we were surrounded by tassled-loafered turks swinging their six-hundred-dollar briefcases into the overheads. The sleek cats in navy suits and cufflinked shirts. What were they to him? I wondered. Some other species to envy for their shiny arrogance and speed? Did he notice the way they whipped out their laptops and squinted at their spreadsheets and schedules, grimly excited by the pressures of the coming day and the feel of their own muscled bodies inside their suits? Did he notice them at all? I couldn't tell.

I tried to read a paperback I'd bought in the airport gift shop.

"Good book?" he asked.

"No," I said.

"I'm working on a book myself," he said. He put the tips of his fingers on the manuscript. "I'm making some changes in a book that I plan to give to my wife."

He placed the point of his Eversharp on an underlined sentence. It read: "Her smoking eyes turned toward ____." He wrote the name Paul into the blank.

"Paul," he said, making a careful row of X's through "smoking." "That's me." He lettered in the word "aquamarine."

"They use the wrong words sometimes and actually have some parts of the plot that are a little too steamy. I mean, if you're going to show it to anyone. My wife, for instance. She is going to want to show this to her sisters and her friend Marla. I know she is. And it would be a little embarrassing as is. So I'm fixing it."

Paul, it turned out, had paid five hundred dollars to someone named George Quintana in Tarzana, California, to furnish him with a personalized book. He had chosen from among five plots and Quintana had sent him the manuscript. For an extra hundred dollars, he could make up to thirty line-edits or deletions. Then Quintana would run everything through the computer and so on, and send Paul a hardcover book with gold lettering for the title of his choosing. This book would star Paul and his wife, Wendy.

"Quintana of Tarzana," I said brightly. Paul waited for me to complete the thought.

Wendy, a Libra, thought she was getting an opal necklace for her thirty-fifth birthday, but Paul had bought this book instead, because he knew it would amaze her.

"The story is basically that my wife is working for a lawyer — she really works for a CPA, but I made him a lawyer — and she is sent to Hawaii to investigate a client's background. She gets into *big* trouble there." He flipped rigorously through the manuscript, scanning. "She doesn't know what to do. She makes mistakes." He flipped some more pages. "This happens, that happens," he said dreamily.

Then he shut the thing and looked at me straight on for the first time. "Basically, the deal is, I'm already there," he said. "In Hawaii. The Big Island. Waiting. I'm already there. And I save her."

# 32

As the plane approached Athens, I grew queasy at the thought of reentering Greece, of showing the Jeanne Thompson passport and feeling a detaining hand on my arm — a look, a room, questions. Surely inhabiting a new self could not be as easy as it had seemed. Surely I had used up my luck. I tried to think about what I would do if the officials looked closely at my forged stamp.

I practiced feeling like Jeanne Thompson and found that I had actually begun to create a person who was distinct from Francesca Woodbridge, who had different tastes, fears, consolations. She seemed in some faint way like Ursula, the Swiss social worker I'd met en route to my island the first time — the woman who seemed to disintegrate by degrees when the Greece of her imagination didn't match the Greece she had found.

When we landed, I signaled to the flight attendant and told her I'd been traveling a long time and felt faint; I had a blood condition that made me sporadically anemic and subject to extreme lightheadedness and medical claustrophobia, a term I used with the firmness of someone who could produce a verifying doctor's note. Could she arrange to have a wheelchair at the gate? She could.

An airport employee wheeled me to customs. He murmured something to the person at the gate, who put me at the head of the line. I let my head tip forward wearily. I took long, studied breaths. The customs officer watched me warily, as if I were going to vomit and that was exactly what he didn't need at that late hour. He asked for my passport. Looked down at it quickly. Quickly verified it against my face, stamped it. Looked quickly inside my pocketbook and small suitcase and asked about the nature of my visit. I told him I was in Greece to shop. That I had heard about the Sifnos pottery, the Santorini rugs. He sorrowfully shook his head and waved me on.

The next morning, before I boarded the ferry, I dressed in the sundress, sandals, and straw hat I'd worn when I left my island and repacked the rest of my Jeanne Thompson clothes in my suitcase. On a street behind Syntagma Square I saw a stationary old man, his white hair in a topknot. His eyes scanned nothing, in a way that said he was either blind or good at pretending. I placed my suitcase next to him and dropped a few coins into the McDonald's cup he held outstretched. *Kali méra,* I greeted him. He nodded elaborately and touched the suitcase with the side of his sandaled foot.

I bought a product that looked as if it might restore my red hair to something like its natural color and boarded a cab that took me to the ferry port. I felt swift, audacious.

And now I am back to the Greece of the sea — to its dryness, the smell of baked thyme, the white and the black and the blue, the austere heat, the dried-gourd agitations of the cicadas, the tiny lizards that seem to be clinging for dear life to a planet of whirring stone.

Mrs. Kouki, my landlady, asked casually about my trip. I went island-hopping as planned, I told her. I went to one island, then took a boat to the next, and became so charmed by the weather, the variety, that I stayed an entire week and a half. I had many adventures, I said. I wouldn't know where to start. She pointed to my red, badly cropped hair. I shrugged, as if the explanation were too elaborate to attempt.

I told her I would swim today at the cove I had told her about before. It was a few miles away, down a rocky path, south of the Castro. It was a perfect place to swim. Then I would leave for good.

A mile from my room is a little chapel flanked by a cemetery. Most of the graves are topped by boxes with windows. Inside the boxes are photos of the dead ones, vases with plastic flowers, jewelry, notes, ribbons. Two crones in black attend the place. One has a mustache and a single front tooth. Their brown hands are permanently curled. They wear wedding rings from husbands a half-century dead. That's my suspicion, anyway. They have that virginal, devoted, sexless look that says their marriages are no more than florid scraps of memory fluttering on the earliest edges of their lives, an almost forgotten escapade of their youth, like the night they all ran to the beach in their nightclothes to make a bonfire and Maria Stavros caught her hem on fire. Like that. And yet those marriages fixed their niches for life. They were born to be widows.

This morning a stocky couple in their seventies walked slowly, self-consciously, among the graves. He wore a gray suit, she a silk paisley dress, nylons, and heels. We greeted each other, knowing before we spoke that we were all Americans, and they turned out to be from Queens, where they had run a restaurant for thirty years. They were visiting their parents' graves. They were here for the island's big festival in honor of the Virgin. The woman in the paisley dress told me the story behind it.

Some miles away at the water's edge, there is another chapel, she said. It once sat at the tip of a spit of land but is now separated by twenty feet of water from the shore. The story begins long ago, when the spit was one smooth knife. One night several young women wearing long skirts knelt in the church and prayed. Candles flickered over their smooth brown faces, their neatly plaited hair. They prayed so earnestly for their secret needs to be met that they didn't hear the pirates until the men were present at the altar itself, as brilliant and gnashing as a fever dream.

The women pulled up their long skirts and ran. The pirates gave chase. One runner did not keep up with the other women. Her long hair came undone. The fastest pirate reached for her, reached for the hair. And at the very moment his fingers touched it, the ground between them split deeply. Water churned up in that space, which grew wider by the second. The pirate stood on one side of the chasm, with strands of the woman's hair in his fingers. She stood on the other, the feel of his fingers in her hair.

"The Virgin saved the woman because of her piety, and that is what the festival celebrates," the lady from Queens told me. I think not. I think the woman was a reluctant runner. I think that the festival celebrates a perfect vision of ambiguous safety — that it celebrates desire.

I said goodbye to the people from Queens and started down the road to the little beach where I had set up my possible disappearance. The pocketbook with my Jeanne Thompson ID and the last of my cash thunked against my hip as I walked. I wanted the day to last a long time. Feel this, I told myself. Feel this.

I passed a lush ravine, a parrot shock of green. The road turned, then ended at yet another chapel. The island has several hundred of them, white boxes with open bell towers. I'll go there and light a last faithless candle, I thought. But when I drew near, I saw a woman standing in front of the tiny church. She faced away from me, toward the water. Her form was solid, plain; she had the no-nonsense look of an island woman past fifty who's still hearty, still strong, still has her own dark hair.

She was all alone. In one hand she held what looked like a large cup. With the other she flung something toward the sea.

There was no car in evidence, no motorbike. No children, no husband, no friend. Just the woman in her plain dark dress standing near a little white church on a rocky hillside, throwing something I couldn't see. She stopped for a moment and bowed her head, then flung her arm again in that gesture of sheer largesse. I turned around and walked away from her, fearful that I would damage whatever was going on.

Around a sharp curve in the road, a shaggy donkey stood inside a fenced plot filled with rocks and nothing obvious to eat. The donkey, though, looked fed, noble, and homely. I touched his muzzle and then we both, for a few minutes, stared down the long hill at the fort town, the Castro. The place like a white skull.

When I reached it, I didn't wander inside as I had before. It had frightened me too much. Instead I walked along the cliff, then began to pick my way down the crooked and rocky trail to the water's edge. It seemed to take a long time. I wasn't entirely sure what I planned to do when I got there.

I heard voices, high young voices chattering in English. Three people in their twenties, two men and a woman, had found my pretty little cove and were returning from a swim. They walked easily, long-limbed and brown and elastic. I passed them and they said hello.

My knee hurt, the one that always does on rough terrain. I felt old. I thought about how I appeared to them, those young animals, in my linen pants and shirt, my pocketbook, my running shoes, my limp. I thought I probably looked peculiar. And I thought, I don't care. I wondered if they had discovered my bundle of clothes, picked over them.

At the water, everything looked undisturbed. There was the broken oar I'd planted in the dirt. There was the big rock. I squatted beside the rock and pushed the oar into the cavity beneath it. If you were looking, the edge of my daypack was plainly visible. I pulled it out. I opened it and examined everything in it: the change of clothes, the flip-flops; lotion, water, and towel. The airline ticket stub belonging to Francesca Woodbridge.

Here she was, Francesca, waiting for me.

This was the moment. I could put the daypack back under the big rock. I could walk the five miles to the ferry port and board the next boat out. I could become Jeanne Thompson from now on.

Mrs. Kouki would enter my room, thinking I'd left for good, and she would find Francesca Woodbridge's identification and money under the pillow, her clothes and suitcase in the narrow closet. She would think she had misunderstood when the American was leaving. She would wait a few days, maybe as long as a week. At some point she would know something was wrong, and she might remember then the place where the visitor said she liked to swim. They would investigate this cove. It would be accomplished.

I retrieved Jeanne Thompson's passport from my pocketbook and examined the photo. I looked strange and old-fashioned with my hair pulled back tight, my out-of-date eyeglasses. I looked a bit like some of the Russian women I'd seen that day at our airport while I waited for Ren to come back from a convention. They deplaned ahead of him and stood for a few moments in the waiting area, scarved and stiff, gazing at the anonymous room as if it held their whole new life.

"My strange one, my traveler," I said to the photo. "My Russian one." I hoisted the daypack onto my back. I closed the passport, made a sweeping discus thrower's spin, and hurled it into the water. It bobbed for quite a long time, then disappeared.

When I returned from the Castro, I dyed my hair back to an approximation of its brown-blond. I let it dry and walked in the dusk down the long hill to town. At the Calypso bar, Nikki was manic. She'd put on Pink Floyd, quite loudly, and was moving among the tables replacing clean ashtrays with clean ashtrays. The real season was just beginning. During my time away, it had begun to happen. There were more people now on the streets, in the bars. The pace of the place had increased. Mercantile alertness was in the air.

Nikki wore her short black skirt and a white lacy top. There was a sheen of sweat on her forehead. She scanned the room, said something to the waiter, and sat down with me for a quick smoke.

"You went on a little trip," she pronounced.

"I went on a little trip to Crete, to some other islands," I agreed. "And tomorrow I return to my home in the United States. To my husband. And my son." As I said it, I remembered that I'd told Nikki I had no children. She nodded vaguely.

"My son and my foster son," I ventured, complicating matters. "Mack and Jimster." Nikki nodded. She stubbed out her cigarette and pulled at the wrinkles in her little skirt.

"And my husband, Ren. I miss them," I said. "I miss them all." It felt like the truth.

Nikki stood up and wished me a good voyage. "Oh," she said as she eyed a tidy pack of Germans chattering at the bar. "You missed the scandal at the Castro."

Three days earlier, the crazy skittering girl had passed the priest as he flapped in his long robes down the narrow covered walkway to the church. The priest who was her reputed father — her reputed father who came back to the fort town but did not speak to the girl or to her mother, ever, though he seemed constantly to be praying for them and perhaps for himself.

The crazy girl had pulled a paring knife from the waistband of her skirt. She leaped at the priest and stabbed him just above the collarbone. The pharmacist from the village was fetched, and he tended to the priest while medical help was en route from a larger island. The priest bled a lot but was not seriously injured, as it turned out.

The girl was sent to Athens and put into a kind of jail for the disturbed, Nikki said. She had done some violent things before.

She poured boiling water on her mother's foot. She stole a tourist's purse. She chased some cats with a nail-studded board.

"And now," Nikki said, "she has left this island for good. We will not see her again."

She put her finger to her lips. "Shhhh," she said elaborately. "This scandal is not for the new visitors to the Calypso. They don't want to know about the crazy girls, bad priests, the slashings on the necks. They want the music!" She jumped up. "They want to dance!"

# 33

It is the quiet afternoon time, the somnolent pause before Athens gears up for the rest of the day. I've checked into a small hotel on Ermou Street, not far from Syntagma Square. It is May 30. My tour group leaves Athens tomorrow, for America. And I, Francesca, go home, go home.

My room is unfussy and clean, though everything about it is contingent. The door feels like cardboard. Wispy curtains ride a small breeze. There is an acrid hint of insecticide. Below, in the narrow lobby, a clerk with a preposterously bushy mustache gazes at a television high in one corner. When he gave me the key to this room, his eyes drifted away from my face toward the soccer game inside the television, then back to me. There was a haughtiness to him, to his movements, as if the actual clerk had temporarily disappeared and he, a far more important man, was simply filling in. He accomplished this with the merest lag in each of his movements — the running of the credit card, the locating of the key — as if each motion involved a process of recall. This does not come naturally to me, he says silently. This is not who I am.

I want to sleep but can't seem to. I'm beyond jet lag. In two and a half weeks I've been several people, traveled 20,000 miles. And now I'm beyond tired.

My room faces a tall building across the street, a narrow Sahara-colored warren topped by a gawky antenna. Some of the windows are shuttered with rotted-looking wood. Some are covered with pastel curtains, peach and mint. One narrow balcony holds a potted tree and a German shepherd. A man in a wine-colored shirt steps onto the balcony, leans briefly on the rail, steps back in. The dog turns around and watches whatever is inside the room. I seem to see the man removing his shirt to join a person on a bed; to slowly, almost absentmindedly run the tips of his fingers down the thin skin of an inner arm.

The building on the corner, next to the dun-colored one, has carved cornices and appears to be abandoned. Shutters are faded, shut. Some hang on their hinges. It looks like a pastiche of nineteenth-century Europe: blank-eyed, genteel, imperious — a ghost of all that. Across the intersection is a white high-rise hung with advertising banners in English: GENE KELLY DANCE LESSONS; YOUNGEST CLOTHES.

A priest moves up the walk, head down and robes flapping. His Orthodox headdress tips forward. He walks rapidly, holding an elaborate purple-and-gold book to his chest. His white beard flows sideways. He reaches the intersection and stands. Head bent over his book, he waits for the moment to cross.

In the evening, on the Acropolis, the streets get quiet. Stone walls border stone walkways, one of which bends sharply at a place called the Tower of the Winds, now a cluster of ancient broken pillars. There is an open-air restaurant near it with red-checked cloths on the rickety tables. Cats slide among them. It's early for dinner. The only other customers are three American college kids. One of them gestures elaborately at the waiter, makes a square with her chubby fingers.

"You take cards?" she calls loudly. "You know what I mean? Cards?"

The waiter has been gazing over the top of her blond head at the crumbled pillars. On one of the low ones, a black cat sits, motionless. Outside the iron bars of a fence, a man aims his camcorder at the cat. The waiter slowly turns to the tanned girl. She wears many silver bangles and a baseball cap with the brim turned backward. He nods with his eyes closed.

My meal is beautiful: a salad of tomatoes, thyme, olives, cucumbers, olive oil, a sprinkling of coarse salt. A little earthenware casserole of juicy lamb that has been cooked forever.

A man and a woman in black business suits walk briskly past my table, their heels clacking on the rock. Up the winding street they go, up toward the higher reaches of the Acropolis, where they have, I think, an elegant apartment, cool and waiting, and a maid who will bring drinks to a lacy metal table in a flower-filled courtyard. They speak into cell phones as they walk. They swing leather briefcases. In the other direction, a young woman in a black, strappy cocktail dress and silver space-odyssey boots talks into a public telephone. She tells an entire elaborate story with her free hand.

The space boots, and above me at the top of the long hill, the Parthenon resting in a pinkish haze. Thin cats on pillars twenty-one centuries old. The tiny electric hum of the camcorder, the cell phones. A murmur beneath it all like underground water sliding on ancient stones, holding itself to itself — waiting for us too to pass.

After my early dinner I meandered down the long hill, stopping here for an ouzo, there to examine some flea market scarves. The air smelled of diesel and charred pretzels and incense.

I heard her voice before I saw her: the clipped English, the aggrieved cheer. She was talking to a vendor who sold cotton dresses to overheated northerners. Ursula held one to her trim torso and examined its length. It was not right; it would not do. Too late, I turned and tilted my sun hat over my face.

"Jeanne!" she called. "You are in Athens!"

"Ursula," I answered. I didn't know what else to say.

"I contacted you from Serifos," she said accusingly. "I wrote you a card to the hotel and told you to come to Serifos because it is a fine place! Many beaches and so clean."

"I was traveling," I said. "I didn't get a card."

She looked much more stalwart than she had when we parted. More planted somehow. Maybe she had found a promising new friendship.

"Oh well, this does not surprise me. Those people where we were, they have the card, I am sure of it. But they did not give it to you." She shrugged elaborately. "So! Where did you go?" she asked. She had the dress draped over her arm. The clerk looked at her expectantly. Business was slow.

"Here and there," I said, tracing a vague oval in the air. "This island, that island. Once I started, I couldn't seem to stop."

"Did you find the good beaches?" she asked dubiously.

"Well, I was more interested in the people than the beaches," I said. "I wanted to get to know some people."

She considered that idea but seemed to find it wanting. "And you did?" she said, only polite now.

The vendor had moved a few steps closer. She wore one of the colorful sundresses and had plaited her dark hair and pinned it on top of her head. She had large green eyes and a mole near her mouth.

"You would like the dress?" she asked Ursula.

"Oh no!" Ursula said, pushing the dress away from her. "This color, it is not me."

We exchanged a few more innocuous comments, and she invited me to go with her to a party at a gallery. Some friends of some friends of hers from Switzerland knew the owner, and they very much wanted her to come. They insisted!

I begged off, saying that I was exhausted. We shook hands awkwardly and said goodbye.

. . .

There they were, my tour group, waiting to go home. Lew looked puffy and exhausted. June, the near-blind woman, looked guarded, as if she carried diplomatic papers. The New Hampshire women rigorously sipped soft drinks. They milled around in one of the airport waiting rooms and seemed surprised to see me.

The waiting area was crammed with people and luggage and had the scrambled, low-ceilinged feel of a room in a much smaller airport. Lew mopped his brow. Janine, the guide, had run out of words. She leaned against a post, arms folded, eyes closed. We all consulted our watches.

Frieda from New Hampshire started to retrieve her map to show me exactly what stops the group had made, but she seemed to have packed it in her suitcase instead of her carry-on, so she told me instead about the best night, the one in Crete when they all went to a taverna and learned the local dances from vigorous high-booted men.

"It's a great little country," Lew intoned. "And it's true about the light. You don't find light like this everywhere."

"Lew got a little carried away at the taverna," said Frieda. "He demolished his back."

Lew lifted his arms and did a stiff little Zorba twirl, then gave me a painful smile and eased himself into a plastic chair. He stared at his shoes. He looked very divorced.

"You didn't get much sun, Mrs. Woodbridge," Janine piped up accusingly. "You didn't go to the beaches, I take it." I saw now that she was furious that I'd left them. "What did you do? Stay in your room? Shop all day?"

"A little of everything," I said pleasantly. "I'm still sorting it all out." She actually snorted.

Waiting together, we were like fish in a tank, darting aimlessly. Lew consulted his big wristwatch. He rolled his eyes.

One gate down, a plane was unloading. We watched the passengers disembark, fresh and eager-eyed. We waited some more, and that area began to fill with departing passengers. I was catching a little catnap when I heard the high call.

"Jeanne! Jeanne Thompson!"

I started. I felt for a moment that I was in a falling dream, that long swoop before your own panic catches you, waking you to live another day.

Ursula's plane was boarding. She gave me a big what-can-I-do shrug and waved again. "Good traveling, Jeanne," she called. I waved buoyantly.

"You know her?" Janine asked.

"Sort of," I said. "I met her on a ferry." Janine looked dubious, or maybe pitying. I couldn't tell.

"She has a friend in Switzerland who looks like me." I smiled indulgently at the departing Ursula. "The friend's name is Jeanne. She thinks it is a funny thing to do, to call me by my 'twin's' name." I laughed lightly.

"Well," said Janine, "there are a lot of strange people out there. You jump into the fray and there is no possibility of avoiding them. The main thing is, sometimes one of them will just glom on." Janine's Arkansas twang was getting more pronounced as she discarded her tour-guide role piece by piece. "And then you've got hell to move to get rid of them."

"I'm sure that happens," I said. "It's a chance you take."

We flew nonstop to Kennedy. A screen at the front of the cabin showed a glowing map of the world. A little plane — us — moved in increments across the hemisphere. I dozed. When I woke again, the little plane was over the black emptiness of the Atlantic. Numbers at the bottom of the screen told us our speed, the time, our estimated time of arrival.

We forged across the wide ocean. The cabin was hushed and dim. The fussy baby had grown quiet. The movie was over. People slept in the ways they could sleep. Some had blankets over their heads. Some lay back, vanquished, mouths open. A woman in the seat behind me muttered plaintively in her sleep. Something lavish in her indecipherable plea made me remember an evening in which I had walked down to the river in my town. The sky was soft gray, lit up on the edges, and the river was fast and brown. There was light on the tops of the mountains, and forked lightning behind them. Two girls on bicycles passed me, looking as if they rode right down the middle of the moment. The first one pumped hard, hunched over her handlebars. The second one had lifted her hands from the bars and was letting them float away from her. She had a striped shirt and long brown hair and she was singing. Not the way you would sing for someone else, but the way you would sing in the shower. It had a pulse, whatever she was singing — a kind of obstreperousness. She was violently off-key. Her hands never touched her bike handles. I heard her even after they zoomed around a corner and out of sight.

It was a good small thing to remember. It helped me to think about my home without thinking specifically about what faced me there: how we all, Ren and Mack and Jimster and I, were going to proceed.

Janine perked up as we neared New York. She handed out evaluation forms for the tour, relieved to be turning us loose soon, and returned to her seat next to Lew. They had been speaking in low tones a lot during the trip, and now I heard the volume in his voice increase happily. Maybe it was painkillers for his blown-out back. Maybe it was love.

We landed in an early-summer drizzle that seemed to push Manhattan lower to the ground, making it too blurred and vague to look like a real destination. Someone passed around a paper placemat and we all wrote our names and addresses on it. I don't even know who wanted them. The near-blind June wrote in a strong, confident hand. She had a day of travel ahead of her. Cincinnati, then Lexington, then a town on the Ohio River where she lived and where she would get her photos printed and enlarged. She would bring them close to her eyes, and her real trip would begin.

At customs, the agent looked up, and a strange ripple of alertness passed over his face, as if he had an invisible earphone that had told him at that moment to take notice. He smiled distantly and asked me to open my luggage. It had to be a quota, I thought. Even in tour groups, one in ten probably gets closely checked. I tried to calm myself. There was nothing strange in my belongings: the cool and tasteful clothes, the face and body creams, the paperback biography of Jennie Churchill, the good camera with two lenses — it all belonged to a handsome, well-off woman in her forties returning from a Mediterranean mini-rejuvenation. I lowered and quieted my voice. I graciously smiled my affront. This wasn't supposed to be happening to this particular me.

The agent bent his head and pushed my clothes around with his fingertips. He asked me to open my cosmetics bag and retrieved a bottle and held it up. It was half full of red hair dye.

"What color does it make the hair?" he asked.

"The color it looks like it makes the hair," I snapped.

He looked at me. He had large black eyes. He smiled. He was furious. Something bad had happened to him that day, that week. Something about me was reminding him of every setback in his life so far.

"I'm tired," I said by way of apology. "It's red hair dye. I thought I might dye my hair on this trip." I smiled again, and remembered a program I'd watched at the Trocadero about wild dog hierarchies and the stylized obsequiousness by which the weaker animals signal their abjection to some alpha that's threatening to tear them apart.

He said nothing.

"I had an idea. I didn't go through with it." I ran my hand across my golden brown hair. "I thought I might surprise my family."

"Really step out there, eh?" he said. He held the bottle to the light. "Half of it's gone."

"I poured it into a bowl," I said. "I was on the very brink. The very brink of a new me." I was trying to get him to smile. "Then I changed my mind. I threw it out."

"And saved the rest for a braver day?"

"I forgot I had it."

He looked at me, head cocked to one side. "I'm trying to imagine you with red hair," he said. His eyes narrowed. "Interesting." He handed me the unzipped bag and signaled to the next person in line. "Sort of."

I zipped it up. He put it back into the suitcase and pushed the suitcase toward me with the tips of his fingers. I zipped it for him and passed through the gate.

# 34

IN SALT LAKE CITY I read a newspaper, then made my way to the gate, just in time to fall in line behind Moira Dennehy. This happens all the time on the flight from Salt Lake to our town. It's rare that you don't meet someone you know.

Moira greeted me as if I'd been gone a year, but that's the way she greets everyone, all the time. A long-lost hug that hasn't a trace of real warmth in it. It's just what she does to seem effervescent.

She was dressed in a sage-green T-shirt and a long narrow skirt, and her chestnut hair looked freshly cut. A wristful of silver bangles set off her perfect tan. She was accompanied by her lanky son, the one who'd undergone the fishing expedition with his father and the hedge-investment guy.

The boy and Moira were returning from San Francisco. They'd looked at small colleges and done some summer shopping. What exactly is summer shopping? I thought. I felt that I had once known, but had somehow let it slip.

"How was Egypt?" she asked, her bangled hand placed confidingly on my forearm. Her son seemed to be monitoring the waiting area for terrorists. He looked rigid and miserable.

"Egypt?"

She tapped her forgetful head with mock impatience. "Greece!" She seemed to search her mind for her file on Greece.

"I'd *love* to go to Greece," she said. "The islands, the friendly people, the water! And those incredible rugs, those white wool rugs that you can get for a pittance?"

"Right!" I said vigorously. I realized I had bought nothing, not even trashy little souvenirs, for my family.

"Greece sounds so *relaxing*," she said, her hand still on my arm. She studied me. "And you did need a rest, right?"

Now I knew that she had been talking to others about me, about Ren and me. I could hear poor Laura Terwilliger at lunch, warning us all about Moira and her evil tongue.

"How's Ren?" Moira asked cautiously. "We haven't seen him in so long. It's as if he's in a foreign country himself, of course through no fault of his own."

We smiled and smiled. Her son looked uneasy.

"He must be depressed. It must be so hard. And that has to affect your own ability to, what, cope?"

I felt fiercely defensive of us both, my husband and me.

"He's actually very much better," I said. "You haven't seen him in a long time. You'd be surprised."

No one from the office had set foot in our house since the shooting. Some phone calls, yes. Warren Evinrude checking in from time to time. But nothing more. I hoped Ren saw where he really stood in their so-called affections.

He was not a player now. He was not bringing in clients. And there was someone out there who might have wanted to shoot him. That was messy. That was something the firm didn't need. Ren had come up lame, I thought, and they were about to leave him out on a winter hillside.

We flew through a violet dusk. I watched the back of Moira's head, ten rows up, and thought, I will probably never speak to her again. I have probably left that life. A child cried for a while, then lapsed into moaning little hiccoughs, then was quiet.

I felt the wired vertigo that can come at the end of a long, long trip, and that scrambling urge to convince myself I'd been somewhere at all. That it hadn't been a trip in a dream. I thought maybe I would have a glass of wine. Then I thought maybe I wouldn't.

A line of fire along the horizon, then deep indigo with severe little stars. The humped shadows of mountains, then nothing but the darkness, then stars on the ground, here, there, and we were descending into our valley, falling gently. This, the flight attendant said, was the termination of the flight.

Mack and Tamara looked small and odd, standing there together behind a clapping, hooting crowd that was meeting a high school athletic team. Mack waved tentatively. He had a crooked half-smile on his face. I wanted to run to him.

I saw very clearly now that I had been playing chicken; daring myself to do something I couldn't finally have lived with. Not if it meant never seeing my son again.

Mack's suit was only half there. He wore the baggy pants and the suspenders but had replaced the wingtips with sneakers, the white shirt with a purple T-shirt. Tamara stood quite close to him, leaning into him, her face a little peaked. They are beginning to unravel, I thought. It is beginning to end. I hugged Mack and then Tamara. They wore the same sweet-smelling gel in their hair.

"Home from the wars," Mack said gruffly.

Tamara tucked her hand under his upper arm. "Was it, like, great?" she asked. "Were there, like, ruins and shit?" Her voice was depleted. Love is so exhausting.

We waited for the baggage carousel to start up. The high school team milled around like muscled ponies, snorting, pawing. One of them lifted a girl, rocked her like a baby, laughed when she shrieked happily. Tamara and Mack rolled their eyes.

Mack drove us home. I had never noticed what a leisurely driver he was. We went slower than I thought we should be going, but I didn't say anything. This might be a new form of resistance, but who cared?

We passed the Trocadero Motel. Through the plate glass window, I could see Gerrald's slick head, bent over his crossword. It was midnight. He'd just started his shift.

"That's that place?" Tamara said plaintively. "That motel?"

"Yeah," Mack said.

"What place?" I asked. "What motel?"

"Where there was, like, a shootout or something," Tamara said. "Two days ago, I think."

"Not a shootout," said Mack. "I don't know. Something. Some homeless people, and that clerk in there was a big hero."

"At the Trocadero?" I said, trying to keep my voice casual. "The Trocadero Motel?"

"Yeah. There was a story in the paper. These homeless people, like bridge people or something, they showed up there in the middle of the night and took the clerk hostage. And they made demands, and a bunch of cops showed up in that jungle camo they like to put on."

"There was a picture of them," Tamara said. "Like, find me a jungle, please?" She was regaining her vitality. Mack turned his head and smiled at her.

"So they had a gun," I said.

"Oh yeah! A major gun. Like, I don't know, a .357 or something. And they pulled it on the motel clerk. It was a guy and a girl," said Tamara.

"A girl of about sixty, it looked like," Mack said.

"And the guy had a really lame name," Tamara said. "Like Cricket or Gerbil or something."

"What did they want?"

"Something," Mack said. "I forget exactly what. The woman, I think, thought her daughter had been kidnapped from her by the cops or the authorities or whatever, and she wanted her back."

"She was younger than sixty," Tamara said. "Her daughter was, like, nine. So she wouldn't be sixty."

"Well, the picture made her look sixty," Mack said.

"Well, she wasn't," said Tamara, a little sexual taunt in her voice.

"What happened?" I asked Mack.

"Well, they had the clerk as a hostage, the night guy, the graveyard guy, and they were making these demands. He just kind of put up his hand, like don't anyone get excited, and then he said something to the, what do you call it, captors. And he just kept talking, with his hand out to the cops, and everyone waited, and then the homeless ones started talking back to him. Then he called out that the woman had something she wanted to state to the cops and everyone should just calm down and hold their fire while she did it, or the guy was going to blow him all to shit. She walked forward and gave this long speech about having this kid she'd lost track of, and it was driving her crazy and she had tried everything and she wanted some help to find her kid."

"I think the guy's name was Gopher," Tamara said. "Actually, I'm sure that's what it was."

Mack went on. "And so they promised this and that, and blah blah blah. And then the guy just put the gun down on the carpet, and he walked forward with his hands up. And that was all she wrote." That last in his Sergeant Friday voice.

"Or Bunny," said Tamara. "I think maybe Bunny."

"*Bunny?*" I said.

Tamara looked at Mack for verification. He shrugged amiably. His life and everyone in it had become water off his back.

There is a frank and lovely tenderness to our town in June. I felt it now, and it was tied to the feeling that now I was really home.

Home is where you recognize yourself. Sometimes that's a place, sometimes not.

The moon was more than three-quarters full, high and bright. The river bounced its light back to it. The air was soft and smelled of lilacs. Summer in earnest was almost here. We drove through the downtown blocks, past bars that had propped their doors open to let the music out, the customers in. Everyone on the street seemed aimless and happily so. A dog with a red scarf around its neck sat next to a parking meter and howled at the bitten moon.

I felt that I now knew this town in a way that was almost carnal. I knew its layers, its crevices, its pockets.

"How's Dad?" I asked.

Mack grunted noncommittally.

"What's the status of things with Jimster?"

"The same, I guess. Supposedly some charges might be filed at the end of this week."

Tamara fiddled proprietarily with the radio.

"Could you stop that?" I asked from the back seat. They looked at each other, said nothing. She turned the radio off.

"This is all a big mistake with Jimster," I assured Mack. "It will be straightened out very soon." I thought of Jimster, how frightened he must be. How alone he must feel.

"Dad thinks it might be a very sobering experience for Jimster," Mack said. "I believe those are his words."

Sometimes anger in me feels as if I've had the air in my lungs sucked out.

We turned down our street. Warm light shone from the ground floor of our house. The lawn had been freshly mowed, and the good smell of cut grass mixed with the smell of the cherry tree in Elise's yard. Everything was silvered by the moon.

. . .

Ren pulled himself up from the wingback chair, grinning a welcome. He walked toward me using only his cane. His face was a little flushed.

"Hi, love," he said. He hadn't called me "love" in a long time. He was trying to be jaunty. He was trying to be reassuring. I saw that, and wondered why.

"Hi, Ren." I wrapped my arms around him and gave him a tentative hug. I felt as if we, he and I, were on the deck of a huge ocean liner that was finally moving out to sea. The water churned. We were launched.

"You look great," Ren said heartily.

"I feel great. I had a good trip."

"That's great."

"Everything's great." I wanted us to laugh at how inane we sounded. The front door opened and Elise strode in, her arms outstretched.

"You're back!" She wore a strange flowing garment like the kind that used to be called a muumuu. "You look absolutely great!"

"If I'd known there was a party, I'd have tried to look more . . . great," I said, looking down at my wrinkled linen jacket and pants. I was beginning to feel lightheaded. I needed to talk with my family. Why were we surrounded like this?

"Well, it's good to see you." I smiled at Elise, nodded at Tamara. "And you too, Tamara. But I have to talk to Ren and Mack alone about something, if you don't mind." I tried to catch Ren's eye, but he wouldn't look at me.

"Did you take a lot of photos?" Elise said.

"No," I said. Then I looked at her and Tamara and decided their presence didn't matter. "What I did, actually, was come to some conclusions. One of them is that it's time to tell the truth about the person who broke into our house. The person who shot Ren."

Ren studied the rug. Mack looked, oddly, as if he were about to cry. Tamara and Elise looked surprised.

"Actually," Mack said, his voice louder than usual. Then he just stopped. "It's your funeral," he said to me.

He thought it was Yuri. That was plain. What does a kid look like on the brink of bad news about a parent? A kid looks like Mack at that moment. Bruised around the eyes.

"I was hoping it wasn't Jimster," said Tamara. "I think Jimster is like just in a really bad place right now, and he hangs out with these incredible losers, and —"

"Shut up, Tamara," Ren said pleasantly. "Let's call it a night."

"You look so tired," Elise said sorrowfully. "Both of you. You need to take care of yourselves."

"You should tell that to my father," Tamara piped up. She had two small dots of red on her cheeks. She moved a few steps closer to Elise. "He says he's having a midlife crisis, and I totally agree. He says he feels like a hypocrite being a minister. He says he wants to get out of this town because he feels like everyone watches every move he makes." She was shouting at Elise now.

Elise looked planted, stoic, ready for the next thing Tamara might say. I thought of Elise and Franklin on a bench by the river, the red sky behind their heads. When did Tamara start to know?

Mack put his hand on Tamara's shoulder and she whirled around to yell at him. "What if we move?" she cried. "What if my parents make me move?" Mack didn't say anything. He just looked at her in a way that made me see that this end of things for them was as much a puzzle to him as it was to her. He was flummoxed.

We stood quietly for a minute, as if any movement would set us off. The big clock in the hall chimed the quarter hour.

"Well, this Jimster business is something that can wait until morning," Ren said.

"No it can't." My voice sounded mechanical to me. "It can't

wait because it has nothing to do with Jimster, as you know."

Ren sat down. He leaned back into the chair and closed his eyes.

"The person who entered the house that night was not Jimster Reece," I said gently to the rest of them. "And it wasn't Yuri Petrov, the man who worked in the garden."

"You can't say that for sure," Mack said. "He had a mask." Ren still had his eyes closed.

"Well, actually, I can say it for sure, Mack. Because the person who entered the house that night, the person who fired the gun, wasn't a young man with a mask. It wasn't a man. In a mask."

My throat closed as I watched their naked faces. I willed it to open, and I placed my index fingers on my breastbone.

"The person who entered the house," I said, "was this person. Me."

# 35

A WEEK BEFORE Ren was wounded, he and I had a searing
fight after a party for the Dennehys' twenty-fifth anniversary.
During the time for toasts, I had risen to offer what I thought was
a complex and interesting salute to marriage in all its ambiguity.
Everyone had applauded, but they were applauding everything,
so it was impossible to gauge what they thought. I sat down and
once again lifted my glass gamely, and discovered that I was crying. Not effusively. Not even noticeably, unless you were within a
few feet of me. And it only lasted a few seconds. And I kept smiling, so the tears could have been taken as a surge of affection
that had splashed briefly over the wall. An errant wave.

But Ren was furious. He froze me out all the way home. Then
he turned to me in the kitchen, his taut face so pale it looked
powdered.

"What are you trying to accomplish, Francesca?" he asked in a
voice so low I could barely hear him. "What is your point, exactly?"

"I have no point," I said, and it sounded so unexpectedly sad
that I had to look at the floor. I wasn't drunk. In fact, in keeping
with recent resolutions, I'd sipped tonic and lime all evening. So
I didn't even have the emotional license of the chemically
skewed.

What I had been feeling that evening was the tyrannical absence of Yuri, a state of missing that wouldn't go away. He had been gone for two long months. Perhaps he was in danger, perhaps not. Perhaps he had simply tired of me. Or tired of the impossibility of us. Perhaps he was dead. Wherever he was, I wanted him.

A friend once told me that the metal pin in her shoulder showed up on an MRI as something called a "vacant artifact." Where there is metal, the machine registers nothing. Nothing in the shape of a pin. Nothing in the shape of my Russian.

"You know what you're accomplishing?" Ren said. His voice was high. He leaned against the cupboard, his head twisted in elaborate interrogation, as if he examined me from below.

"You're drunk."

"I wish that were the case," he said. "If that were the case, I might find myself in a jollier and more forgiving frame of mind."

And then he imitated, perfectly, my toast. And everything that had sounded to me wry and insightful became moronic and plaintive. The point made, he said, "This is what you're trying to do, Francesca. You're trying to get me booted from the firm. You are quite obviously a loose cannon. And you know they won't tolerate a loose cannon, even in a spouse."

"Boom," I said.

"It's easy for you, isn't it?" His voice had become ethereally bland. "You just issue your little pronouncements on everyone and everything that I pour my energy into, day after day. It's easy for you. You could do it in your sleep."

"They're snakes, Ren," I said. "They're vicious little scramblers, Warren and his pals, and you are not one of them, and I don't know why you would care if they voted you out."

Ren put both of his hands on my shoulders and brought his face close to mine. "I care," he whispered, almost tenderly, "because I like my work, and I like the life it has bought *us*" — he gave my shoulders a small shake — "and because I don't think your protracted indulgence of your own mysterious miseries is a reason for me to change my life."

"You've changed it already," I said. "You are beyond recognition." My voice sounded like cardboard.

He shrugged elaborately. I hated him at that moment.

It went on for a while. At one point we were both nearly shrieking. Mack, thank God, was at Tamara's.

A few days later, as we silently watched the news, an announcer made a ridiculous blooper and we both laughed, which had the effect of a match held to damp paper. There was a little flicker. But it would need long tending, gentle breaths, and it still might go out.

October in our town is a crisp and gaudy time, piquant and full of sap. The Chinese maples in our neighborhood flare into crimson as if every previous phase had been a rehearsal, just getting lines down. The other trees back them up in gold, and the whole show — the trees, the kids leaping into piles of them, Mr. Puermutter raking ecstatically, sleepy-eyed students ambling toward the university, frosty-breathed, carrying their coffee cups, kicking at leaves — can feel like pealing brass bells.

A week after our fight, on the morning of the day in which everything would change for our family, I fed the cat and kissed Mack on the crown of his hat. He ambled off in his suit, stopping to light a cigarette when he knew he wasn't officially watched. After he got out the door, anything I saw and didn't like was my problem. His slightness, his suit, his springy tough-guy bounce, made him look from behind like a Halloween gangster.

Ren had already left because he was taking the Audi to the mechanic out on the strip for some serious work on the transmission. The dealer would give him a ride to work; Jim Dennehy at the office would get him home and pick him up the next morning. When he left, I kissed him crisply goodbye. He backed the

Audi out of the garage and closed the door with the opener, then opened and closed it again because it had stalled briefly the day before and he was convinced someone had been tampering with the mechanism.

My plan was to drive that day to Seattle. I had called Siobhan the week before. She was taking a long weekend off work, and the little guestroom on her houseboat waited for me.

When I said goodbye to Ren, I told him I'd call sometime that evening and leave a message that I had arrived safely. It was our practice. He had a football game he wanted to watch, and there was no need to talk in person, I said. I was punishing him more and more with I-don't-need-you messages. I see that now.

We were still brittle and careful with each other, polite in the way that feels like a holding action against further damage.

The drive takes nine hours. The day was gorgeous, high-colored and dry. I'd be there by late afternoon. Siobhan and I would sit on the deck of her houseboat if the evening was clear, and we'd have a few drinks and talk and watch the skyscrapers at the foot of the lake light up.

I left at nine, and I thought I was on my way. I truly did.

At the freeway, I headed west. I put in a tape Siobhan had sent me — stern and mournful Japanese shakuhachi — and adjusted the seat to long-haul position and went into freeway mode, which seems to me like parking the car to watch the scenery glide by. Our little city, off to my left, glided by like a Rockwell painting: red and gold trees punctured by a church spire, a courthouse clock tower, with the glint of a river prettily bisecting it all.

A few miles west of the city proper, I decided I had to use a restroom and get another cup of coffee for the trip, so I exited onto the stark new commercial strip and pulled into a Quik Stop across the road from a Best Western. I used the restroom, bought the rancid coffee, sipped it, and threw it out. And then I just stood there, trying to think of the next thing I wanted to do. It seemed I'd had another reason for pulling off the road, for breaking the trip's rhythm so soon. I leaned against the car and consulted my Seattle shopping list. It was fairly long. I planned to be away two days, plus a driving day on either end, and now there didn't seem to be enough time for everything I wanted to do when I got there.

I parked the car in the lot of the Best Western and went inside with my list. I smiled in a familiar way to the clerk and helped myself to some okay coffee from the hospitality room and sat down in one of the overstuffed lobby chairs to think. As if I were waiting for someone.

It all seems very peculiar now, but it didn't that day. Not at the beginning. Sitting there in the motel felt like a simple pause before the trip went forward.

I consulted my list. I sipped my coffee. I thought about the details of arrival: how Siobhan would pour us icy martinis with two olives, then retrieve savories of some kind from the oven, and we'd sit on the narrow deck in the red sunset as the water grew molten. She'd bring me a cashmere shawl and one for herself, and we'd wrap them around our shoulders until the chill drove us inside. I thought about what she might bring from the oven. Piping hot cheese pastries, maybe, or minipizzas she makes with rosemary and fennel. Or mushrooms stuffed with prosciutto and spinach and garlic. Maybe those.

Sometimes — rarely — we can watch our own minds. Sometimes, for a few moments, we can watch ourselves thinking. As I sat there, I was stunned by what I saw myself thinking. Food. What food would I enjoy with my martini? I felt suddenly so embarrassed for myself that my face grew hot. Not embarrassed at the content, but at the scale. I was peering at a pretty wildflower while the ground around me fissured and steamed.

I would sleep alone tonight in a narrow bed on a boat, having diverted myself with vodka and chatter, and Ren would sleep alone tonight, having diverted himself with television football. And as I pictured the separate two of us, twelve or so hours from now, we stood on small dirt islands in black blindfolds, listening to the large water, clueless that we were within shouting distance.

I couldn't lose that picture. And when I knew I couldn't, I simply checked in to the motel.

The clerk looked up as if I were a guest whose face he should remember, and I told him I needed a room for one night. I felt expectant and careful, as if I were on the verge of unwrapping something that would make a large difference to the rest of my life. I walked carefully to my room, as if the wrapped object could slip from my arms.

When the Challenger blew up, there were a few moments in which it seemed to be performing an elaborate trick. A column of dense smoke broke off from the main column of smoke and looped downward, making a lazy Y that seemed to rest against the sky before the disaster was clear. I saw that now — that smoky *why?*

I locked the room and put a DO NOT DISTURB sign on the door, and I pulled a chair closer to the window, opening the curtain just enough to see a sliver of sky, sign, concrete.

I slowly began to unwrap whatever it was I needed to see, and what I saw was Ren. Not the furious, white-faced Ren, or the Ren who looked so contained and smug the day the workmen wired our house against intruders, and not the Ren who marched Jimster Reece out to the garage and returned with Jimster out of our lives.

I saw Ren and his white-haired father at our wedding, that soft day in the early summer of 1980. Twenty of us assembled in the main courtroom of the courthouse, and a nice old judge made us legal. I remembered the way Ren held my waist as we promised thick-or-thin until death, and how he seemed to be sending waves of confidence and hope through his fingertips, through my skin, to my innermost self and to the beginnings of Mack.

He seemed amplified that day, and newly serene, as if he had solved a problem that had been nagging him for a long time. He bent his head to my mother as we walked into the restaurant afterward, and they laughed. Before we left for the motel, he walked his father to his car, his arm very frankly across the shoulders of the man who had been his ally through so much sorrow. They looked like victorious soldiers. Life had turned a big corner.

I saw Ren in the bathtub with tiny Mack, his hair in wild damp curls, singing his idea of an aria. And Mack's big toothless grin.

There were times when I woke in the night and was unable to distinguish where I stopped and Ren started.

There was the way he used to wave his arms around when he was arguing politics, when he was indignant over duplicity and greed on the part of fat cats or bureaucrats — how he almost windmilled.

The way he put my bare feet in his lap and told me, always as if he'd just noticed, that I had the most beautiful dogs on the planet, and how I laughed every time he said it.

His radiant teary face when Mack was born.

The way he looked after his father's murder. As if every inch of him had been flogged. And the way he cried so bitterly that long night, that one time, and told me I was all that kept him alive. How that confession seemed to line my veins with lead.

You can't live on escape. I sat in that chair in that motel and looked back on the last few years, at the way I had tried to file off my sharp sorrows with fantasy, with alcohol, with my long elaborate game of concocting a new identity — Jeanne Thompson! — who would spring out when I needed her and take me to a new life.

And where was Yuri Petrov in all that? Was he another kind of running? Perhaps. He took me away from my attraction to Jimster. He took me away from my sad self. And then he himself went away. And I had, I realized, always known that he would go. Perhaps that is what I needed, more than the actual man — someone who could be counted on to guarantee unrequitedness. The way Stephen Lovano had. Someone who was always just out of sight and who therefore, in a peculiar and enduring way, affirmed that the unseen realms are the ones that count the most.

When you choose marriage, you choose coherence over yearning, the living world over the imagined one. When I knew that, I knew too that it was time to choose. And then I knew that I had halted my trip in order to halt the final unraveling of my marriage. It kept getting unknitted, and we were both nearing a point after which we would be unwilling to knit it up again. If I ran this time, we had no further chances.

I called Siobhan. I lied. My car had developed a frightening knock deep in the engine, a few miles out of town. I couldn't proceed.

She didn't believe me, but she let me think she did. She asked how I was. She let me assure her that all was fine, apart from the deep knocking, and we'd see each other soon. I paused before I hung up, some part of me wanting to tell her I felt in the midst of a crucial decision. But there was no way to describe it accurately, so I told her I loved her, which I do, and hung up.

I took a long bath. I slept for an hour. I walked a few blocks and had a reuben sandwich at one of those places that's always a fun Friday-after-work place, or tries to be. The sandwich was made with a bizarre sauce that tasted like fish.

I drove up the mountain to the ski area, the afternoon light so bright that the spindly lodgepole shadows that cut across the road created a strobe-lit, migraine effect. A caretaker at the lodge was fixing some pipe. He waved hi, watched me guardedly as I walked around the empty parking lot in my slacks, sweater, good raincoat. I waved to him before I left, as if we'd had a long conversation and solved some things.

The light was lengthening. The motel had taken on a kind of luminescence that carried it out of time and place. I felt extremely grateful for it.

Mack would have come home by now, and left again to go to Tamara's. He'd asked me to bring some crab home from the fish market in Seattle. He'd make crab cocktails for his and Tamara's monthly anniversary dinner later this week.

It was nearing dusk. Ren would be home. He'd said that he wanted to watch the Raiders game, that he planned a quiet evening. Just himself and his socked feet and the cat and a beer. He looked forward to it, he had said.

I gathered my things and checked out, suffering the clerk's shadowy little smile.

Then I thought, This is not a time to rush. Ren and I will retrieve the car tomorrow, when we are restored to ourselves. So I locked my suitcase in the trunk and began the five-mile walk through town to my house. I needed the movement. I do this all the time. When I'm agitated, when I need to think, I walk. It was dusk. When I got there, it would be dark.

Light rain began to fall, a mist really, an invigorating spritz. I moved into a residential area that had a thin haphazardness to it, the frail houses angled oddly, the garages sagging, too many loud dogs. A few more blocks and things smoothed out, improved. The houses and yards got larger, more confident.

I'd go to my house, call out to my husband. He'd answer, startled, come rushing out of his study, fearing some harm to me. An accident, a mishap, something. I'd smile quick reassurance, and then I'd say to him, Ren. This is our big chance. This is our time to save ourselves.

I would say, Please.

He would turn the game off. We would go up to our big bed

and draw the bedroom curtains against the rain that would by then be washing down, washing the last of all the gold leaves off the trees, and we would drape blankets across our shoulders and we would talk. We would become as pared, as stark, as the stripped branches.

He would tell me how something at the core of him simply froze when his father died his terrible death. Who can think about a decent old man tortured and killed, made into an emblem of the effects of pure evil, after so much patience, so many years of it? After refusing bitterness for himself, how can a man have to die that way?

And he would tell me how much angry women terrify him. How his mother's rages in her cage of a bed rained upon him like daily poison and built barricades in his heart.

He would say that he decided sometime after his father's death against faith or fairness, decided in favor of sheer gamesmanship. That his work with Warren Evinrude was the game that seemed most able to engage him.

He would tell me how I seemed sometimes to go away, or to retain a presence that was too extreme, too dangerous. How I had behaved badly, scarily. But this time he would ask, Why? What is wrong, Francesca? he would say. And then I would try to tell him.

All of it? I didn't know.

If he must know?

Then yes. No more lies.

Real rain now, and the streets looked freshly oiled. I smelled smoke, probably from a fireplace, but it had an underscent that flooded me with nostalgia. It was the smell of burning leaves.

I heard footsteps behind me, fast. Running steps. Rasping breaths, timed to the footfalls. He jogged past me, a slim man in a hooded sweatshirt, a bandanna around his neck. He wore gloves, said nothing. He sounded almost agonized, but his body moved with a young man's spring. He shrank as he ran down the tunnel of trees. Round the corner. Gone.

Elise's car is in her driveway and her house is lit. Our house stands white and square and solid. In the dark, it seems to glow. Here is where we will start over. We have barricaded ourselves. We have become unhappy inside our white fort. Now we will begin again. A warm light glows from behind the shade in the den.

I'll bring us wine and cheese.

Light from the television skitters across the shade.

I see the two of us stretched on the big couch watching a movie, his hand slipped into the back pocket of my jeans.

I walk around back, through the trellis Yuri made from willow branches, to the kitchen door. The television is loud enough to hear. Ren likes the aural tumult, can't understand friends who watch games with the sound muted.

I let myself in with my key. The alarm is on, of course. If Ren isn't going out and Mack is at Tamara's for the night, he sets it early so he won't forget.

I call gently, "I'm home." But my voice gets lost in a roaring crowd and Ren's happy shout: "Run, you bastard!"

I walk across the kitchen and turn off the alarm. I almost reset it, then think, No. This is ridiculous. We're hiding. We don't need this. A locked door, period, not this wiring that summons a security team. That would be a small first step.

I'm calm. I feel that some kind of readjustment has already occurred between Ren and me, some kind of corner has been turned. I kick off my sodden shoes. I want something to give my husband. I want something in my arms to present to him, some kind of peace offering — a hope offering. But I can think of nothing but my whole self.

I pad down the hall to the den.

Then that sound of no-noise. The no-noise of a dive into deep water, that extinguishing of the world's busy sounds. The house holds no sound. And then the light ahead of me dims. The hall grows shadowy. I open my mouth to call out.

And then I seem to hear that happy cry again — "Run, you bastard!" — and I know why something bothered me about it. It didn't seem to be the exclamation of someone who was alone. It carried the verve of a communication. There is a listener with him.

What does jealousy feel like? Like walking off a plank you thought was longer, your legs stepping through air..

Perhaps Elise sat with him on the couch, watching the game. The idea quite suddenly made a kind of inevitable sense. I would walk into — the antique word came to me — perfidy. In just a few seconds, the two of them would stand to face me, and I would, I now knew, feel killed.

He calls out. Mack? There's guilt in that voice, fear. I wait for Elise to chime in. Mr. Mack? So as to sound casual, offhand, as she scrambles to look temporary. Just passing through, just dropping by.

I stay silent. Sweat a little, I think. You're caught. Sweat just a little. I keep walking, soundlessly.

He faces the far door of the den, away from me. He is alone in the room. He wears his old cashmere sweater, his slacks, his socks. His whitening hair flares around his head. There is something odd about his posture.

At first I think he has his hands folded in front of him, at his stomach. Then he turns. And in the dim room he faces me, vulnerable and amazed, holding a gun.

"Ren?" I keep walking. He holds the gun on me as if he doesn't see me. He sees someone, but I don't think he sees me. I don't know who he sees.

His mouth does a funny little thing, a kind of fake grin, very quick, gone in a second. The gun quavers.

"Ren!" More sharply, like someone trying to wake a sleep-walker.

He steps forward. "What?" It sounds strangled.

A silver gun hangs in the air between us.

It's the fright of encountering a violent sleepwalker. Or a baby with the night terrors, like Mack had for a while. Such people are not entirely asleep or entirely awake. They are terrified, and they don't seem to know you.

What had we done with Mack? I scrambled to think. What had worked?

"Ren," I plead. "My love."

This is dissecting all the parts, spreading them out, giving them room. I am talking actually about a couple of seconds.

"Put it down, Ren." He clenches it tighter. His face is the face I will see later in Greece, in the Castro. The look on the skittery crazy girl. The look of just-before. Just before revelation. Just before being struck. That absolute alertness.

He isn't seeing me. He's seeing something else, just for those few seconds. He's seeing the callers who phoned threats after the Recon spill. He's seeing Jimster, come back to steal something else. He's seeing his son, mocking him in a lawyer suit.

He's seeing the hitchhiker who demolished his father.

He's seeing the Russian who slept with his wife.

He's seeing the wife.

I jump at him, at the gun, grab it by the barrel, and wrench it sideways. Very fast; oddly strong, I am. But he doesn't let go of the stock, and we fall to the ground, both holding it.

We roll. He grunts. We gasp.

Who are we?

I catch the quickest flash across his face and know then that he knows me. And now we are both trying to save the other from the gun. And it fires.

It deafens us. The metal jumps in our hands like something alive. The gun flies across the floor.

．　．　．

Ren is laughing softly, as if he has just wakened from a night of squirrely dreams, as if he is freshly amazed at what the brain will do on automatic. He sits on the floor, his back against his big desk. I kneel, unable to get a full breath. Trying.

"Could you hand me the phone?" he says quietly, almost gently. I stand, my lungs still grabbing for air, and hand it to him. He gives me a thin smile of thanks. Presses buttons.

"Yes," he says. "We need an ambulance right away. Now. Seven fifty-five Dogwood. White house, black shutters." He listens. "Renton Woodbridge." His voice sounds as if his stomach is cramping badly. Another pause. "D-o-g-w-o-o-d." He closes his eyes. Opens them. "I've been shot," he explains.

He falls over sideways, very slowly, the phone under his ear like a pillow. His eyes stay open. They follow me, mild and alert. There is a tiny urgent voice inside the phone. Then there isn't.

# 36

As I described what had happened the night Ren was shot, each person in the room reacted differently. Ren's face flushed. Even after I had finished, he kept both hands on the seat of his chair, as if braced for a heavy blow. Mack, sweet Mack, looked incredulous. Incredulous and relieved. Tamara gaped like a nine-year-old. And Elise tilted her head, as if trying to examine me from a new angle. She looked interested and sympathetic, in a willed way, like a bored scientist at a colleague's lecture.

"But I was there right afterward," she said. "And you weren't."

I told them the rest. How Ren had whispered, "Run outside, Francesca. Flag them down." How I, crying, had tried to hold him, to keep him intact, and how he had urged me again to go outside, to show the rescuers quickly where he was.

So I did. It was pouring rain. I wore no shoes. In the street, I waited for the tiny sirens to grow, hearing an echo of their thin wail far back in my throat. As moving lights appeared at the end of my street, the wailing became unconsolable, then bleeped and stopped.

Porch lights went on. Next door at Elise's and across the street, down the block. They joined the lights of the ambulance and now the fire engine, and were so bright I was blinded. I backed into the black shadow of the big spruce and waited for my eyes to adjust. My yard, my house, was full of rapidly moving people who seemed to know exactly where to go. They were a movie of a large disaster, the camera niftily cutting here, there, all of the confusion a way to make the watcher attend with jagged alertness. Where will the next thing come from?

An empty stretcher slid out the back of the boxy white truck and athletic young people in jumpsuits ran it to the door of my house, where another jumpsuit relayed some kind of information about what he had found. The stretcher and the attendants disappeared inside. A policeman kept the neighbors back. Elise seemed to argue with him. He shook his head, took her elbow gently, and escorted her a few steps away.

Now I would step out. Now I would step into those lights to touch my husband, who was emerging from our house on the white plank with wheels, one of the attendants bent low to him as if he whispered something urgent.

It was time for me to step out, to say my lines, to become the apparition, the surprise, to crawl into that white truck with my wounded husband. He had surely said something to them. He had said, My wife went outside to wait for you. She is out there. But no one seemed to be searching for the wife who was supposed to be out there. Maybe Ren wasn't speaking.

That's when I wanted to freeze the moment. The moment held hope. I could believe that Ren was conscious, that he was not dying. But if I walked into that moment, information would replace hope, and I didn't know if I could bear that. They would see me soon, there in the shadow of the tree. But the scene was so flashing, so charged, that I thought they must be night-blind. If I walked out, I thought, they might become confused and incompetent. I might find that Ren couldn't speak.

And so I simply let the scene darken, as the vehicles pulled away one by one and the neighbors dispersed to enter their softly lit caves and turn off the porch lights.

"We'll lock it," the last policeman called to Elise as she moved toward her car. I assumed she had already given them Tamara's number; Mack might already be on his way to the hospital. "I have a key," she called back. "I'll watch things."

She got into her car and drove away. The policeman drove away. Now everyone was gone and my house stood white, empty, acted upon.

I began to walk, then run, down the rain-shiny sidewalks, under the tilting maples, toward the hospital a mile away. The rain had begun to freeze. My feet were in stockings.

I turned back to the house. My key was inside, so I had to find the one under the rock. Hands and knees on the wet grass. The flat rock next to the planter. No, the small rock next to the flat rock. I felt blindly for the piece of metal and finally found it.

Numbly I put on dry clothes and shoes and called a cab. It took me to my car outside the Best Western, and I drove to the hospital.

"I'm his wife," I told them at the nurses' station, and they showed me where to sit.

"Your neighbor Elise Prentice just went to call your son," one of the nurses said.

"My car developed a strange knocking sound," I told her. She looked at me mildly. "Way inside the engine," I said. "I came back."

Elise returned, tears rivering her face. She ran to me and threw her arms around me. I told her I had come home, seen the blood.

"He's going to be all right," she said over and over. "I'm so glad you're here. Mack and Tamara are on their way." We sat on the plaid loveseats of the waiting room.

Mack showed up with Tamara. He looked white-faced, very young.

"Why are you here?" he said. "Why aren't you at Siobhan's?"

"I didn't go," I said. "I got down the road, then didn't like the sound of the car and came back." Now I was going to tell him the rest. I wished Elise would go away, but it didn't seem likely to happen, and so I drew a deep breath. The four of us were sitting on two loveseats, facing each other. At that moment, a baby-faced man in a pinstriped shirt appeared.

"You're with Renton Woodbridge?" he asked us all. "Yes," we said, all together. I identified everyone for him. He identified himself as the resident on duty.

"He was conscious when he went into surgery," he said. "He's there now. He has a bullet near his spine, but we don't think there has been profound damage. He has some loss of feeling in his extremities, but we can't say yet what that means. They'll remove the bullet and try to assess its route, and then we'll know where we stand. His vital signs are good."

"What happened?" Mack said. "Who shot him?"

The doctor didn't hesitate. "An intruder," he said. "Your father says the guy let himself into the house somehow and lunged at your father's gun, and they wrestled and it went off. He had a mask. Seemed young. He wanted us to tell you right away what happened. So you wouldn't sit here and wonder."

Elise gave a little moan.

I felt like a cool glass bowl. I said nothing.

Lies get installed. They skitter into place like a panting child late for the first day of class, unsure if she's got the right room. Heads turn. Where did *she* come from in all her strange dishevelment? A half-hour later, head bent and scribbling away, she's always been there; she's never been gone.

"So," I said now, "I was the intruder, and Jimster is starting to take the fall. He had nothing to do with anything that happened that night."

Our big clock intoned the half-hour. Ren cleared his throat. "I have no intention of cooperating in any kind of case against Jimster, Francesca," he said in an almost kindly tone. "I've never had that intention. Jimster is getting asked some fairly tough questions about his friends and his whereabouts and what he's been up to in general. And I, for one, don't think that a few days of those kinds of questions are going to hurt him in the least. He'll know that the authorities have an eye on him, that they know he has some passing familiarity with burglary and God knows what else. It won't hurt him to get a wake-up call like this."

"For God's sake, Ren," I snapped. "He didn't do it." I said the words very slowly.

"And that is exactly what I'll say when we are interviewed in more detail," Ren said. "I can offer specifics that won't fit Jimster. No charges have been filed, and no charges will be filed."

"We know what happened," I said, my voice climbing. "We tell them what happened. All of it."

Ren leaned back in his chair and closed his eyes. I will never forget him at that moment, because it was the last time in which he was recognizable to me. It was the final time I could look at him and think, Whatever else has gone on between us, we are allies. We are partners.

He seemed to think for a long time. Then he opened his eyes, his decision made.

"There's still the question of who the guy was, if it wasn't Jimster," he said quietly. The whole room seemed to rearrange itself.

"What are you talking about?"

"I'm saying that you tell stories, Francesca. And in this case, you've outdone yourself. In some ways I understand your need to put yourself at the center of this little disaster." He glanced almost involuntarily at the cane resting against his knee. "And I can understand that you might want to deflect attention from an intruder whose identity you knew, a person who had knowledge of our security arrangements, so to speak."

Mack stood up abruptly, turned his back on all of us, and left the room. "You're insane," he called over his shoulder. "You're both insane. And I'm tired of listening to it."

I watched him go. Tamara and Elise followed him.

I lowered my voice, trying to make myself very reasonable. "You are keeping this lie intact because you don't want to revise your own story," I said. "You can't redescribe what happened and keep any personal or professional credibility, is that it?"

"Would *you* hire me?"

I patted him goodbye on his knee. "No," I said. "I wouldn't hire you."

# 37

I LIVE NOW in Seattle. I'm between apartments and am houseboat-sitting for Siobhan. The rain pours down. The boat rocks gently, creaks quietly.

I like the moisture here. My skin feels younger; my hair springs into exuberant waves.

Siobhan is gone much of the time. Her company sends her to Tokyo, to Moscow, to Frankfurt. She has become an expert on jet lag, having virtually eliminated it through a sophisticated combination of timed naps, melatonin, odd-hour exercise, Saint Johnswort. She is quite something — one of the new self-contained people. Her own small planet. She has one set of coordinated clothes for fall and winter, another for spring and summer. The first are black and brown, the second white and a silvery slate. They are expensive and elegant and minimal — just a few pieces, really. She chose them carefully, and looks severe and wonderful in everything she puts on.

When she goes someplace, she takes her carry-on, her laptop, her cell phone. That's it. She's ready to go anywhere in the world, stay for any length of time. Nine tenths of her conversations are by e-mail, maybe more. I couldn't begin to describe her job with any precision. All I know is that it has something to do with resetting the world's computers to register the turn of the century accurately. She helped develop a simple verification procedure, and saved untold numbers of companies untold amounts of money. She pulled them gently from the brink of disaster, and now she goes around in what is largely a role of reassurance. The nurse's cool hand on the recovering patient's brow.

She is in the process of eliminating everything in her houseboat that isn't essential. She gave away all her books, for instance, except for a dozen first editions. The rest she can retrieve from libraries. That's what libraries are for, she says. She has subscribed to a philosophy of lightness.

For my fiftieth birthday, she express-mailed a Provence picnic to me, from Provence. It arrived with the cheeses and pâté impeccably chilled, the bread baked that morning, the ratatouille at room temperature, the wine bought a day earlier from a wonderful old winery that has never exported a bottle beyond Toulouse. Siobhan has decided to take the fullest advantage of what planes plus money can really do.

Ren e-mails her once in a while to check on my whereabouts, my general well-being. I've moved often since I landed in Seattle, and make no effort to contact him. Mack lives near the city, in a suburb, with his most recent girlfriend, and he talks to Ren about once a month on the phone. Between Mack and Siobhan, Ren remains assured that I'll be no trouble.

I spoke this morning with my brother, Skip, asking him to tell our parents again that I am okay, though still between things, as Skip likes to put it. When we were all kids, Skip had a furtive wild crush on Siobhan. Even now, with the sounds of his hearty family in the background, he will figure out a way to bring her up in conversation. "Is she still flying across the world at a moment's notice?" he asked today.

"Absolutely," I assured him.

I became very unhappy. I let my own child drift away. I had an affair. A passionate affair. The man went away. I reembraced my marriage — twice, I reembraced my marriage — but it was not there anymore. It's an old, old tale, and I offer it only because my version has certain embellishments and blind corners that I continue to find curious, even amazing. What if I had been told, for instance, that meeting Stephen Lovano when I was in college would set in motion the demise of my long marriage to Ren Woodbridge thirty years later?

Because it did. Stephen Lovano, a shadowy, double man, convinced both Ren and me that exhilaration has virtually nothing to do with loyalty or kindness and everything to do with the experience of your own powers. I felt amplified beyond description with Stephen, and can only replicate the experience with someone as unknowable and fleeting as he. Ren too felt all his own possibilities with Stephen, and can only try to replicate the experience by linking himself with someone as adrenalinized and ruthless as Warren Evinrude.

It's frightening to think that our deepest sense of what is fair and generous gets tossed aside so quickly in favor of a powerfully racing heart.

Here in the city where we lived three decades ago, I keep remembering Ren and Stephen in the sky, falling one after the other from a tiny whining plane, their miniature forms spread-eagled. I count the long seconds, and then the chutes puff open with a soft whump. Another figure sometimes appears with them. My Yuri. A third falling one. And sometimes his chute opens and sometimes it doesn't, but by then I've turned my eyes away and fixed them on the rest of my life.

At my alma mater, I major in art history. My special interest is ceramics and pottery, particularly that of the Greek settlements of southern Ukraine, which made the news a few years ago. It's the farthest from home the ancient Greeks ever settled. I'll have my master's degree in a year, my doctorate down the road.

I work at a store that sells tiles, expensive imported tiles. I have a knack for knowing how certain tile treatments can make a room come alive. I'm a consultant; I advise customers with decorating dilemmas. Most of them have piles of money, new homes, and parents my age.

Ren and Elise were married last year. Elise sold her house for four times what she and Roger paid for it, and she now lives in my former house with my former husband. Mack tells me they entertain a lot, an idea that doesn't affect me one way or another unless I imagine them entertaining in the garden. That's what I ache for sometimes — the garden. What does it look like now?

Mack tells me they hire professional yard workers to keep it up. They took out the circulating pond and reseeded the area with grass, and they spray every week for anything untoward that might pop up. My straitened garden is evolving without me. I think about Yuri's initials carved into the cinnamon-colored willow of the trellis, assuming the trellis is still there. Mack said the yard crew had ripped up my irises and replaced them with some strange, hyperdurable shrubs that look almost like cacti.

Ren is a senior partner at Evinrude, Terwilliger, Dennehy, and Fleet and recently made it to the state semifinals in squash, his vehement hobby. He has fully recovered from his injury, except for the faintest of limps when he is particularly tired. He and Elise take pricey vacations to places where they can learn something. Their most recent adventure was a Shakespeare tour to England — London, Oxford, Stratford, and Warwick. They saw a play at each stop, then ate a meal from the sixteenth century as interpreted by a crack panel from an international food magazine. They vote for progressive Republicans or law-and-order Democrats, and back up their state-of-the-art security system with two Doberman crosses they bought from the state's top breeder after the demise of Elise's poor Roberta.

I got the cat, Ragamuffin. But she's on her last legs and spends most of her time asleep. She's proven to be incredibly adaptable through my moves, or else she's just comatose and doesn't care. I can't tell.

Franklin Klemenhagen has left the ministry. He and Krystal both went back to school for a while and now do couples counseling. Mack tells me that Franklin and Krystal renewed their wedding vows in some kind of ceremony by the river, with Elise and Ren in attendance. I think about Franklin and Elise on the bench by the river, their voices falling silent as they waited for a stranger — me — to pass. I don't know if his family ever knew he was assaulted with a knife. I never heard it mentioned. I spoke with Franklin a few times before I moved to Seattle and he said nothing about seeing me that day by the river. He thinks, perhaps, that he imagined me.

Tamara started junior college somewhere in California, then surprised everyone by hiring on with a business that runs households for moneyed, frantically scheduled couples who don't have time to do it themselves. She and Mack broke up shortly after Ren and I had our confrontation upon my return from Greece. My real return, my return as Francesca.

Gerrald's bravery and wit during the hostage situation at the Trocadero made the national wires, and there was even a rumor that he was going to appear on a morning news show. His neighborhood association recruited him to be a liaison between the association and the police, and he was so intelligent and effective that he was elected last year to the city council. I sent him an anonymous note of congratulations.

The homeless ones, Bunny and Ruthie, underwent psychiatric evaluations after the hostage incident with Gerrald and are both at the state hospital for the foreseeable future.

When Ren next spoke with the police, he told them that the intruder was significantly taller than Jimster Reece, and that he had blurted out a few words that Ren now realized were Spanish. He was very firm about all this. Jimster was dropped as a suspect, and the unanswered question simply remained in place. How did the burglar know the security code?

I did not go to Captain McDean with my story. If I told the truth, it would be my word against Ren's, and Ren is the one who would be believed.

For all I know, the silver box with the volcanic ash still waits in Andrej's garage, unnoticed even by him.

I have no idea what Mack decided about the break-in. I told him my version again when we were alone, and he listened carefully. I told him I could prove I had checked into the Best Western, prove I had called a cab from our home. He said he needed no proof. He is friendly to Ren, friendly to me. He looks out for himself.

When he and Tamara broke up, he quit wearing his big-shouldered suits, his fedora, and began to dress in an ordinary and unremarkable manner. He is attending a community college to get his grades up and wants to go to the university. He looks uncannily like Ren did when he was Mack's age. They have the same curly hair, the same eager grin, even the same gift for mimicry.

Jimster Reece was killed last year in a three-car pileup on black ice. He was a passenger in a car driven by his father, who was drunk.

I last saw Jimster shortly before I moved to Seattle. He was at the mall, leaning against the wall as if waiting for someone. He had dyed his hair blond. He wore a leather jacket and torn jeans and stared out from under his brows in a detached but wakeful way, as if he were on patrol. His arms were folded. As I got closer, I noticed small stitch marks tattooed onto his cheek in a semicircle, along the very line that the dog's teeth had left, that the surgeon had erased.

I greeted him warmly, put a hand on the leather of his jacket.

For the flicker of a second he looked trapped. Then he seemed to examine me, to look a little more closely. And he grinned faintly in a way that seemed affectionate and complicit, as if I'd just helped him steal something small, for kicks.

Jimster's survivors included his new wife, the young woman with the white hair that Mack had seen with him. She is a Russian named Natalya. Their daughter was six months old when Jimster died.

I have been regularly in touch with Natalya, and she is planning to visit me with the child when I get settled in my new apartment. They may stay a while, because she intends to look for work here.

When I heard about Jimster, I was unable to speak for several days. Siobhan took me to her houseboat and canceled a business trip to stay with me. When I began to talk again, I told her the whole story about myself and that boy, and then we both cried.

That week in my town as not-me? That was the strangest thing I ever did, or ever will do. That was the pivot of my life. And what did it bring me? Awakeness, I hope. I am more awake to my life. I see it, in all its jagged and uncertain beauty.

Siobhan understands. She told me a story she heard about mules in the old days who spent their lives down in the mines, hauling the cars of ore. At the end, when they were brought up and turned out to pasture, they couldn't see. Their lives had made them blind. I don't want that. That is what I dread.

But I carry my conditions with me, and one of them is that passion for the unrequited. A desire for desire. I'm hoping to channel it into something constructive, but it's possible that that won't happen. It may be my religion, my way of insisting on the existence of some unseeable truth.

It may also be a way of going blind. Of missing what's best when it's right before your eyes.

. . .

I know now that there was a shard of a moment, when Ren and I held that gun, in which we both were murderous. I know too that I have loved him, and he me.

There are people who seem to achieve love and contentment within the forms, who seem to know what is true and who view their roiling dreams, morning sweats, sudden moistenings with equanimity, like pets that can be sent back to obedience school. I know I am not one of them.

I think of the invisible lake that once filled our valley. It has risen again to the tops of the banks. I stand on new ground.

Someday, perhaps, I will go back to my town and walk along the river, holding the hand of a little girl, Jimster's daughter, Sophia. Her mother, Natalya, will be glad that the girl and I like to spend time together. It gives Natalya a freer life.

Sophia is five or six by then. She is blond and skinny, as I was at that age, and she is full of questions and stories. I am an aging woman in a cardigan sweater. My hair is turning gray.

We will watch the river, as people do, telling each other tales. The one I will tell her has both of us in it. I am sent to a strange country to do some very dangerous work. I get into trouble. I make mistakes. My very life is in danger. This happens. That happens. I describe it all in detail, then stop on the brink of the direst danger.

"Don't stop!" she cries. "You forgot about me!"

"You?" I draw it out.

"Me! You get in trouble, but I'm already there. I'm already in that country."

I shake my head. I act confused.

"I'm already there," she shouts. "And I save you!"

It's one of our stories, but only one. In others, she is the one in danger. In some of them, Mack is present. He will become a friend of ours, a close friend of mine, and we will all see each other often.

Mack walks with Sophia and me along the banks of the glittering river. He remembers aloud how Yuri, that summer long ago, made a garden in our yard. How his English at the beginning of the summer was so much more awkward than it was at the end. Mack will sound exactly like Yuri when he illustrates the point.

There was a day. I was talking on the phone outside while Yuri waited to discuss where we should place the iris bed. Mack lounged in his suit, waiting for me to hang up so he could call Tamara. Yuri crouched to run his fingers through the dark, damp soil, assessing it. The leaves on the maple were barely unfurled, the newest green.

I clicked off the phone and handed it to Mack. Yuri stood up, smiling.

Mack remembers this moment as we stand by the river. He walks toward me with Yuri's long stride. He places his hand on my forearm. "Come, Mrs. Woodbridge," he says in Yuri's accented voice, "time is melting."

# 38

About a year after I moved to Seattle, Ren sent a newspaper clipping to Mack, and Mack brought it to me. There's a photo with the story. Half a dozen men mill around an ambulance, looking as if they are trying to know what to do. A stocky man is pointing at the edge of the river, which appears to be roaring along, carrying chunks of ice. There is a thin sun. The contrast is poor. All depth is rubbed out.

The river through our town was swollen that day, the story said. Ice jams had broken loose and unleashed walls of muddy pent-up water. Snow on the mountains was turning to rivers.

The photo again. The stocky man, Andrej, has sunglasses that puncture the whiteness. He has a new mustache that covers his mouth. He stands at an angle to the camera. The river behind him looks black.

He and his cousin had been walking in the early morning hours, he told the police. They had been walking because there was a full moon that night, and they'd had some vodka and were reminiscing about the Russia of their childhood. The whiteness and the snow had made them remember how far they were from home.

They had been singing, he said. That was the detail that told me he lied, the embellishment that turned the whole picture false. Because Yuri would never sing along with Andrej. He might talk with him, argue with him, but he would never sing with him.

They had been walking along the banks of the river near the place where a canal runs parallel to the bigger water. Yuri Petrov had said, quite suddenly, that he would take a quick run onto the ice of the canal and be back on shore before it could break through.

Andrej said he warned him against it — because of the cold, because of the hour, because the ice did not look thick enough — but Yuri didn't listen. He stepped onto the ice and began walking as fast as he could, and suddenly broke though to his knees, to his thighs. Then, said Andrej, Yuri somehow slipped beneath the ice and was pulled under and away. He said it happened so fast, he couldn't believe what he was seeing.

Andrej said he slid onto his stomach and peered frantically into the place where Yuri had crashed through. But he could see nothing, nothing at all, so he ran for help. Across the nearby footbridge to the all-night supermarket, the outdoor phone. But he could not make the phone work, and so, in a state of delirium now, he ran back to his car and got it started and tried to drive to the police station. But he got stuck in the heavy snow, and then he couldn't find the station. It wasn't where he had thought it was. He eventually made his way home and called from there.

The canal where he said Yuri had disappeared is perhaps fifty yards long and ends in a concrete wall that blocks it off from the river. A body should have been found. Could Yuri have somehow surfaced to float over the wall and into the swollen river? It seemed unlikely.

A body was not found. Not that day, or the day after, or the day after that. The curious gathered in larger crowds each day on the bank. Rescuers brought machinery — hooks, backhoes — and searched every foot of the canal.

Nothing. Nothing to this day.

I think that Andrej lied. That he had a role in making Yuri disappear a long time ago, and that the river story is his way of lending drama and finality to his cousin's absence. I also think it's possible that Yuri manages to be alive somewhere, far from Andrej. But I will never know.

It's a vivid story that Andrej told, one that's hard to forget. The bank, the river, the ice — they stay in the mind. A face beneath the ice, open-eyed and young — it stays forever in the mind.